BENEATH THE SURFACE

ABBI COOK

BENEATH THE SURFACE BLURB

I was born and bred to be a killer. It's all I'm supposed to be.

I take no prisoners. Until Lily. For her, I make an exception. But only for a week.

When I walk in, time starts ticking down to zero. Her father has seven days to save her.

Until then, she's mine. Mine to have. Mine to take.

Mine to keep.

Beneath The Surface is a work of fiction. Names, characters, places, and events are the products of the author's imagination. Any resemblance to events, locations, or persons, living or dead, is coincidental.

Published in the United States

ISBN: 978-1-7345173-3-0

*C*ason

One look into my father's office and I know something's off. Fuck. The vibe in the room feels all wrong. The usual people are here, so it's not that, and a quick glance around the place tells me nothing's really changed. The office looks just as meticulous as it always has. That's one thing about Victor I still can't figure out.

The guy's a neat freak. Considering what he spends his days and nights involved in, you'd think a little dust and some papers laying around wouldn't bother him.

My mind drifts to how strange he gets about even a single scrap of paper being out of place, but my attention is quickly ripped out of my thoughts and back to him when he barks, "Cason, get the fuck in here!"

I step into his office and stop as my cousin Jaxon and one of the new guys named Scotch turn to look at

1

me. I scan their expressions for some sense of what the hell is going on but glean nothing from either of them. They look like they usually do.

Like we all do. Like guys who do the work we do.

"What's up?" I ask in a low voice, suddenly feeling like I need to be even more serious than I usually am.

He twists his face into an ugly grimace and shakes his head. "What's up is I have a job for you and you're nowhere to be found. Where the fuck have you been?"

The real reason for why I'm later than usual flashes through my mind, but I don't think explaining that I got wrapped up in some show about Jack the Ripper and lost track of the time is going to go over well right now. So I come up with a lie as quickly as I can and blurt it out.

"Sorry. After the other day, my shoulder's still pretty stiff. I guess I stood under the hot water a little too long today."

All three men around me nod their understanding, and I know I skated by on that question. Anyone who does what we do knows the job comes with aches and pains. Sometimes we get it back at us.

And three days ago, I got it from some asshole who thought it would be cute if he pulled a fucking gun on me in some pathetic attempt to avoid the inevitable. He caught me by surprise, which, of course, was my fault, but I wrestled the gun away from him fast. Unfortunately, the motherfucker went all kung fu fighting on me and got a few hits in before I took him out.

I did my job, but my shoulders and back took the brunt of the whole damn thing. Since then, I've truthfully felt like shit, but I can't let anyone here know that. A big part of my usefulness is that I can take a beating and still do what's necessary for the business. If I suddenly turn into some candy ass who can't deal with a little pain, then things will change here for me, and not for the better.

My father's sympathy runs out quickly, and he waves me closer to his desk. "Well, toughen the fuck up. I've got work for you to do today."

"You give the word and I'm on it," I say as I stop a couple feet from the corner of his desk.

"Good. That son of a bitch Harry Pinto thinks he can get away with not paying me the money he owes. You need to go to his place and show him the errors in that kind of thinking. Got it?"

I stand there stunned as he hands me a slip of paper with an address on it. Collecting money from some nobody? My father has other people to handle that low-level shit. Why is he making me take care of this?

He stares at me for a long moment and then shakes his head. "Got it? I expect an answer when I ask you a question."

"Yeah, I guess, but why have me go over to collect money from someone like Harry? He's penny-ante shit. Unless you're looking for me to take care of him, I don't see why you'd have me do this."

"Don't question me. Just go! And impress upon that stupid fuck that I'm not a bank. If he doesn't pay, he doesn't get extra charges tacked onto his account. The currency we deal in is far pricier."

I know what he's saying. He doesn't have to spell it out for me. Get the money or take it out of him in a way that gives him the chance to pay it back but makes it clear things are going to get a whole lot fucking worse if that repayment doesn't happen in the next few days.

What I don't understand is why he's sending a killer to do an errand boy's task.

This isn't my first time doing this kind of job, though. I've worked for the family for years, and I started out collecting money, so I know how it goes. Hurt him but don't kill him until you get the word. I'm nothing if not a good soldier.

In fact, I'm one hell of a soldier. It's just that I usually do the killing of a soldier.

As I turn to leave, out of the corner of my eye I catch Jaxon smiling. Curious, I stop and ask, "Something funny?"

"Just wondering if you finished watching that Jack the Ripper show you were talking about yesterday," he asks with a chuckle.

He's busting my ass because he knows the real reason I'm late. We're like that with each other. The only thing is I don't need my father knowing the truth in the mood he's in. That doesn't mean I can let Jaxon's ass busting pass, though. I like giving my cousin a hard time, so I throw him the middle finger and laugh.

"Yeah, and you'd be surprised at how much

information on his technique they explained. Watch yourself or you'll get a taste of some Jack the Ripper modern-day style, fucker."

Jaxon opens his mouth to snap back at me, but Victor barks, "What the hell is this, PBS news hour? Enough talk about Jack the Ripper! Cason, get the hell out of here and get my money from Pinto. Now!"

As I hurry out of his office, I hear Jaxon snickering behind me. I'd stay to have another verbal go-round with him, but I've got more important things to take care of at the moment.

STANDING ON HARRY PINTO'S PORCH, A MILD MID-September wind blowing against my skin, I look through the tiny window in his front door into his house. The guy's not poor. It's not a brand new home, but the place isn't a shithole. He's got nice furniture, decent rugs, and collectable plates displayed where I can see them. They aren't any kind of things I'd want, but they show he's got some money. Hell, I bet if he just cashed in a few of those goddamned plates he'd probably be able to pay off his debt in one fell swoop.

Instead, he drags his damn feet so we have to send someone over to see him every month for the past three months and do this same song and dance shit with him. Makes no sense to me at all.

But even more, I don't understand why the fuck I'm stuck doing this bullshit job. Who sends a killer to get some asshole's payment? Talk about using a cannon to get rid of a fly.

For a second time, I bang my fist against his front door. Scotch has been handling this, and he's never had to rough up Harry in the past, as far as I know. He's got to be in his mid-fifties, for God's sake, and he's small. It wouldn't even be a challenge for somebody like Scotch, much less a fair fight for me.

Not that I'm in the business of making anything fair for the likes of him. He knew what he was getting into when he took my father's money. As he said, he's no fucking bank. It's not like he didn't know the penalties he'd face if he didn't pay up when it was time.

Footsteps shake me out of my daydreaming about beating the hell out of Harry, and I peer in through the window to see him shuffling toward the door. He looks older than mid-fifties, and although I'm not certain he doesn't always look sort of hunched over, his body seems curled up.

He opens the door, unsurprised to see me, and nods his grey head. "You one of Victor's guys? I figured I'd see you sometime today."

Before he has the chance to ask me to come in, I walk past him into his house filled with knick-knacks. "You know why I'm here, Harry. Victor isn't going to wait forever."

As I look around the place to make sure he isn't going to stupidly spring something on me, I think to myself that this small talk seems unnecessary. We aren't friends. We aren't even acquaintances.

Harry closes the door and pauses before walking past me into the living room and its walls covered with more of those damn plates. They all have some blue design on them I can't make out, but hell, they're everywhere now that I look around.

For a moment, he straightens up only to have his body collapse down on itself again. It's like his slight shoulders are too heavy for his small body.

"I just need more time. Just a little more time. A week or two, maybe."

That right there is why I never missed leaving behind this errand boy bullshit. The excuses. The reasons that inevitably lead to the pleading. If we were close or even casual friends, I could see why someone might think that would work.

But we're not. I'm an enforcer, muscle for the man he owes money to. I don't judge the right or wrong of this situation. I just go where I'm told to go and do what I'm told to do.

Usually, it's killing someone. To be honest, I prefer that. At least with that kind of job, I don't have to put up with all this fucking chit chat.

He's goddamned lucky I'm not here to do my usual job. Then it wouldn't be a matter of him pleading for more time. All he'd get is a shot to the head and my day would be done.

Today, though, I'm here to get money. This isn't difficult. Harry knows this too, I'm sure. He took money from us and promised to pay it back. That time has come.

I don't like this little dance he's forcing me to do. I

don't want to talk about why he needs more time or what he hopes will happen to make it possible for him to pay his debt. I don't care. I just want to get what I came here for and leave.

"No more time, Harry. You know how this works," I say flatly, careful to not let a hint of emotion creep into my voice.

That will only make him think he can plead his case. He can't.

His eyes grow wide as I watch him try to come up with something that will put off the inevitable. "Just a couple weeks. That's all I ask. Two weeks and I'll have it all for him. No more than that."

Goddamned people who get in over their heads.

I don't want to have a conversation about this, but before I can stop myself, a question about all these damn plates hanging on the white walls around me slips out. "Harry, why don't you just sell some of these plates and get this over with?"

He shakes his head like that's the most ridiculous thing he's ever heard in his life. Or even more, the most horrifying suggestion he's ever heard. "Sell my plates? I can't."

Now that we've started this, I can't not ask the next logical question. Pointing to the far wall with ten plates hanging in a row about two feet from the ceiling, I say, "What's going on with these things anyway? Why the plates all over the place?"

Smoothing his grey hair back off his face, Harry proudly stands a little taller as he explains the deal with them. "They're Danish and German collectible plates. They're my pride and joy."

I narrow my eyes and take a good look at the one closest to me. It's blue and white with a winter scene painted on it. Not beautiful but not ugly. Just nothing I'd ever want littering up my place.

Turning back to look down at him, I shrug. "Then just sell as many plates as you need to pay Victor back and we'll be square."

"No! I can't do that!" Harry says, suddenly very perturbed by my suggestion. "I borrowed money off him so I could buy more. It would defeat the whole purpose if I then sold any of them to pay him back."

My curiosity about the whole plate thing sated, I'm quickly running out of patience. Taking a step closer to Harry, I glare down at him and hope he doesn't force me to rough up someone half my size and more than twice my age.

"Let me explain this to you. I'm here to get your payment. That's it. I can't renegotiate the terms of your loan with you. I'm a courier here, and you need to give me the money to take back to him. Now. Or I'm going to have to take matters into my own hands."

From behind me, I feel someone hit me in the middle of my back. "Get away from him! He's just an old man, for God's sake!"

My brain registers the sound of a woman's voice, and I spin around to see a blond girl who looks like a teenager glaring up at me. She's at least a foot shorter than I am and tiny, like if I wanted to, I could flick her away like a bug with almost no effort. She's also beautiful, like stunningly beautiful to the point that I doubt she could be related to Harry. Is it possible she's got an old guy fetish and he's banging her? Dressed in black yoga pants and a pale green T-shirt that highlights a nice rack, she's easy on the eyes, if not on the ears.

"Don't you touch him! Do you hear me?" she says in a voice far tougher than she looks.

Harry hurries around me and wraps his arm around the girl. "Lily, please. We don't need to act that way. Everything's fine."

She doesn't take her brown eyes off me but answers him. "It's not fine, Daddy. Nothing's fine, if the way this big lug was talking to you is any indication."

Her pathetic attempt at insulting me makes me chuckle. Harry's daughter? My eyes dart from her gorgeous face with big brown eyes and a mouth that makes me think of things I shouldn't at the moment to Harry's grizzled old face. Impossible. Or maybe she looks like her mother and not him?

None of it matters, although I do have to admit she's a nice distraction for a few moments.

"Little girl, your father and I have business to attend to, so why don't you run off and go play with dolls or something?"

Finished with her, I return my focus to her father, but she isn't done. Stepping out of her father's arms and toward me, she stops not a foot away and cranes her neck to look up at me.

And then she fucking pokes me right in the chest!

"Don't talk to me like I'm a child. I'm a grown woman, and even though I'm not a giant like you, I won't let you hurt my father. Now leave us alone!"

Stunned by her bravery, even if it is a mistake, I stare down into her eyes and see she's deadly serious. I'm not used to people not being afraid of me. Being six foot six and as big as I am, I'm just naturally feared. It's one of the reasons I'm so good at what I do.

But for some reason, this little slip of a woman, or so she claims, doesn't seem frightened at all by me or my size. I'm not sure what to do about that.

Never taking my gaze off her, I lower my voice and say, "Harry, I'd warn your daughter to keep her nose out of things where it doesn't belong."

"I don't need to be warned," she snaps at me, her eyes filling with anger I've only seen from men.

But Harry understands the perilous position she's put herself in and quickly pulls her back away from me. Wrapping his arms around her, he kisses her on the cheek.

"Honey, it's okay. This man and I are just discussing business. There's no need to get excited. Why don't you go into the kitchen and make me some of that banana bread that I love?"

Still, she doesn't divert her angry stare leveled at my face. "I think I should stay right where I am, Daddy."

Fuck. Who does this little woman think she is?

I consider threatening her to get her to leave so we can get back to the business at hand, but Harry again suggests for her to go make him that bread he likes and finally she stops glaring up at me and turns to look at him.

"If you're sure, Daddy," she says in a wary but sweet voice I have to admit suits her much better than the snappy one she's used since she walked into the room.

Harry kisses her on the forehead and smiles. "It's okay, Lily. I can't wait to have some banana bread for lunch."

After throwing me one last nasty glance, she turns to leave. As I watch her walk away, I have to admit the body is as nice as her face.

Once she's out of earshot, her father says in a low voice, "I'm sorry about that. She's got her mother's fire in her. She's usually a very sweet girl, but you know how children can be when it comes to their parents."

I want to tell him I have no idea about children or parents. I just want to get the damn money I came here for and go on with my life.

"Now what's it going to be, Harry? You give me the money, or you force me to do something you don't want me to do. To be honest, I don't care one way or another, but you're a little old man and I'm sure you're going to be hurting if I do what I have to."

He looks up at me, pleading with his eyes. "Just two more weeks. I swear I'll have all the money then."

We're getting nowhere with this, and I'm tired of talking about this shit with him. I'm not against roughing up anyone, but I've got a better idea.

"Okay, Harry. I'll just take a handful of your

plates. That seems fair," I say as I move toward the winter plate to grab it.

"No! Please! I need them to be able to convince the seller I'm worthy of his plates," he cries out. "Don't take my plates. They're all I have, other than Lily."

His words echo in my brain, and suddenly, I know what will get him to pay up. Nodding my agreement to his offer, I march past him. "I'll take her then."

Shock registers on his face and he starts to beg for me not take her, but I don't have time to deal with his pleading anymore. Ignoring him, I walk into the kitchen and see her standing at the counter.

Turning to look at me, she gives me another one of her nasty glares. "What are you doing?"

I don't bother answering her before I lift her up into my arms, tossing her over my shoulder. "Time to go. Say goodbye to Daddy."

"You can't do this!" she screams, pounding my back with her fists.

"Yeah, I can. Now behave yourself."

I call back to her father as I head for the front door, "You have seven days, Harry. Seven days to pay up or you don't get your daughter back."

What's left unspoken is what will happen to her after those seven days are up if he doesn't pay back the money he owes. Knowing my father, those could be the last seven days of her life.

CHAPTER TWO

*C*ason

Her fists pounding against my back barely register as I walk out to my car. She's sort of amusing with all this protesting and threatening me.

"You won't get away with this! Let me down!"

I glance around the neighborhood to see if anyone is listening to all of her caterwauling. I see no one at first, but as my gaze drifts toward the blue house at the end of the street, I see someone peeking through their front window curtains.

Not that they'll do anything. Harry lives on a typical American street, and in the middle of the day, the only people around are third shift workers fast asleep and nosy housewives who will gossip about what they're seeing me doing with Lily right now but won't call the cops.

Lily starts doing swimmer kicks with her legs, barely missing my head. I tighten my hold on her and snap, "I swear to God, you hit me once and I'm going to knock you out."

My threat has no effect on her at all. She lets out a grunt and directs all her attention to pummeling my shoulder blades again in her futile attempt to get free.

I reach my car parked on the street in front of Harry's house and fling open the back door. Tossing her into the back seat, I quickly look around as she sits stunned at how hard she landed. I hadn't planned on kidnapping anyone today, so I didn't come prepared.

My eyes scan the car floor, and I see a rope poking out from under the passenger front seat. That'll do. I lean over her to grab it, and that's when she takes her opportunity to kick me hard in the side. The point of her sneaker jabs directly into my skin.

Rage erupts inside me as stabbing pain spikes in my ribs. Fuck! On the same side as my sore shoulder too, damnit!

"Sit still!" I bark as I move to tie her wrists and ankles together.

"I thought you said you were going to knock me out."

I look up at her just as I finish securing her ankles. Does this girl have a death wish or something? I've threatened grown men and watched while they pleaded for mercy, crying like babies. This girl doesn't seem to understand how much I can fuck her up.

"You seem to want me to hurt you, little girl. Don't test me. I'm not some gentle giant. I'm a vicious one, and I will knock you out if I have to."

"Fuck you! You're a monster and nothing more."

I finish tying her wrists together and smile. If she thinks being called that will hurt me, she's missing the mark.

"Try again, sweetheart. Being called a monster doesn't bother me. I am monster, and now you're my boss's captive until your father pays his bill."

She doesn't answer this time, and I see in her eyes she's frightened. Good. Maybe that means she won't scream and beg all the way back to the estate. I move to close the door so we can get going and realize her feet are right behind my seat. Hell no. There's no way I want her kicking my back for the entire drive.

Pushing her across the back seat to the passenger side, I fight her wriggling to get the seatbelt around her. She's a fighter, but I'm bigger. As I've found with most things in life, size matters. In fact, it wins over nearly everything else.

"Now sit there and keep quiet."

I climb into the front seat and start the car. Looking up toward the house, I see Harry standing in his front doorway. Fucking coward. What kind of man lets someone take his daughter away like I just did? I'm no honorable soul, but if anyone tried to do that with my kid, I'd break them in half first.

As if on cue, little miss thing in the backseat starts with the bravado as we drive away. "My father won't let you get away with this."

Glancing up at the rearview mirror, I see her courage hasn't reached her eyes filled with fear at what's about to happen next. "Your father just let me walk out of your house with you. He was more protective of those plates of his than he was with you. Harry's not going to do anything other than pay back the money he owes."

I give the car some gas as she asks in a terrified voice I know is truer than that brave one she just tried, "What if he can't get the money?"

Once more I glance up at the rearview mirror, and our gazes meet. She deserves the truth, even if it frightens her. She clearly doesn't know the truth about her father, who did worry more about those goddamned plates than about her. She likely thinks he's just some sweet old guy and not someone who gets involved with the likes like Victor Varens.

"Then my boss will decide what to do with you. Now shut your mouth so I can have some peace and quiet."

Lily obeys me for about two point five seconds before she returns to asking me questions I don't want to answer. I don't know what my father will do to her if her father doesn't pay up. I suspect he'll get rid of her. She wouldn't serve any purpose to him. He already has a wife and women he keeps around for whatever he wants, and with how much this one talks, I can't imagine he'll like having her under foot for more than a few minutes.

She also wants to know where we're going. I don't bother to explain that either. She'll figure that out when we get to the house. What does she want? A fucking address and zip code?

"Why won't you tell me where you're taking me? Don't I have the right to know that?"

I jam on the brakes to stop at a red light and spin around to look at her in the back seat. "Don't you know how to listen? I told you to keep quiet. What about those fucking words don't you understand?"

My voice echoes off the sides of the car and the windows, and she shrinks down against the seat, finally frightened enough to shut up. For a moment, I watch her, expecting to see the tears welling in her eyes begin to spill out onto her cheeks. But she holds them back.

"I'm sorry. This is my first kidnapping. I guess I'm not very good at this."

I sigh in frustration. Even her apology is full of sass.

"Just sit there and be quiet."

The guy in the car behind me blows his horn, and I swear to God I want to march back there and rip his fucking head off. I throw him a death look and spin around to see the light has already turned green.

"What the fuck are you in such a hurry for, asshole?" I grumble before slamming my foot on the gas.

We take off like a bat out of hell, my body pushing back against the leather seat the speed hits so fast. I want to get away from that impatient jackass, but all of a sudden, I feel like I want to get away from this whole thing.

Harry. Lily. Jaxon. My father. All of it.

I don't know where I'd go or what I'd do since I've never had any job but working for the family. This is the first time I've ever even thought of leaving this life behind, so it's not like I've formulated a plan or anything like that. It's just after dealing with Harry and his fucking stupid plates, Lily and her need to constantly talk, and everything else today, maybe it might be nice to go somewhere else and start over.

Daydreaming about that lasts for about a minute before Lily interrupts my thoughts with another goddamned question. I swear to God this woman has a death wish.

"What's your name?"

The way she asks that sounds different than every other time she's talked to me. Before, every word out of her mouth came with a razor sharp edge. Even her fucking apology. But now, she sounds gentle and sweet, like she truly cares to know the answer to her question.

I look up at the rearview mirror and see her staring at me, her eyes filled with curiosity. Something deep inside me says I should tell her since this is the first nice thing she's said and maybe keeping her happy will make her stay quiet.

But then another part of me says don't. She and I don't need to share names or anything else. She's nobody to me and never will be. She's a hostage, a payment for her father's loan that will be replaced by money in a week or less. Nothing more. In fact, I probably won't see her after today since I imagine my father will take her and do something with her that suits him.

So, no, she won't get kindness in return for hers.

"Shut your mouth and keep quiet."

The frustration—or is it hurt?—that comes off her nearly fills all the space around us in the car. I quickly look up at the mirror and see her pouting back there. Returning my focus to the road, I can't help but wonder when the hell the last time I saw someone pout. Christ, it has to be twenty years.

Then a flash of fear races through me. Is it possible she really is just a girl and not a grown woman like she said back at the house?

"How old are you?" I ask into the brief silence of the car without looking back at her.

"Oh, so now you want to chat? You won't even answer me when I ask your name. Why the hell should I answer your question?" she answers in that razor sharp way once again.

Now I look back at her and see the pout is gone, replaced by a smug look like she's caught me at my own game. *Little girl, don't test me. That's not where you want to go.*

"Because I want to know. Now answer. How old are you?" I ask in a more threatening tone than before.

"No."

I suddenly feel like I know exactly how every father in the world has felt when they said to their kids, "I swear to God I'll stop this car if you don't behave." She's like a fucking child. If I have to pull this car over to get her to give me the answer to my question, then so be it.

With a sharp yank of the steering wheel, I pull off the road and slam my foot on the brake. Even I go flying forward it all happens so fast.

Spinning around in my seat, I look back at her and point my Glock at her head. She's tugging on her seatbelt, which nearly choked her when I stopped so short.

"Look at me."

For once, she obeys my order and stops everything else to look at me. Her expression fills with hurt and then utter fear, but I don't care. I want an answer, and I want it now.

"Last time, and I swear to God if you don't give me what I want to know, I'm going to hurt you. Now tell me, how old are you?"

I wait, expecting her to give me an answer full of her usual attitude, but an answer nonetheless. A few seconds pass, and all she does is stare at me. I can't tell if she's getting ready to tell me what I want to know or to continue playing this game that can't end well for her.

In her eyes, I recognize the real fear she's trying to hide. She can't, though. I've hurt enough people in my life to know what true fear looks like.

Even though I don't do it intentionally, I find myself holding my breath as I wait for her to tell me what I want to know. I've beaten and tortured enough people to understand that getting answers from people takes patience. Only rookies and psychotic assholes jump right to the end game.

Finally, she opens her mouth and sighs. "Fine. I'm eighteen. Happy now?"

As I turn around, I let myself enjoy a tiny smile she can't see. *Yes, I am happy, Lily. Kidnapping a child wasn't in my game plan for today, so finding out you're of age is great.*

Neither of us say another word the rest of the way to the estate, and when I park the car, I'm thankful that I'll be done dealing with her in just a few minutes. My father will take her off my hands, and I'll return to my job that usually contains a lot less frustration.

I open the rear passenger side door and unhook her seat belt. I consider untying her but quickly decide against that as the memory of her fighting me when I first got her in the car flashes through my mind.

Nope. Keeping her tied up will be a hell of a lot less hassle.

"Time to go meet your new babysitter," I say with a chuckle as I pull her out of the car and toss her over my shoulder.

After kicking the car door closed, I head to the office with her as she once again begins to ask more fucking questions. What is with this woman and her questions?

"Who? You mean you aren't going to be the person taking care of me this whole time?" she asks in a strange way that makes her sound almost disappointed.

"My boss. Don't worry. He'll like you, as long as you learn to keep your mouth closed."

"And if I don't?"

Who the fuck asks this many questions?

"Then he won't like you. Now shut up."

My hands hold her tightly against me, and I can't avoid feeling the swell of her very nice ass against my fingers. Turning my head, I see she's got great legs too. Victor will probably be very happy to have her for the next week. She's gorgeous and has a great body, and if she stays quiet, she's practically perfect.

Maybe I'll get a raise out of this. That is, if he stifles all her talk by gagging her.

The office door is open, so I rap my knuckles on the doorframe before walking in. "So the visit with Harry didn't go as well as expected. He says he needs more time to get the money, and since I didn't figure you'd want me to kill him before that time was up, I took his daughter."

My father stares up at me, and his mouth drops open. "What the fuck are you talking about? Who the fuck is this?"

I lower her to the ground and steady her for a second so she doesn't fall over since her ankles are still tied together. "This is Lily, Harry's daughter," I answer proudly as I watch his gaze roam over her very nice body, pausing on her tits.

"What the hell am I supposed to do with her?" he asks when he's finished inspecting her finer points.

"Whatever your heart desires. I told Harry he has seven days, so for the next week, she's all yours to do whatever you want."

Lily inches a step closer to me and hides her head behind me, although I can't imagine why she thinks that's going to do anything for her. My father leans back in his chair and folds his arms across his chest before shaking his head.

"It looks like she isn't mine to have, if you ask me.

You take care of her for the next week, but keep her out of sight. I knew Harry would be a hassle. Why can't he just pay like everyone else?"

While he wonders aloud about Harry's poor performance as a borrower, his words about my having to be responsible for Lily echo in my brain. A whole week with this person? What the fuck am I going to do with her for seven days? She never shuts up, and every word that comes from her mouth is like poison.

"Don't you think she'd be better off with you?" I ask as Lily manages to hide all of herself behind me.

Why the hell does she think I'm her savior now? I've threatened her half a dozen times since I met her less than an hour ago.

My father smiles and shakes his head again. "Not from where I'm sitting, no. There's not a lot going on for the next couple days, so take some time off and enjoy yourself. It looks like you're halfway there already."

I look back to see Lily staring up at me with terror in her eyes and can't imagine what the fuck my father is seeing. All I know is now I'm stuck babysitting an eighteen year old with too much sass for the next week.

"Fine. I need a few days of vacation anyway," I mutter under my breath, hoping to hide how much this arrangement pisses me off.

Once more, I lift Lily over my shoulder and head back to my car. Furious about how all of this has turned out, I don't even bother putting the seat belt around her after dumping her into the back seat.

If I'm lucky, she'll give me a chance to knock her out and maybe she'll stay unconscious for the next seven days.

CHAPTER THREE

*L*ily

Already tired of being carried around like an unwanted sack of potatoes, I cringe when this behemoth reaches into the backseat of his car and throws me over his shoulder yet again to carry me up three flights of stairs to his apartment. It's like he's a Cro-Magnon man and this is all he knows to do.

"I can walk, you know," I say as I bounce off his back with each step he takes.

He ignores me and doesn't respond, which to be honest, isn't a horrible thing. He's cruel and has spent nearly every minute since we met threatening me. It's just that I hate this thing he has with carrying me like some meaningless, inanimate object.

We pass a woman on the second floor with strange blue hair and a round face. Her eyes open wide as we walk by, like she can't believe what she's seeing. I'm right there with her. I can't believe this either.

My instinct is to make a joke of the whole thing so

I don't look like pathetic prisoner of this guy's, but then a flash of brilliance hits me. If she thinks I'm in danger, maybe she'll call the police.

So I quickly whip up some tears and begin to sob while I stare directly at her. "Please help. Call someone and tell them I'm not here of my own volition."

His reaction is to spin around so fast I nearly throw up and snap at the woman, "Tell anyone about this and it'll be the last time you'll see anything. Understand?"

And with that little bit of viciousness from him, my one sure chance of getting help disappears as quickly as it presented itself. I watch the woman hurry into her apartment and slam the door on me and my plight, my hopes dashed completely when I hear her lock her deadbolt.

Still, my captor doesn't say a word as he continues to march up the steps with me slung over his shoulder. By the time we reach his apartment, my ribs are killing me, and all the blood has rushed to my head.

He practically kicks the door open, and once we're inside, he slams it so hard I expect it to come off its hinges. I take a quick look around my new temporary home and see he clearly doesn't spend much time at this place. No pictures hang on the bland white walls, and other than a couch and a TV tray, there is no furniture in the living room. A heavy bag hangs from the ceiling in the corner of the room, not much help when it comes to relaxing. Then again, I don't get the sense this guy relaxes. There is a TV, though, so at least I won't have to sit in silence the whole time I'm here.

As I'm studying his apartment, he plants me onto the floor. Dizzy from hanging upside down for three flights, I sway left and then right before falling backward into him. My problem only serves to irritate him, and he once again stands me firmly on the floor, in the process squeezing my arms so tightly he surely leaves marks.

"Ouch! That hurts!" I cry out as I attempt to rub the pain out of my biceps.

His dark eyes flash pure rage at me. "Stand up straight. I'm not your fucking nursemaid. You're lucky I didn't toss you over the stairs onto the ground after that stunt you pulled with that woman. I swear to God you have a death wish, little girl."

"My name is Lily. What's your name? Maybe we could call a cease fire and start by using our proper names."

He hesitates, and I have the sense that he doesn't intend on telling me his name, so I force a smile and do what I can to smooth things over. "If I knew your name, I might not be so terrified and want to accost strange ladies on the stairs. I know you're all about threatening me with bodily harm, but I am just a way to make my father pay up, right? Your boss doesn't get what he really wants if it's anything but money."

His expression so full of rage morphs into something that resembles confusion or disgust. Or maybe a mixture of both. At least it's not that pure anger that terrifies me.

"Do you ever shut up? You talk more than anyone I've ever met," he asks in a tone that tells me it's disgust he's feeling at the moment.

I can maneuver around disgust better than rage, so I answer, "I just want to know what to call you. At the moment, all I have is Cro-Magnon since you've spent nearly every moment with me carrying me on your shoulder."

He explodes for some reason I can't figure out, his face contorting into a monstrous look that instantly makes my blood run cold, before he bellows, "Cason! Are you happy now? My name is Cason! Now shut the fuck up or I swear I'm going to end up killing you."

Okay. The whole thing with him yelling so loud that the walls shook wasn't great and him threatening to kill me another time wasn't terrific either, but at least now I know his name.

Cason. I've never heard of that name. My curiosity makes me want to ask him about it, but after he quickly unties my ankles and wrists, he storms away toward the kitchen and I decide against it.

Maybe later.

I stand there in the middle of his barely furnished living room considering what my options are. Fighting him doesn't seem to have worked very well. He appears to be someone who approaches every situation with anger as his base emotion, so fighting likely won't get me far.

Crying hasn't worked well with him so far either. That's not surprising since he's so angry. He's probably been the cause of so many people crying that seeing tears doesn't even affect him anymore.

As much as I hate to admit it, giving him the silence he wants seems to be my only option. The problem with that is I can't make him consider me a person and hopefully not want to hurt me, or worse, if I can't get him to talk to me. I've seen enough movies with bad guys who take hostages to know it's key he sees me as a person and not just some thing to be traded for something else.

The clanking sound of pots and pans banging against one another pulls me out of my thoughts, so I poke my head around the wall into the kitchen to see what he's doing. Cason is standing at the counter with enough cookware to make a meal for an army spread out in front of him, but he's shaking his head.

"Excuse me, Cason? Can I help?" I ask in a tiny voice I hope won't send him into a rage.

He shoots me a nasty glance and shakes his head. "What did I tell you about talking?"

Most people would walk away and give up around this time, but the mere thought of getting something to eat makes me more desperate than I should be, so I take a step into the kitchen and stop a few feet away from him. He glowers down at me with nothing but hatred in his eyes, so I force another smile I hope might melt at least a tiny bit of that hate in him.

"I'm a great cook. Whatever you want to eat, if you have the ingredients, I can make it for you," I offer as sweetly as I can possibly get my voice to sound.

He lets out a heavy sigh, so I quickly add, "Having

me cook will keep me from talking. It's a win-win for you, it seems."

I don't get the pleasant thank you most decent people would give in response to such an offer, and he storms past me as he snaps, "There are eggs in the refrigerator, along with ham, onions, and peppers. Let's see if you know how to make a Denver omelet."

Silently, I answer his challenge. I can not only make a Denver omelet, but I make an incredible Denver omelet, Cason. Prepare to be blown away.

Ten minutes later, two omelets better than anything he could get served to him in a restaurant are ready. He seems to have disappeared, though, and when I look around for him, he's nowhere to be found.

"Cason? Your omelet is ready," I call out toward what looks like a bedroom.

Silence.

As much as I want to see the look on his face when he takes the first bite of my delicious meal, I can't help but wonder if this is my chance to escape. If I could get down the three flights of stairs before he caught up with me, I'd be home free. I saw a neighborhood grocery store about a block away as we drove here, so all I'd have to do is reach there to get to a phone and call the police.

"Cason?" I say far more quietly than a minute ago and wait for any response.

Again, silence.

So I take the chance and move to leave, but he appears out of nowhere in the doorway to the bedroom just in time to see me reaching for the doorknob on the front door. I freeze, my fingers still on it, as he stomps toward me in all his terrifying glory.

Bracing for him to yell again or even finally hit me, I'm surprised when he stops next to me and simply stares down at my hand on the doorknob. No yelling. No lashing out. Just a simple question I don't know how to answer.

"Planning to go somewhere, Lily?"

"I called for you to come to eat. I made the omelet you wanted. It's probably cold now, but I can make another one. There are more eggs. Maybe not so heavy on the peppers, but I think it would still be okay," I say, my thoughts quickly tumbling out of my mouth because of utter terror.

"Then let's eat," he says in a low voice tinged with impatience, still staring down at where my fingers remain on the doorknob.

Lifting my hand, I nod and follow him into the kitchen. This Cason is even more frightening than the Cro-Magnon version I've experienced up until now, if that's possible. I don't know why he isn't screaming at me or threatening to kill me again. At least with that Cason, I thought I knew what to do. This one unnerves me to the core.

So I do what I always do when I don't know how to act. I do the one thing he hates most.

Talk.

As he picks up his plate and begins eating standing at the counter, I say, "I hope you like it. I had to learn to cook very early in life after my mother died, so I've gotten pretty good at it. Omelets aren't my specialty, but I have to say that I make a pretty good one. I'm better with meats than I am with eggs, but I think you'll enjoy it. Do you use ketchup on yours?"

He doesn't say a word in response but turns to look at me after taking his second bite. I know I'm aggravating him, but it's almost as if I can't stop myself.

"No, I guess not. I don't use ketchup on eggs either. It sounds really disgusting, to be honest," I continue to ramble while reaching around him to get my own omelet.

Maybe if I stuff the whole thing in my mouth I'll be able to shut up. Cutting a piece off, I quickly start chewing, hoping he likes his food and hasn't decided to kill me already.

The two of us stand there in silence while we finish our Denver omelets, him focused entirely on his food and me focused entirely on biting my tongue so more words don't come flying out. When he finishes, he sets the plate and fork in the sink and runs some water to rinse them off. I expect him to finally say something, but when he does speak again, I'm shocked.

"Lily, do you have a death wish?" he asks so earnestly that I can't mistake how honest the question is.

After swallowing my bite of omelet, I shake my head and fight back tears as terror courses through my brain. Did he just have me cook him a meal that he's decided is my last one before he kills me right here? Did I finally push him too far with my talking?

"N-n-no. Why?" I stammer out.

Cason shrugs. "Just wondering. By the way, you make an incredible omelet. That might be the best one I've ever had."

A sob escapes my mouth as the realization that he doesn't plan to actually kill me right there in the kitchen at the counter where we've just shared a meal settles into my brain. He stares at me like he doesn't understand what's wrong with me, and for possibly the first time in my life, I can't explain what I feel.

When he leaves me standing there in shock at the first kind words he's said to me, I can't stop myself from crying. I muffle the sound of it, but whether it's because of all that's happened or how I've never felt more terrified than I did at that moment when he asked me if I had a death wish, I can only cry.

I hear his phone ring and quickly finish my meal before the next shock comes at me. The running water to wash the dishes drowns out his conversation, and when I'm done, I turn around to see him standing there behind me.

"Time to get settled in. Come with me."

The relief I felt a few moments before when I believed he wouldn't kill me evaporates as I follow him into the living room. There waiting for me is a single orphaned wooden chair from some dining set long gone from his apartment. It's placed in front of the TV, but just the sight of it makes me feel like I'm going to throw up my eggs.

"What's going on?" I ask, unable to stop the words from coming out.

"I have to go back to work, but you're staying here," he explains as he steps behind the chair. "Come here."

Staying here? Alone? He trusts me to stay in this apartment alone? For how long?

I do as he orders and stop next to the chair, still not understanding what he's got planned for me. "How long will you be gone?"

Pointing down at the seat, he answers, "A few hours. Sit down. I won't be gone so long that you'll be uncomfortable."

Now he cares about my comfort level? What's going on? He hasn't cared one bit about me being comfortable since the moment he hauled me out of my home hours ago. Why now would he care?

My hands begin to shake, but I do as he says and sit down on that old wooden dining room chair. It creaks when I put all my weight on it, and then I realize he's leaning over the back of it so his face is next to mine. In his expression, I don't see anger or rage or anything I've usually seen in it up until now, further confusing me.

"Cason, what's going on?"

I hate how scared I sound, like a frightened little girl being forced to do something for the first time and not sure she can handle it. I want to be brave. I want him to think I'm strong. But at this moment, I'm anything but and feel like I'm going to burst into tears at any second.

Out of the corner of my eye, I see the rope for the first time. All of a sudden, everything makes sense.

The chair. Where it's positioned in the room. His concern about my comfort.

Terror races through me, and then faster than I could ever imagine a person could move, he wraps the rope around my wrists, my ankles, and my chest, restraining me to the chair even worse than he did to ride in the car. His large hands move deftly, proof that this isn't his first time tying someone up.

"Cason, I swear I won't do anything. Please don't tie me up like this. What if I have to go to the bathroom? Please," I beg, but to no avail while I tug against my restraints.

All he does is shake his head and smile. "I won't be gone for long."

And just as I think this couldn't be worse, he pulls out a red bandana. Holding my head still, he stuffs it into my mouth. Looking down at his handiwork, he moves his hand next to my face and gently caresses my jawline. I want to shake my head so he can't touch me like that. I want to cry out past the piece of fabric pushed into my mouth.

But more than anything else, I want to cry.

His hand slides down so it circles my neck, his fingers pressing just hard enough into my flesh to be an unmistakable warning. "Be good, Lily, and I promise you'll be happy you behaved. Try to scream or cry out for help, and I swear to God what I do to you will be beyond your wildest nightmares," he says in a low voice that sounds almost like a lover's.

If he wasn't threatening me.

His expression is emotionless, but in his eyes, I see

something I can't place. It's not anger or even unhappiness. If anything, the look in his eyes is one I've seen before in men.

The look they get just before they get off. That's it. He's enjoying this. This thrills him some way.

Sobs overwhelm my urge to tell him to fuck off, and he walks over toward the TV to turn it on. How nice of my captor.

Pointing the remote at it, he flips through the channels and says, "I'll put something on for you to watch so you don't get bored. I won't be long. Remember, be good, Lily."

He leaves me sitting there tied up to that chair with his words echoing in my head. Be good, Lily.

It's all I've ever been, and look where it's gotten me.

CHAPTER FOUR

*E*ason

Some issue with one of our rivals takes up my first fifteen minutes back at the estate, so by the time I get to find out what my new job is, Victor's as wound up as a spinning top. That's never a good thing. My father rarely makes my life easy when he's like this.

I watch him pace back and forth across his office from his desk to the French doors and back again no less than ten times. His hands flail around in front of him as he mumbles about Duke and how much he's going to fucking make him pay.

Halfway through this show, I consider making my way out of the office and coming back later, but he sees me standing there, so there's no escape for me. I know better than to interrupt him when this madness of his settles in, so I prepare myself for the wait and the eventual explosion when he comes out of this.

I do have to wonder why he doesn't just strike at Duke, for fuck's sake. He and that asshole he has working for him, a psycho named Tap who acts like all this fucking job involves is killing, have crossed him twice this year. I don't know all the details about what happened since Victor likes to keep his business to himself, except for these bouts of craziness he sometimes shows all of us, but I do know that Duke guy has it coming.

My father stops midway through one of his passes through the office and turns to face me. Beads of sweat cover his forehead, and his cheeks are bright red. Christ, he looks like he's going to stroke out at any minute.

"What's going on with Harry? Any movement on his end?" he asks in a strange voice that sounds almost pleading.

Shaking my head, I wonder why he thinks there would be any change from just a few hours ago. Maybe he is having a stroke. Just what I fucking need. I need to get the hell out of this office before I get stuck in the middle of some health crisis with my father. That's the last thing I want today.

"No. He said he needs a week. I figure having the girl will put a rush on how fast he gets you the money, though."

"The girl?" he says like he has no idea what the hell I'm talking about.

"Yeah, the girl. Harry's daughter. Lily."

He stares at me for a few seconds like he still can't figure out who I mean but then nods his head and smiles. "Oh yeah. She's not bad. If I wasn't busy with so much, I'd have kept her here."

"She'd drive you nuts. All she does is talk. I swear to God the woman is a non-stop talking machine. Even threats don't work with her. She even tried to talk to one of my neighbors when I took her back to my apartment. Like I want to have to threaten the old lady on the second floor because she can't stop herself from asking strangers to call the cops."

"Maybe you should hand her over to your brother. She's young, close to his age, I imagine. He seems to like chatty girls."

Balling my hands into fists, I silently correct him. My half-brother. Your other son from your wife, who is not my mother. Fucking Michael.

I don't give a fuck about what happens with Lily, but what I do goddamned care about is handing anything over to that asshole that has even the slightest possibility of bringing him even a single moment of happiness.

"He's busy with his girlfriend, remember? That's the reason he's been down on the island instead of here with us," I bite out through clenched teeth.

I can barely hide how much I hate his other son when I say that. It must be nice to be the golden child who doesn't have to do anything but lay around getting high and blowjobs at our private villa in the Caribbean while everyone else does their job.

"That's right. He won't be back for a couple weeks, so that doesn't work."

"Not to worry. I've got this covered. It's only seven days. I can handle her."

My father chuckles. "Well, then fine. That works with what I called you about anyway."

I wait for him to continue, but all he does is start pacing again. Does he mean he wants me to bring her back here so he can have at her? That would make my life infinitely easier since she can't seem to follow the only goddamned direction I've given her so far. Not that I think she'll be much better with him, but then again, maybe she will since he'll probably slap her around the first time she starts running off at the mouth.

Finally, after another two passes through the room, he points at me like he's ready to tell me what the hell he wants me to do. "I have a job I need to you to take care of. It's out near the country house, so why don't you take the girl there? Handle what I need you to do and keep her away from people. The last thing we need is her making noise. The nearest house is miles away, and I'll have Sanderson send a few guys out so if she gets away, you'll have backup to grab her quickly."

"The country house?" I ask, not believing he's sending me out there while I have to do a job.

"Do I fucking stutter?" he snaps.

"No."

"Good. Keep her out there for the week so I don't have to deal with it."

I'd worried as I watched him spiral out of control for the past fifteen minutes that what he called me back for would just add to the shittiness of my day, but this might not be horrible. I don't like having to go out to the house, but Lily will be kept away from the rest of the world for the week so I don't have to constantly have my eyes on her, and I'll be able to take care of whatever my father wants done.

"Fine. I'll head out there as soon as I leave here. So what's the job?"

Running his hand over the top of his head, he takes a deep breath in and sighs. "Creighton. He's become too much of a liability. He needs to go. Take care of it and make that problem go away. Then you can have the rest of the week to play house with the girl."

I know what he's referring to with play house. The sly smile he gives me to punctuate his last statement tells me he thinks I should enjoy the one thing Lily has to offer since I have to spend time with her anyway. I chuckle like I agree and plan to do just that, but the truth is as much as she's gorgeous and I can think of half a dozen things I'd like to do with that beautiful mouth of hers, the one thing I want from her and her mouth is some peace and quiet.

Too bad that doesn't seem very likely to happen in my future. A week in the country could be relaxing, though. The place has the best of everything, so it's more like a week at a luxury resort than it is a cabin in the sticks. But a week in the country with her is likely to make me as crazy as Victor seems today.

"I'll let you know when it's done."

As I head for the door, he mumbles something

about having a good time and returns to pacing and cursing out Duke for whatever the hell he's done. I hurry out before he stops me and forces me to listen to more crazy talk. I don't need any more of his chatter either.

TWO HOURS OF UNEXPECTED SILENCE ON THE DRIVE out to the house in the country makes me wonder if I'd been all wrong about Lily. True, she tried to escape when I finally let her out of those ropes back at my place, and I had to threaten her again, but maybe it's finally sinking into that pretty little head of hers that I would do it.

I kill the engine and turn around to look at her tied up in the back seat. Her eyes widen as she looks out the window at the new place she'll be staying at for the next few days, and I can't avoid noticing she seems far more innocent than a grown woman should be at this moment.

Pushing that thought out of my head, I explain the realities of the next week to her. "I won't be keeping you tied up while we're here, but don't put it past me to tape your mouth shut if you won't stop talking."

Lily turns her head to face me and grimaces. "Nice way to ruin all the beauty."

Fucking smart mouth.

"As for the beauty, feel free to enjoy it. Just know that in case you're thinking it's the perfect chance for escape, it isn't. Guards watch every square inch of the property, and the fence that marks the edges of it is electrified. Even if you try to get past it, you'll get a jolt of electricity that if it doesn't kill you will slow you down enough so security finds you. And they'll bring you right back to me."

"Charming. So I can walk around outside and get some fresh air without being tied up?"

I nod, happy to imagine her spending all her time outside. Hell, maybe I can find a tent for her somewhere so she can camp out at night. That would give me that peace and quiet I want.

"Feel free to spend every minute you're here outside. You aren't going to be able to escape, so get all the fresh air you want."

I turn around to get out of the car, but as usual, she has more questions.

"What will you be doing then while I'm outside all the time? Will there be other people here with us? Do people live in this house and we'll be guests?"

I close my eyes and take a deep breath, letting it out slowly as her questions hang in the air between us. Why are there always so many questions with her?

Looking back at her in the rearview mirror, I answer them one by one. "I'll be working or trying to relax. There won't be any other people here, except security and they stay somewhere else. And no, nobody lives here, but yes, we are technically guests of my boss, who owns this house."

I stop for a moment and then add sarcastically, "Any other questions?"

Her gaze fixes on mine for a long moment, and in her dark eyes, I see hints of what could make a man go crazy for her. Beyond the beautiful face and the hot body, those eyes can look so incredibly innocent that even a corrupt soul like me could want to protect her.

"No. I think that's it," she says with a smile that lights up her face and erases that innocence that was there just a second ago. "Thank you for answering my questions, though. That was very nice of you."

I ignore her attempt to ingratiate herself with me and push the car door open to get out. Innocence my ass. Whatever she is, I can say with certainty that she is way too damn crafty to be considered anything close to innocent.

By the time I get over to where she's sitting in the back seat, she's ready to jump out the door and start enjoying that fresh air she's so interested in, even though she's still bound at her wrists and ankles. Fidgeting like a kid who's had too much sugar that day, she hums some silly song as I untie her and step away from the car. She bounds out like that jacked up child and stops to stretch her arms out to her sides and breathe in the air.

Turning back to look at me, she smiles. "You don't have to worry about me running away from here, Cason. Your bigger problem will be making me leave this place to go back to my father's tiny old house. Your boss must really like you to let you stay here with me this week. This place is incredible!"

I glance up at the house and cringe as memories of my time at this place pass through my mind. The cream colored stone French Provincial façade in front of me conceals an ugliness that's woven into the fabric of my family.

As I march past her up the grey and cream stone walkway toward the front door, I say, "Feel free to stay outside here as long as you like. Remember, the guards can see every move you make out here, so don't do anything stupid."

Behind me, I hear her say, "Who would do anything stupid in such a beautiful place?"

"People do stupid things everywhere," I mumble as I climb the steps. "I don't see why this place should be any different."

Whatever she says in response to that I don't hear, but she yells, "Are those stables over there?"

I stop at the front door and turn around to see her pointing toward the garages. "No. Used to be, but now all you'll find in there are cars. No horses."

The happiness drains from her face, and her shoulders sag in disappointment. "Oh. Okay. This place is still pretty great, even without horses."

Answering her seems pointless, so I turn back to the front door and push it open. "I'll make sure to let my boss know you approve of his horseless house," I mumble as I slam it shut behind me.

After I get myself settled into one of the six available bedrooms, I sit back on the bed and close my eyes for a minute. Thankfully, the drive wasn't filled with Lily's endless talking, but even silent the two hours here has wiped me out.

Not that there's any hurry in getting to Creighton. He's hiding out at a house about fifteen miles away thinking no one has any idea where he is. Little does he know one of his buddies gave his old friend up to my father last week. Since then, it's been a matter of when, not if, he'd take care of business with him.

I've got eyes on him to let me know if he tries to move, but I don't expect it to happen. He has nowhere left to run after burning all his bridges. Signing a deal with Victor was his first mistake. His last was reneging on it.

You sign your name on the dotted line, you better be prepared to do whatever you pledged you would. Now he gets to find out what happens when you don't.

Before then, though, I plan to relax and maybe eat a nice meal, assuming there's anything in the refrigerator since the last time Victor and his wife spent time out there last summer. That can happen later, though. Now, I just want to close my eyes and enjoy the peace and quiet.

"Cason! Where are you? Are you up here?" Lily yells, breaking the silence.

All I want is for her to stop intruding on the only thing I want in this world. How can that be so fucking impossible?

I know she'll keep yelling for me if I don't answer, so I open my eyes and bark back, "I'm in here. Go find yourself a bedroom and make yourself at home!"

There are six bedrooms in this house. Five of them aren't the one I've chosen, which means there is no reason for her to come in here where I am. Yet, a second later, that's exactly what she does, flinging the door open and walking right in.

"Go find somewhere else to go, Lily. I'm working. Go away."

Ignoring my order to leave, she looks around the room, examining it. "This is gorgeous! Is this where you usually stay when you come here?"

"This isn't a hotel. I stay where there's a room available," I answer as the reality that there will be no peace and quiet for me in my immediate future fills my brain.

"Do all the rooms look like this?" she asks as she continues to study the pale blue-green walls and the dark wood bedroom furniture that has been here since I was a child.

"Why don't you go check them out for yourself?" I ask in frustration, already wishing this house was twice its size and she'd get lost in it.

My question makes her stop looking around the room, and she focuses her attention on me once more. "I get that you're the guy holding me hostage and all, but do you have to be so nasty all the time?"

"Would you rather I tie you up again and stuff the gag back in your mouth like I did back at the apartment?" I pull out my gun and point it at her. "Or maybe remembering who I am might help you figure things out?"

The last question makes her eyes well up with tears. She stares at me with a look of pure hurt in them before storming out and slamming the door behind her, leaving me confused.

Setting my Glock down on the nightstand, I wonder if this is how she plans to convince me not to kill her, if that time comes and her father won't pay up. Does she think making me talk to her is the way to stay alive?

If she does, she's wrong. Dead wrong. I kill people. That's what I do. That's who I am. And no one is going to change that. Not even a beautiful girl with innocence in her eyes and a mouth I can't stop thinking about and how it would feel wrapped around my cock.

CHAPTER FIVE

*L*ily

My feet pound against the polished hardwood floor of the hallway as I march toward some unknown destination. I can't think straight. My mind fills by the second with hate and loathing for that man. I try to be nice. I try to make the best of the situation we're both stuck in, and what does he do?

Fucking threaten me!

I swear to God the man has a one track mind. Someone's difficult with him? Threaten them. Someone's kind to him? Threaten them. Someone's merely existing in the same world as him? Threaten them.

What a jackass! Fucking barbarian.

Halfway around the second floor, I stop, unsure where I am in the house. "I'm sure he'd love it if I just got lost in some study or something and he never had to deal with me again," I mumble as I look around for where to go now.

It's the middle of the goddamned day, so it's not like I want to sleep. Not after being tied to that chair for God only knows how long. I want to stretch my legs and move around. I want to breathe in the fresh air of a beautiful September day. Unlike Cason, I'm not an old bastard who needs to nap during the afternoon. Some mob guy he is. He probably falls asleep during a hit.

My brain swirls with questions as I head toward the door to go outside and enjoy myself while I can. Who knows when he'll change his mind and tie me up to a goddamned chair again?

Do mob guys do hits? What is a hit anyway? That's killing someone, isn't it?

I shake my head as these questions clog my thoughts. What do they matter anyway? I'm definitely not a hit. Am I? No, I can't be. I'm not important enough. Either is my father. He's just an old man obsessed with his plate collection. Too bad he was too stupid to understand you don't take a loan out with mobsters.

Not that he's the one suffering. He and those fucking plates are safe and sound, while I get to spend time with the crankiest hit man ever.

Suddenly, I stop on the stairs as a terrible thought pushes every other one out of my mind. My father is safe, isn't he?

I turn around and run back to Cason's room. He's still lying back against the pillows on that enormous bed, his eyes now closed like he's asleep. I don't care. He needs to wake up and tell me what's happened to my father right now.

"Is my father okay? I need to know."

For a few seconds, Cason doesn't open his eyes. Fuck, is he really asleep in the middle of the afternoon? How old is this guy anyway? My father naps in the afternoon, but he's in his fifties. I didn't think Cason was that old, but I'm beginning to think he just looks good for an old guy.

Creeping across the floor, I stop a few feet from the bed and yell. "Cason! Wake up! I need to know if my father's okay."

My screaming doesn't startle him, oddly enough, and he slowly rouses, opening his eyes to glare at me. "Why the fuck are you screeching like a fucking animal?" he asks in a calm voice, utterly wrong for the moment.

"I need to know if my father's okay. You took me to ensure he'll pay back the money he took, right? That's how this goes, isn't it? Nobody went over to the house and hurt him, did they?"

"That's not how it goes. People in my business don't hurt people. We kill them," he answers flatly, like all of this concern rushing out of me bores him.

"Stop being such an asshole! Just tell me if my father's okay or not! Try being a decent human being for two seconds for once. Is he okay or not?" I scream, tears forming in my eyes as I grow desperate to get a straight answer from this guy about the most important person in my life.

My emotional explosion seems to unnerve him, and he stares at me like he doesn't know what to say. It's an easy fucking question, jackass. Is he okay or not? This isn't rocket science or brain surgery.

I want to strangle him for every second I stand there waiting for some coherent answer that will tell me what I need to know. Finally, he nods his head and shrugs. I'm asking about someone's life, and this guy shrugs. I can barely contain how much I hate him right now.

"My boss wants the money Harry owes him, so I'm sure he's fine."

Even though his words filter through to my brain and I know my father's okay, I still can't stop the whirlwind of emotion inside me. Hearing the answer I'd hoped for doesn't calm me at all. I'm still just as furious as I was before he told me that. I want to hit something. Someone. I want him to feel as terrible as I just felt for the last few minutes when I didn't know if my father was alive or dead.

"You know, none of this is okay. Taking someone as a hostage to get your stinking money. Hurting people like you do. Acting like what you do is fine because the people you hurt deserve it. Well, I don't deserve it. I've never done anything to you or your boss. I don't deserve this, and I don't deserve to be tied up or threatened all the time or any of it. And the fact that you think I do shows there's something wrong with you."

The entire time I'm unraveling right there in front of Cason, tears stream out of my eyes and down my cheeks, making him turn into a blurry, watery version of himself. I can't see how he reacts because the tears make it impossible to focus on his expression, but I don't care. I watch to make sure he doesn't get off the bed and lunge at me or point that damn gun of his at me again, but other than that, I don't care how he feels about what I have to say. I don't care because at least I know my father's okay.

I also don't care because this person sitting on the bed in front of me—this hazy, watery thing with no feelings and no heart—means nothing to me.

If he has anything to say to my outburst, he doesn't voice it before I spin on my heels and storm out of his room. I run down the hallway, still blinded by tears, and take the stairs by twos to get the hell out of that house and out into the fresh air and only freedom I have now.

My emotions stay limited to my screaming at him and crying until I get outside, but it takes only seconds for them to completely spill out once my feet hit the soft grass in the front yard. It feels so cool against my skin and so perfectly natural, unlike the rest of my existence at that moment, that I collapse onto the ground as my emotions overwhelm me.

Squeezing my eyes closed, I still can't stop my tears from coming as thoughts of my father sitting in our little house wondering what's happening to me mix with memories of my mother and how much I wish I'd had more time with her. If I had, maybe I'd know how to be the kind of person who could handle what I'm going through instead of bumbling around in the dark, unsure of how to deal with Cason so he doesn't finally follow through on his threats and kill me that one time I say the wrong thing or look at him the wrong way.

I don't know how to be the person I need to be to stop someone who thinks it's okay to take a person hostage, threaten them, and tie them up like a bunch of unwanted papers you set out for the garbage. Maybe I'm too young. Maybe I'm not smart enough. I don't know.

All I do know is I have to find a way to make it out of this alive. The problem is how?

"You know, they treat that grass with chemicals."

Lifting my head, I see the person who said that, and it's not Cason. I quickly scramble to my feet as the tall man with dirty blond hair standing there watching me smiles.

"I didn't mean you had to get up. I just figured I should mention that. You know, in case you didn't know about the stuff they put on the lawn."

His gaze drifts down my body, so I follow it and see I have a few blades of grass stuck to my pants. I brush them off and look up to see him still smiling at me.

"Who are you? Do you live here?"

"Nate. I'm one of the security team here. We stay in the shack at the front of the property. I was just coming up to find Cason. Is he in the house?" he says very politely.

"I have no idea where he is," I answer far less graciously than this Nate person deserves. It isn't his fault that I hate the man he's looking for.

My rudeness ends our conversation, much to my regret, and Nate's smile fades away. Instantly, I regret how I've acted toward him and apologize.

"I'm sorry. I didn't mean to say it like that. It's just..." I hesitate to tell the truth of my situation, but if this guy works here, he's probably seen someone like me under the same conditions before, so it won't be any surprise to him.

"You know, I'm not here as a guest," I say, finishing my idea with something far less obvious than I'd intended.

I want to tell the truth—that I'm being held against my will—but I remember how Cason acted when I tried to get help from that lady at his apartment building. Better to choose my words far more carefully this time.

Nate doesn't answer for a long moment before smiling once more. "I know why you're here. Don't get your hopes up. I'm not going to help you get away. I value my own life far too dearly."

Immediately crestfallen that he's just another Cason, I turn away and mumble under my breath, "How heroic. Good to know chivalry isn't dead out here in God's country."

I leave yet another person who doesn't give a damn that I'm being held against my will and walk off to explore the property. Cason's warning about the electrified fence around the perimeter never leaves the front of my mind, but I enjoy the ability to at least have some measure of freedom.

It's not true freedom, but for the time being, it's all I have, so I plan to make the most of it.

FOR TWO HOURS, I BEHAVE LIKE A TRUE CHILD OF nature. I walk across the cool grass, loving the feel of every step I take. I climb a large tree for the first time in my life and sit on the branch to look out over the landscape like I assume boys do when they climb trees. Power surges through me, like I'm the ruler of some tiny kingdom containing only me and the nature surrounding that tree, but that power feels better than anything I remember in a long time.

When I grow tired of ruling from my branchy throne, I climb back down to Earth and roll around on the grass. So what if they use chemicals on it like that Nate person said? I don't care. The softness of the grass feels good against my skin.

And anyway, this may be one of my last days to enjoy grass and trees and fresh air, so why not take advantage of every precious second I can to revel in all of it? That's the truth I can't escape from in those hours alone wandering around the grounds. If my father doesn't pay the money he owes Cason's boss, I'll be dead at the end of seven days.

That reality colors every blade of grass I touch, every branch I cling to, every breath I take into my lungs. It ruins me, and then it strengthens me.

Cason will kill me at the end of this week if my father can't pay the money back. I understand that on my travels around the property, and now as I walk back to the silent house I'm to spend my time in for the rest of that week, I accept that fact.

He will kill me. He's threatened it more than once already, and I have no illusions that he's a man who will do anything other than what he must. No amount of sweetness or tears will help me.

So I come to a decision out there in nature where no one tells me to shut up but still I say nothing. I will give him what he's wanted from me since he dropped me into the back seat of his car. He'll get his silence.

Nate is nowhere to be found as I walk up the stairs after looking through each room for some sign of him. Not that I expect him to be here. It doesn't matter if he is. He's already made it clear that he's no one who will help me, so he can stay wherever the security guys belong.

My curiosity about Cason and if he's still in his bedroom nearly makes me check. It's my nature to be that kind of person. I don't know if I've been that way since birth or if losing my mother and having to take care of my only remaining parent made me that way, but I've always liked to know where everyone in my life is at all times. It's made me a careful and doting friend, probably a smothering one to some people.

As much as I hate the idea that someone like Cason is in my life, I can't escape that truth either. For good or bad, he is, and that makes me want to know where he is.

I don't check his bedroom, though. I won't be able to keep silent if I see him, and that's what I need to do now. So I walk past his room and peek into the one next to his, cracking the door just a few inches to take a look.

Unlike his room with its blue-green walls, this one's walls are painted a cream color and the furniture is a light wood. The bed and windows have been decorated in a brown and black geometric pattern that seems far more masculine than the room Cason chose. The rectangles and triangles make me uneasy with their sharp edges, so I close the door and move on to the next room.

As soon as I open the door, I see pale pink walls and white wood furniture. The rug in the center of the dark hardwood floor is a matching pink, and I run in to feel its softness on the soles of my feet. Whoever decorated this room with its pink walls and matching draperies and bedspread had to be a woman or know what women love.

I spin around on the soft pink carpet, spreading my arms out wide and closing my eyes at how welcoming this room feels compared to the one next door with its jagged edges. I'll stay here with my silence, far enough away from Cason to avoid him but close enough to hear when he comes and goes.

As much as I don't feel tired in the least, I throw myself onto the bed and relax in what may be the most beautiful bedroom I've ever been in. Some of my friends had rooms like this in their homes when they were little girls, but I never did. My room remains the way it was my entire life with its tan walls, brown carpeting, and twin bed I've slept in since I moved from my crib.

Closing my eyes, I revel in the feel of the king size bed I now get to rest on and let my mind wander to a place where I'm not a hostage of Cason's, he's not in my life, and my father and I are safe and living in a home like this. He wouldn't have to worry about having to sell any of his belongings to afford things, and he'd get to be the man he's always dreamed of being with his collectable plates and the prestige that comes from owning them.

And then, just as my brain succeeds in pushing everything awful out until only my fantasy about that future remains, Cason's voice rings out, ripping me back to reality.

"Lily, where are you? Answer me."

I don't want to answer him. I don't want to speak to him. I don't want to give him that so he can complain that all I do is steal his precious peace and quiet.

He doesn't knock, instead flinging open my bedroom door and stomping in like some invading barbarian into my pink sanctuary. I stare at his face with all the disgust I have inside for him and his intruding on the only happiness I've had since he took me from my home.

My nature is to ask him what he wants since he's standing there looking at me, but I promised myself I would give him that silence he's berated me for over and over. So our gazes lock while neither of us says a word. It's strange and awkward for both of us, and finally, he gives in and breaks the silence.

"I called your name. Why didn't you answer?" he asks with more than a hint of impatience.

I want to tell him I didn't care to answer him, but I say nothing and simply shrug. It's far more difficult saying nothing than I imagined, and more than once my lips part to let the words out before I catch them and swallow them down, entire phrases in my throat nearly choking me.

He wanted silence. Now he can have it.

CHAPTER SIX

*C*ason

I swear this woman has some kind of split personality. One minute she's rambling on about whatever pops into her head, and the next she's as silent as a statue and looking at me like I'm the one invading her privacy.

"Lily, where did you go?" I ask, not even really interested in knowing the answer but wanting to assert some control over her.

Finally, she says, "Out."

And that's it.

Somehow, the girl who couldn't stop talking now has nothing to say. All the better. Maybe I'll get some peace and quiet now. Suddenly, the week ahead doesn't look so grim.

"Well, good. I didn't mention it earlier, but there's no staff, so you're going to have to do the cooking while we're here. I'm going out now, so have dinner ready for six."

I know she wants to say something in response to my command. I see it in her eyes as she glares across the room at me. I wait, but still she says nothing.

"Do you understand?"

"Yes."

Turning to leave, I glance back at her and see that look in her eyes that tells me whatever she's doing with this silent treatment is practically killing her. With a chuckle, I head toward the hallway, but just before I open the bedroom door, she starts talking again.

"Am I allowed to socialize with the other inmates in this prison? I met that Nate guy before, and except for him being as mean as you are, at least every word out of his mouth wasn't a threat."

Her mention of the security guard who came up to relay a message from my father a couple hours ago sets my teeth on edge. I've never liked him because he's a kiss ass and fucking brown noser. He'd stab me or anyone else in the back to get ahead in even the smallest way, and in an organization like Victor's, that shit gets you noticed and for all the wrong reasons.

Looking back at her, I shrug. "Feel free. He's exactly the kind of guy who'd love to hear your constant chatter."

Before she can say anything, I walk out of the room. Let her go talk that dick's ear off. All the better. At least that will keep her out of my hair since I have work to do. And after I take care of Creighton, the rest of the week will be my own to do as I want.

~

His house looks vacant from where I'm sitting on top of a ridge overlooking the valley. A thorough assessment of the place's security tells me he doesn't value his life much. The property has more than a few acres, but he has no set up to keep anyone out.

Then again, maybe all the men he had working for him fled when they heard Victor had decided to move on him. It's not like he kept it a secret from anyone. In fact, he seemed to want Creighton to find out.

"Better to keep him on edge and never know exactly when the end is coming," he said with a chuckle when Jaxon asked him about not keeping his intentions quiet.

That was last week. As I stand up from my perch where I can see every inch of the property and the house, I wonder how fucked up that made Creighton. The guy is probably half out of his mind by now. My father has never been known to be a patient or subtle man, but this time, he's surprised everyone.

Even me.

The memory of him looking half out of his mind himself earlier that day flashes through my brain as I begin to make my way toward the house below. Whatever's going on with Duke isn't going to end well. I want to think we'll come out on top, but shit's been getting uglier in the past few months between Duke's crew and ours.

But that's not what I need to focus on right now.

I've got a job to do, and I want to get it done before nightfall.

With every step down the grassy hill, I get closer to ridding the world of this fuck. Just another asshole who couldn't understand you don't fuck with the people who helped you and you don't turn on your friends. This guy had been as close as close can be with Victor once upon a time. I actually heard he worked for him back in the day.

Then all of that changed when Creighton got himself in too deep with the one vice he never could shake. When his luck dried up and there was nothing left in his bank accounts, his family deserted him and he turned to his old friend for help. He'd known my family for long enough to understand that help always comes with a price.

Maybe it's that he's gotten soft in his old age. Or maybe he thinks Victor has and would cut him some slack. The problem is my father has gotten harder as the years have gone by, and when it came time to pay back what he owed, Creighton ran and hid.

As if he thought we'd never find him out here in no man's land.

He got away with it for a while, I suspect because somewhere in his black heart my father still remembered the old days with his good buddy. That ended, though, so now I get to send his old friend off to the next life.

A single light in a lower room of the two-story old farmhouse house flickers on just as I move toward the back door. For a second, I wonder if he knows I'm here. No, he couldn't. Whatever Creighton used to be or may still be at this moment, he's never been particularly clever or sly. That I do know.

I take a step onto the rotting wooden porch and hear it groan at the weight of my foot. I freeze and wait to hear any movement inside the house, but there's only silence.

A minute later, I've made quick work of the basic lock Creighton put his faith in to protect him and this house and walk inside. The twilight casts an orange hue on the old country kitchen, making it look like one of those Americana pictures I remembering seeing on a trip to a museum in elementary school. Every one of those pictures looked like it had been done by the light of sunset with their oranges and yellows.

With each second that passes, the daylight shrinks behind the horizon, so I don't have time to waste. The last thing I want to do is have to search this old house in the dark to find him.

I head down the hallway, checking each room as I move toward the room with the light I saw from the hill. "Creighton, you knew I'd be coming. It was just a matter of time, now wasn't it?"

He doesn't answer, but I can feel his fear. It comes off him in waves and fills this home that's been abandoned by everyone but him with a tightness that presses down on me.

"All you had to do was do the right thing. You knew that, and still here we are. Don't make this worse on yourself. Be a man when it counts most," I say in a loud voice sure to make it to wherever he's hiding.

And then I hear a creak from the floor not from my own boots hitting the wood and know he's nearby. That whole be a man when it counts most crap always works to unnerve guys like Creighton. That kind of thing matters to them, for some reason. It means something to him that when I report back to my father that I say he died like a real man and not some sniveling piece of shit coward.

That nonsense wouldn't work on me. I wouldn't get all twitchy and give away my position because some guy tried to call me out on being a man. My days of worrying about someone's opinion of me ended when I became the man I am now.

You can't kill and give a fuck about what people think. The two are wholly incompatible. One requires no conscience, and the other requires too much of one. Mine left me the first time I put a bullet into someone and I watched them take their final breath in this life.

When my time comes, it won't be because some asshole tries to guilt me into being something I've never been. If Creighton and guys like him were being honest, they've never been that either.

I stop right before the last room and look down at the floor to see the light shining under the door. Did he actually make this easy on me and put out a light to show where he is? I thought he was smarter than that.

Or maybe he's just accepted his fate. That I could admire. Fuck that shit about being some kind of man he's never been. Just be a stand up human and face what's coming for you with the strength you pretended to have when life was easy.

I push open the door and see him sitting in a chair next to the light. His grey hair hangs over his forehead, giving him a haggard look. I imagine he's been sitting in this very spot for what seems like ages waiting for this moment, the tension of knowing it will happen but not knowing when carving those worry lines deeper into the skin around his mouth that's stuck in a permanent frown now. He's a far cry from the man I heard about from my father and uncles when they talked about him and how much the women fell at this guy's feet.

I guess that falls away like everything else over the years. Fortune, friends, and even fucking women.

His gun rests in his lap, the wrong place for it if he's thinking about making one last stand in this life. I take a step into the room and he fumbles for it, practically dropping it onto the floor.

With unsteady hands, he points it at me and says, "This isn't right. You know it as well as I do. Victor and I were friends."

"And now you're not, Creighton."

"I'm not going without a fight," he says as his hands shake almost uncontrollably.

At this rate, even if I couldn't overpower him, he'd never be able to take a shot at me. At least not one that could have a snowball's chance in hell of hitting me.

"Decided not to take the manly route? So be it."

Before he can answer, I lunge at him and take him to the ground. The gun takes a few hops across the wood floor and comes to a stop too far away for him to have a chance to grab it.

Creighton looks up at me and then over in the direction of the gun as I see reality settle into his expression. Unless he's got another gun and steadier hands, his time is up.

"What are you going to do?" he asks, his eyes filled with utter terror.

It's a stupid question, really, but one someone like me gets more often than you'd think. Maybe they all want to know what weapon will take their life from them. Or maybe they mean how fast will they go.

I don't know, but every time those words hit my ears, I can't help but hope I don't ask something so fucking stupid when my time comes.

"This is the end, Creighton. You know what I'm going to do."

He puts his hands up in front of his face and shakes his head. "Not the face. Just don't do the face!" he begs in a panicked voice.

Vain fuck. It would serve him right if I did mess up his face.

I stand over him and sigh in disgust. "Fine. I won't do your face. Now shut up."

Squeezing his eyes shut, he nods and stiffens his entire body. "Okay. Do it then."

So this is what being a coward looks like. I've killed a lot of men, and never once has one behaved like a frightened little animal before. Most fight me. Some seem resigned to their fate once they see me. No one has ever sniveled like this guy, though. Makes me wonder how my father could have ever called him a friend.

None of that matters, though, so I pull out my gun and aim it at his head for a moment, amused by the idea that he won't have the lovely looking face he so desperately wants for his mourners. Considering the fact that he's got nobody left in life, I question whether anyone will even show up for this fuck's funeral.

After a second or two, I slowly move my aim to his chest. He relaxes his body and peers out from behind his hands just before I pull the trigger, like he thinks I've changed my mind about doing what I've been sent here to do.

No. That's not how this works, Creighton.

One shot and then another into his heart and he's gone instantly. Slumped onto the floor, his hands no longer hiding his face, he exists now only in someone's memory. His expression in death is even uglier than the years marked on his face, but it seems only right for someone so concerned about how he'd look that he'd beg a hitman not to fuck up his face.

I consider going back on my word and shooting him right between the eyes, but I decide not to. Let whatever mourners who bother to attend his funeral get that face as the last thing they ever see of him.

Stepping over Creighton's dead body, I put my gun away and walk out the same way I came in. Some guys like to leave a mess to make it look like someone broke in and killed the guy. Why bother? Most cops aren't going to spend a whole lot of time on an old dead guy nobody gave a damn about by the end of his life. I don't need to construct some fucking story for why he got shot.

People who know him know why, and people who don't know him won't care. That's how it is for everyone. Why the fuck would Creighton be any different?

By the time I get back to the house, I'm hungry and hope to God Lily has made food and isn't in the mood to talk now. Before I may have wanted to for a minute or so, but now I just want silence. I don't know if it's just the way I am after a kill, but I never want to sit around having a good time after one.

I like to think that's maybe my way of respecting the dead, even though I'm the one who made them that way. Maybe not. Maybe I just have nothing to say after putting a few into a guy. All I know is I'm not like other guys who love to brag about that kind of shit after they do a job.

There's nothing to brag about. I did what I was supposed to do. He's dead. And now I get a few days off. Period. End of discussion.

As I open the front door, I hear her laughing and for some reason, rage bubbles up inside me. I don't know why, but I don't want to think about it either.

With every step I take toward the kitchen, my anger builds until I'm ready to pull out my gun and kill someone because she's fucking laughing. When I step into the room and see her sitting at the island with that dick Nate, it takes every ounce of willpower inside me not to shoot the whole fucking place up.

"Having a good time?"

He looks over at me and nods, as if I was talking to him. What an asshole. Lily at least has the good sense to quickly jump off the bar stool and hurry over to the stove where something is cooking. In my rage, I can't seem to smell anything, which is disappointing since it's not a good sign of what my dinner will be like.

"Hey! You're early. Lily said you wouldn't be back until six," he says casually, like we're all friends hanging out for dinner.

I don't bother answering him. I wasn't talking to him anyway.

Lily turns around and gives me a tepid smile as she continually stirs something in a pot. "It's almost ready." She stops herself as she begins to say something else about dinner and points at me. "What's all over your jacket?"

Confused, I look down and see splashes of Creighton's blood on the front of my blue windbreaker. Before I can answer her question, Nate lets out a laugh.

"That's blood. Our boy here had a job to do this afternoon."

I shoot him a look as the urge to pull out my gun and put a couple into him surges inside me. Do I need this jackass's commentary on my job?

Lily turns to face him and shakes her head. "What do you mean?"

Now it's my turn to answer since I have no

intention of letting him talk for me. "He means I had a job to do this afternoon. Kill someone. I did it, so now I want to eat and enjoy some quiet."

She recoils at my answer, backing up into the stove and knocking the pot over so all the red liquid spills everywhere. Lily jumps as it hits her arm and runs out of the kitchen crying.

"Dude, I don't think you needed to say it like that," Nate says as he gets up to begin cleaning up what looks like spaghetti sauce spilled on the stovetop, the countertop, and the floor.

"Why are you here? Don't you have some security shit to handle somewhere else?"

I don't wait for him to answer me before I turn to walk upstairs to my room. As I walk past Lily's, I hear her crying, but I can't help her. She's upset because I'm exactly who I've always been.

Her being around isn't going to change that. She can wish it would, but it won't.

CHAPTER SEVEN

*C*ason

No dinner, thanks to Lily and that asshole Nate. He needs to stay the fuck away from me or risk me sending him off to his maker like I did Creighton.

Stripping out of my clothes, I toss them on the floor in the bathroom along with my blood-stained jacket and kick my socks and boots into the corner. Maybe a shower will make me feel better.

Ten minutes under the scalding hot water and I can at least think straight again. I hate that walking in on those two made me so crazy. Why shouldn't I be happy that she's bothering someone else with all her useless chatter?

It's that Nate shithead. He's the problem. I don't give a fuck about who she talks to, but just having him in my space pisses me off. He needs to go back to wherever he and the rest of the security guys spend their time and leave us alone.

She's a hostage, for Christ's sake. It's not like it's

supposed to be a vacation at fucking Club Med for her this week.

Maybe I should call my father and tell him we need to return to my place. I can keep her tied up for the next six days and be sure she stays out of trouble.

As I rinse the shampoo out of my hair, I remember why staying there was a problem in the first place. She already tried to get that woman on the second floor to call the cops. She'll try again if I take her back there.

Fuck. So we'll have to stay here, unless I can take her back to the estate and give her to Victor. Then she'd be out of my hair and out of my life for good.

Pushing my wet hair back off my face, I tilt my head to crack my neck. He doesn't want her at the estate. She'd only cause problems there, too.

I lean against the white marble shower wall and sigh as the smoothness of the tile presses against my back. We'll have to stay here. Fine. But if that's the case, Nate has to go back to where he belongs. I don't need to have to watch out for two people for the next week.

I don't trust him. That jackass being around might end up with him thinking he can score points by doing something with her. The two of them together spell nothing but trouble. I feel it in my gut.

Turning off the water, I step out of the glass shower enclosure and look straight ahead at the mirror, but it's covered from the steam. I grab a towel and wrap it around my hips before leaning forward to wipe my hand across the mirror to clear it. It's a strange action since I already know what I look like.

It's not like I've forgotten since the last time I checked myself out in a mirror.

"Cason?"

I turn to see Lily standing near the doorway to the bathroom staring in at me like I'm some kind of zoo animal on display she's never encountered before. Her dark eyes are wide like saucers, and her mouth is hanging open.

"What?" I answer, not sure if I should be bothered by how shocked she looks right now.

"I was calling your name. I didn't realize you were in the shower. I didn't mean to bother you," she explains and then looks down at the floor.

"What do you want?" I ask as I push past her into the bedroom.

When she doesn't answer me, I repeat myself. "Did you come up here for any particular reason or just to see me getting out of the shower? What do you want?"

She lifts her head but avoids meeting my gaze. "I wanted to tell you I fixed everything and dinner's ready. It's waiting for you in the kitchen."

"Good. I'll be down in a minute."

"Okay. I won't bother you while you're eating. I'll stay in my room."

Lily makes a move to leave, but I grab her arm, my wet hand catching on her soft skin. "Nope. You'll be there, too. But not good old Nate, so if he's still around, tell him to go back where he belongs."

After a few seconds of hesitation, she says quietly, still not looking me in the eye, "Why do you want me there when you eat?"

"Because you're my hostage, and I need to keep an eye on you."

Finally, she looks up and I see the confusion written all over her face. "And Nate? What's wrong with him staying? He doesn't seem to have a problem with my talking as much as I do, so he'd probably be a good person to keep around if you don't want to have to deal with all my senseless gibberish."

"I'll decide what I want to do with your gibberish. Just make sure he's gone before I get downstairs."

As I let go of her arm, she shrugs like all of this means nothing to her, but I know she's still confused. To be honest, I don't know why I want her around. She can't escape the property, and her talking does get on my nerves. After the day I've had, I don't want to think too deeply about anything, though, so whatever the reason is to keep her close, I'll figure it out some other time.

"Okay. I'll tell him to go."

We stand there silently looking at one another, and I wonder why she isn't leaving. Then it dawns on me. I just told her she's my hostage. She thinks she needs to wait for me to tell her to leave.

I grab hold of the knot in the towel near my right hip and smile. "Unless you want to see me as God made me, you can go."

Her eyes grow wide after a moment, and then her gaze zeroes in on where my hand rests as my meaning becomes clear. A deep pink blush instantly covers her cheeks, and she shakes her head, embarrassed.

"Oh, okay. I better go."

As I watch her scurry away into the hallway, I can't deny she's much cuter when she's like this. Not as difficult and definitely cuter.

At least my cock thinks so.

LILY WAITS AT THE KITCHEN ISLAND WHERE SHE AND jackass were sitting when I came back from the job. Thankfully, Nate is nowhere to be found, so I can eat in peace.

Well, relative peace. Even though she's silent as I eat my first forkful of spaghetti, I know that won't last for long.

As if she can read my mind, a second after my thinking how nice the quiet is, she starts in with the questions. I swear it's like a disease with her.

"Do you know that some people cut their spaghetti instead of twisting it like that?" she asks like it's the most interesting goddamned fact she's ever learned.

I stare at her for a moment, unsure if I want to encourage this conversation, but then I nod as I begin twisting my spaghetti around my fork for a second time. "They sound like animals if you ask me, but I guess it takes all kinds."

Her shoulders sag like my answer in some way deflates her. She returns to being silent for another few minutes and then brightens up to ask me yet something else.

"Do you like it? The spaghetti and sauce, I mean."

The food's not bad. I probably have had better pasta

meals, but she is a good cook like she claimed earlier today. I look up and see her dark eyes full of hope staring at me as she waits for my answer to her question, and for the first time, I don't want to be cruel to her.

"It's very good. Thanks."

And with just those four simple words, her face lights up. "I'm so happy you like it. I wasn't sure if you were a sweet sauce person or a more bitter kind, so I tried to walk a line right between them. My mother always loved very sweet sauce. My father says every time I make mine that it needs more sugar. I guess I tend toward the more bitter kind."

I watch as her emotions dart from happy to worry in a flash as soon as she mentions her father. Her eyebrows draw in toward her nose, making her look like at any moment she's going to cry.

Although it's not my nature at all to be nice to anyone, that expression on her face makes something inside me want to do whatever I have to so it will go away. It's a strange feeling I don't exactly know what to do with, so I stuff more spaghetti into my mouth and wait for the next thing she says.

And when she speaks, her words barely reach a whisper, like she can't bring herself to say them any louder.

"Have you heard anything from your boss about my father paying him the money yet?"

Only someone so completely innocent about the world could even think of asking that question. Her father asked for a week or two because it's going to take him at least that long to raise the money. He didn't just pick a number out of thin air.

I shake my head but don't answer because she doesn't want to hear the truth. Or maybe she does and I don't want to be the one who has to tell it to her right at this moment after I've finished a plate of spaghetti and for the first time today I don't feel like shit.

"Would you tell me if you did?" she asks.

It seems like an odd question. Why wouldn't I tell her if her father paid off his debt?

"Yeah. Why not?"

Shaking her head, she gets that expression again that makes her look like she's about to burst into tears. "I don't know. I don't know anything about this kind of thing. I've never been taken away from my home, tied up, and kept hostage, Cason. I don't know how to act to make sure you don't kill me for doing something wrong or saying something stupid. Well, I guess that's obvious, isn't it?"

I push my plate away from me and take a step back from the island. "I'm not going to kill you for doing or saying something stupid, Lily."

For a moment, I silently congratulate myself on being kinder than I usually am, but she can't let that be. She needs more.

"But you are going to kill me, aren't you?"

Christ. Why can't she just let that be something that stays unspoken?

"Not if your father pays back the money he owes my boss," I say flatly, hoping my obvious disinterest in this topic makes her stop.

"But if he doesn't, that's what you'll have to do," she continues, refusing to let this go.

I've never been someone to want to protect people's feelings, but even now as I try to, she's making it impossible. I don't want to look at her and tell her that yes, I will have to put a bullet in her fucking skull if her father is so stupid to not pay his goddamned debt, but as she stands there staring at me and waiting for my answer, I have no choice.

"That's what I do. It's who I am. Let's hope that I won't have to do that with you, okay?"

She seems to be satisfied with that and silently takes my plate and fork to the sink to wash it. As much as I don't want to keep going with this conversation, I don't leave. I can't explain it, but something about her makes me want to be around her now. Maybe it's because I've accepted all her talking.

Fuck, that didn't take long. One day and I'm a convert.

I don't know what it is, but I feel like I don't want to leave our time together with me explaining I'm a fucking killer. It's true that I am, but for a few seconds, it felt nice to be something else.

When she finishes washing the dishes from dinner, she turns around and looks at me with shock. "I didn't realize you were still here. I didn't mean to be rude. I would have said something if I knew."

This thing with her and talking suddenly strikes me as funny, and I laugh for the first time today. "It's not rude to be silent. If that's the case, I must be the rudest person in the world."

"Well, your manners leave a lot to be desired, speaking as someone you tied up and gagged not an hour after you met me," she says with a tiny smile.

"If I had the sense that you wouldn't run down to my second floor neighbor and try to get her to call the cops, I wouldn't have had to do that."

Lily's mouth opens and closes once and then twice before she shakes her head. "I don't even know what to say to that, to be honest. Punishing me because I want to escape being a hostage seems pretty fucked up, but what do I know?"

The way she says that makes her seem like she's more experienced with the world than a few minutes ago when she naïvely asked about her father paying the money back early. One minute she sounds like a child, and the next she sounds like a grown woman.

As my brain tries to process this difference, she asks yet another question. "So what do we do now here in this place in the middle of nowhere?"

"I don't know," I answer honestly. "I've never been here for more than a few hours at a time. At least not recently."

"Isn't this your boss's house? You don't get to come out here regularly?"

And there, once again, she sounds so innocent, like I'm some businessman and my company has me out here regularly on some ridiculous retreat with other businessmen.

With a chuckle, I shake my head. "Not exactly."

Lily narrows her eyes in confusion and tilts her

head. "Then why did he send you out here with me now?"

Victor's words run through my head, and with a smile, I repeat them to her. "He sent me out here to play house with you."

"What does that mean?"

I consider explaining my father's intention but decide against it. Nothing good can come of that anyway.

"Nothing. I think this place has TVs in each room, so I'm sure you can do that for the rest of the night."

"What are you going to do? Are you going to watch TV all night and then go to sleep?" she asks with a hint of something definitely not innocent in her tone.

I take a step toward her and stop. She tilts her chin up defiantly, like she wants me to see she isn't that weepy girl who was just standing at the kitchen island with me a short time ago. I can't deny she's beautiful. Even after the day I've put her through, she's still stunning, and in her eyes, I see a curiosity growing that wasn't there before.

It would be nothing to do exactly what my father suggested for the next few days. But she's eighteen and only a girl, no matter what she likes to pretend. At that age, I knew more than she did but definitely not what I know now at twenty-seven.

Still, she's legal and my prisoner.

"I don't know what I'm going to do," I say as I take another step closer to her. "It's been a long time since I

ABBI COOK

had a few days off. Maybe I'll just lay around in bed for the next few days."

Lily's eyes open wide and then narrow as I suspect she begins to understand my meaning. Pursing her lips, she smiles in a way that's perfectly wicked.

"Well, then maybe I'll do the same. I am stuck here for the duration, so I don't really have a choice, do I?"

I shake my head as my brain fills with thoughts of what it would be like to play house with her. Glancing down her body, I silently admit I have nothing else I'd rather do for the next six days than take advantage of what's right in front of me. I don't generally make it a practice to sleep with the people I may have to kill just days after fucking them, but then again, maybe her father will do the right thing and pay his loan off.

Walking past her into the hallway, I hear her make a sound like her breath hitching in her chest. Someone else seems to have more than watching TV in mind for the next few days too.

CHAPTER EIGHT

*L*ily
      I know what he's thinking. He's a man. Of
course he's thinking that. I'm not stupid. I'm
young. They're not the same.

It's not like I haven't been with men either. Most of
them were technically boys, but it's the same process
whether a guy is sixteen or sixty. I'm not a virgin, and
if sex is what it takes to keep Cason from killing me,
why wouldn't I?

He's not hideous, by any means. In fact, once I saw
him standing there in his bathroom in only a towel
barely clinging to his hips, I made up my mind to use
what my father likes to call feminine wiles. The way he
usually talks about them makes it sound like they're
bad things, but desperate times call for desperate
measures.

Now I just have to figure out how to approach
him.

These thoughts bounce around in my head as I

climb the stairs toward my room. I don't have any sexy clothes to change into. Looking down at my green T-shirt and black yoga pants, I can't help but be worried that I'm not looking my best to seduce a man holding me hostage. If only I had a dress that showed some skin, I'd feel better about my chances.

Maybe someone left clothes in one of the bedrooms. I can't check the closet in Cason's room, but there are a bunch of others, so hopefully a woman stayed here at some time and left behind a nice dress. Much of the house looks like a female had a hand in decorating it at some point. I just hope she didn't take everything when she left.

I start with my own room, but when I open the doors to the walk-in closet, I'm disappointed by the emptiness in front of me. Not even a single hanger left on the rod. A check of the dresser drawers offers the same.

Nothing but empty space.

Oh, well. Onto the next room.

I make my way to the pointy geometrical design room and open the door as doubts that any woman would want to spend a single minute in this room fill my head. Certainly, this room wasn't designed with any female in mind. That's for sure.

The closet is in the far corner of the room, so I head there as I silently comment about how ugly this room is. The pattern of triangles and rectangles is bad enough, but the brown color makes this a bedroom I could never sleep in.

One glance inside the closet and my guess is

confirmed. Nothing for a woman to wear, but there is a single black and green striped tie draped over a wire hanger. It looks like the kind of tie my father wears to funerals.

Just the thought of someone dying makes my situation all too real once more. Before I close the closet door, I run my fingertips down along the tie and quietly plead with my father to pay Cason's boss before it's too late for both of us.

"Daddy, please do the right thing. For once, do the right thing," I whisper into the silence around me.

I feel the tears begin to form in my eyes, but I push them away, shaking my head. No more crying. I have work to do because even if my father pays his debt, I need to ensure Cason isn't going to kill me like he killed that person this afternoon.

Just as the first bedroom I checked, this one also has a dresser full of empty drawers. Didn't anyone ever leave a stitch of clothing behind when they left this place?

Room after room offers nothing but empty closets and dressers, and with each one I check, I lose a little more hope that I'll be able to have anything other than the clothes on my back to lure Cason to feeling more for me than he does right now. As it stands, I'm little more than a nuisance who talks too much. I need to change that if I ever expect to be able to save myself.

By the time I reach the last bedroom, I've convinced myself all I've done is enjoyed a tour of the house and not much more. Other than an ugly tie, I haven't found anything else, not even an old winter coat left behind.

The final closet has another singular tie much like the other one I found, except this one is red and blue striped. It sort of looks like someone bought them both off the same table at a discount store. Not exactly the kind of thing I'd expect to find in a house this nice.

I pull out each dresser drawer to find the same thing in each one. Nothing. Bending down, I check the last possible place someone could have left anything and see a white T-shirt crumpled up in a bottom drawer. I grab it and shake it out in front of me. It's a wrinkled mess, but it's clean.

Lifting it to my nose, I inhale a deep sniff to make sure it doesn't stink. The last thing I want as part of my seduction is body odor. So not sexy. Thankfully, it smells like it's fresh out of the dryer. This can work. A T-shirt and underwear combo is much sexier than what I've been wearing all day, and I've never met a guy who didn't love seeing a girl wearing that.

A quick but very hot shower will take the wrinkles right out, so I hurry down the hall to my room and strip out of my clothes quickly. Hanging the T-shirt over the towel rack, I turn the water on and step into the glass shower enclosure.

I close my eyes and let the water hit my back, pricking my skin with the scorching heat that makes me flinch. It feels good in some distorted way, but I imagine it's turning my skin beet red. As long as it makes the wrinkles disappear from that T-shirt, I don't care.

A lick of excitement jumps inside me as I remember what Cason looked like in that towel. I knew from being tossed over his shoulder that he had a great body. His muscles and cut abs didn't surprise me. Him being covered in tattoos and his pierced nipples did, though.

My first boyfriend was pierced like that, and I don't know why it thrilled me so much since I didn't even have my ears pierced because my father wouldn't let me do that, but from the moment I first saw those silver barbells through his skin, all I wanted to do was fuck him. Fifteen year old me sneaking out to be with a nineteen year old I knew my father would kill me for dating couldn't get enough of everything about that guy, and his being pierced only added to my need to do whatever it took to have him.

I turn around to face the water and my eyes fly open at how hot it feels on the front of me. Quickly, I move to adjust the handle on the cold water to make it cooler before my face turns bright red. With no makeup here to fix that, I need to avoid that problem. Blotchy skin isn't going to help me with what I'm trying to do in a few minutes.

The momentary shock of the burning water behind me, I soap myself up as I return to thinking about Cason. I know I shouldn't even consider trying to seduce him. He's clearly someone who's had many women in his life. No man with that body hasn't slept with dozens of women in his lifetime.

Maybe hundreds?

I shake my head to push that intimidating thought

out of my head. It doesn't matter how many women he's fucked before. This isn't about love or even him liking me.

It's about him not being able to kill me if and when the time comes. Nothing more. I have something I can use to protect myself, and damnit if I'm not going to put this body to work to make sure I'm alive next week when he and this whole thing are just a memory I want to forget.

It could be worse. I could have to sleep with a man my father's age to save myself. Even worse, I could have to sleep with someone like Cason's boss.

A HALF HOUR LATER, I'M STANDING IN FRONT OF THE bathroom mirror trying to make my hair do something more than just hang straight. Perfectly straight, like not a single wave to be found. No matter how many times I scrunch it, my blond hair falls right back where it was, straight as an arrow.

I look down at the white T-shirt that thankfully isn't as wrinkled as it was before my skin-peelingly hot shower. Oddly sexy, it'll work. It has to.

With one last look at my naked face, I thank God for getting my mother's eyelashes that are naturally long and lick my lips. "It doesn't matter, Lily," I mutter to my reflection. "Men will sleep with anything willing. You know that, so use it to your advantage. You can do this."

I have to do this.

After repeating that mantra another half dozen

times on my short walk to Cason's room, I stop in front of his door and listen for a moment. I hear nothing coming from inside. Is it possible he decided not to watch TV after all?

Disappointment makes my shoulders sag, but I still knock on the door and hope he hasn't fallen asleep or gone out. What kind of guy lets his hostage just stay in a house alone? Yes, the property is guarded, but more than once I've wondered if his electric fence claim was all just to scare me.

As I ponder whether it's possible that I could actually escape this place without getting fried, the door opens in front of me. Standing in jeans and a black T-shirt, Cason twists his face into a look of confusion, as if he can't imagine what I'd be doing knocking at his door.

Like he seems to all the time, he doesn't say a word, so I quickly fill the dead space with my own. "Are you busy?"

Instead of saying yes or no, he answers my question with one of his own. "What happened to your clothes?"

I smile and smooth the T-shirt against my body, making sure to push my breasts out so he can see I'm not wearing a bra. "I'd been in those clothes all day, so I figured when I found this T-shirt that I'd wear it to bed. So you didn't answer my question. Are you busy?"

His eyes narrow as he shakes his head. "No. What do you want?"

Perhaps I was wrong when I said men will sleep

with anything. I know I don't look my best, but is he actually planning to send a young and very willing woman away instead of taking the bait I'm dangling in front of his face?

Undeterred, I smile. "I was bored. What are you doing in there?"

He doesn't give me a smile in return. Instead, he leans in close to me and takes a deep breath in, letting it out slowly as an ominous hum reverberates in the space around us. "I don't know what you're doing, little girl, but trust me, you don't want to tease a man stuck out alone in the country."

"You're not alone. I'm here."

Cason's gaze travels down my body and back up again to meet mine. His lids heavy, he looks at me hungrily. "You're playing with fire here, Lily. You're going to get hurt."

My knees shake at how intimidating he sounds, but I press them together and flash him my best fuck me smile. "I'm not a child, Cason. It's not like I don't know things."

"And what do you think this is? Do you think if you get me to fuck you that I won't want to kill you when the time comes? Is that what you're thinking?" he asks in a low voice, his warm breath drifting over my ear with each word he practically hisses out before he steps back away from me.

My heart sinks at how callously he dismisses my plan, but I can't let him see how frightened I am at this very moment. This can work. I know it can. I just have to see it through.

So I take a step closer to him, close enough that I can feel the heat coming from him through that black T-shirt that fits so perfectly over his toned body. I look up into his dark eyes and swallow hard. "What I was thinking was I didn't want to be alone, Cason."

The words hang in the sliver of space that separates us as I wait for him to respond. He just needs to say yes and I can do this.

He looks down at my T-shirt, and then his hand touches my hip, sending need dancing through me. "I'm not one of those boys you tease to get your own way, Lily. This is your one last chance to go back to your room and pretend this never happened because if I let you come in, the word no doesn't exist in here."

Every word drips with a threat of something he thinks I can't handle, but I don't care. Whatever he is inside that room, at least I'll be alive there at the week's end.

"Okay."

I don't know what else to say. Unlike in the movies where women always seem to say something snappy, I can't think of a single clever thing at this moment. All that fills my brain is a mixture of fear, desire, and curiosity regarding the man in front of me.

Cason doesn't answer and steps back to open the door and let me in. I walk across the threshold with the sense that something has changed the moment the door shuts behind me. The blue-green walls and matching rug look the same as before when I stood in that room and filled my eyes with the vision of him wearing only a towel, but unlike then, I don't feel like

I have the same ability to leave now. He hasn't said I can't, but there's a sense all around me that he controls what happens in this place, and I will play my part in whatever that is, willing or unwillingly.

"So what do you want, little girl?" he says as he stops behind me.

Staring straight ahead, I fix my gaze on the slightly wrinkled bedspread that shows all he was doing was sitting around before I knocked on his door. "I want you to stop calling me little girl," I answer softly before turning my head to look back at him.

His eyes meet mine, but he doesn't say anything. Instead, his strong hands slide around my waist and then drift down to my hips. When he pulls me back against his body, I nearly stumble at the feel of his hard cock pressing against me.

"Feel that? I can't deny you have an effect on me. But I like things rougher than those boys you're used to. You should have thought twice about coming in here."

A shiver races down my spine at the first touch of his lips to the back of my neck. His mouth is soft and teases my skin with things to come, but his words rattle around in my head as his hands tighten their grip on my hips with each second that passes.

My head flops forward when his tongue touches me, the tip of it flicking against my skin. I close my eyes and don't even try to conceal the moan that escapes from my throat. There's no use. Whatever this is in this room, whatever we are to one another here, I have to see all of it through to the end.

My life depends on it.

I feel Cason's hand slide up over my left breast and then clamp around my throat, making my head snap up instantly. He chuckles behind me, moving his mouth away from me to speak.

"You had fair warning, Lily. I told you I wouldn't be like those boys you're used to."

"I'm not afraid," I squeak out as the pressure of his fingers pushing into my skin sends waves of need coursing through me.

His other hand slides up my body from its place on my hip, and he pinches my right nipple between his thumb and forefinger. I press my lips together to stop the moan that wants to come out so badly and squeeze my eyes shut as I struggle not to look so inexperienced that a single touch from him can arouse me this much.

"Your fear is coming off you in waves. I can practically taste it on your skin," he whispers ominously against the back of my head. "What are you afraid of, Lily?"

That you won't care what I do and still will kill me at the end of this week.

That I'm not enough to make you want to save me.

Those thoughts race through my brain, but they're quickly replaced with another more urgent fear I can't deny.

That you're not like all the others and will use that against me.

"I'm not afraid," I lie for a second time, but my words come out shaky and unconvincing, even to me.

His fingers pinch my nipple again, harder this

time, and I can't stifle the moan the pain forces out of me. It sounds like pure need, and I can't help but be embarrassed.

"Maybe it's not only fear I'm smelling after all," he says like he's amused by my reaction.

He takes a deep breath in and holds it, letting it out with his own moan. "No, fear doesn't smell like that. I've smelled fear and it definitely is different from what's coming from you right now. That tells me all I need to know."

I try to stop myself, but a single word slips from between my lips. "What?"

Tightening his hold on my throat, he presses a kiss against my ear and answers my question. "That if I slipped my finger inside you that you'd be fucking dripping wet already. Right, Lily?"

A shudder moves through me, and I close my eyes. He's right. There's no way I can deny it.

My silence confirms his assumption, and he hums his satisfaction. "Nothing to say now?"

I open my mouth to speak, but instead of words a sigh comes out. "I'm not sure what you want me to say to that."

Behind me, he looms large, like a presence that controls everything that's happening between us. I want to sound unafraid, but my fear pours out of me without my permission, confirming all he believes about me.

His fingertips press against my throat, exciting and terrifying me. It would take nothing to stop my breathing, yet in the same vein, he can thrill me merely by his touch. My body fights against trying to escape and craving more of him.

Slowly, he turns me around, and for the first time I see his entire face since I walked into this room. He looks different now, like a darker version of the man I've spent the day with. His gaze roams over my face, studying me as if I'm some strange creature he's never encountered before.

"Tell me, Lily, what do you want coming here tonight?" he whispers just inches away from my lips.

Just the way he says that makes me feel like I'm drowning in humiliation, and from somewhere deep inside me where fear of him doesn't exist come the words I never would have believed I could say.

"If you don't want me, just say so. You don't have to be cruel at this too."

For a moment, he stares at me. I feel like he's memorizing what I look like right before he follows through on every threat he's made to me today.

In a deep voice that hits me like a fist to my chest, he says, "I'm nothing but cruel. Now you get to see the real me."

CHAPTER NINE

*C*ason

My eyes fill with the sight of this girl—this woman—and I can't decide if she simply doesn't fear me or if she's just too innocent to understand she should. Staring up at me, her eyes fixed on mine, she doesn't look away. I've made grown men cry and beg for mercy, yet this girl either doesn't know to or refuses to do those very things.

I can't explain the effect she has on me. Maybe it's because she's so beautiful and so willing, standing in front of me offering herself up to the one person who holds her fate in his hands.

Touching her face, I slowly drag my fingertip along her jaw she's defiantly tilted up to prove to me she's strong. I want her to be strong. I'll be disappointed if she's not. I want her to be the first person under my control who forces me to reckon with their power against my own.

She winces, probably because she thinks I'm going

to hit her. I've threatened her enough times today for her to believe that. But still, she doesn't pull away and doesn't avert her gaze from my face.

I like that. Now I want to see if she'll remain strong when I take all her power away.

My hand drifts down along the column of her neck and over her collarbone I could easily snap she's so much smaller than me. I don't want violence like that tonight, though. I've killed today. Maybe tonight I can do something that feels good.

I hook my fingers under the collar of the T-shirt and tug hard down between her tits, ripping the shirt down the middle. Glancing up, I see her eyes grow wide and fill with fear.

Don't go soft on me already, little girl. We're just getting started. Stay with me and prove you're as strong as I think you may be.

My hand cups her full breast, perfectly fitting against its heaviness like two puzzle pieces made for one another. Her hard nipple pokes against the base of my thumb, teasing me with how perfect she truly is.

Perfect and mine for as long as I choose tonight.

"Why did you rip this?" she asks, grabbing the two ragged sides of the shirt in her hands. "I would have just as happily taken it off over my head."

I don't want to hear about the shirt or what she wanted to do with it, so I pull her to me and kiss her hard. Her lips soften almost instantly, yielding to the pressure of my mouth as I take this first taste of her. My tongue slides into her mouth, and the feel of her giving in to me makes my cock harden like steel.

Stuffing my hand into her hair, I tighten my grip on the soft strands and tug her head back. She doesn't fight me at all, reaching out to run her hands over my chest and down my ribs.

Her need comes off her in waves, and it's nothing less than intoxicating. But it's not enough for me. I want her to beg.

So I pull my mouth away and look down at her to see her eyelids flutter open and her beautiful brown eyes staring up at me. Filled with confusion, that slowly morphs into a look of hurt, like she can't believe I wouldn't want her.

"What's wrong?" she asks, every word laced with the same emotion that now fills her eyes. "Why did you stop?"

I know what she's thinking. I can see it in her face, hear it in the panic that clings to every word. She's set all her hopes for living on being able to make me want her. Smiling down at her, I can't help but laugh at how wrong she is.

She can offer me her very soul, and it won't change a thing. If her father fails to pay back that money by the seventh day, I'll do to her what I've done to everyone else marked for death.

What I did to Creighton just hours ago.

And not even the best fucking sex of my life can stop that from happening.

"Let me hear what you want, Lily."

Pressing her lips tightly together, she seems unwilling or unable to voice what she wants me to do to her. That needs to change. Now.

With a sharp tug of her hair that makes her wince, I give her a taste of what will happen if she doesn't obey my command. "I told you once you come into this room, no is not allowed. So I repeat, let me hear you say what you want, Lily."

In a tiny voice, she whispers, "You."

But her eyes tell the real truth, what she wants more than anything else in the world, and it's not me. It's to stay alive.

For a moment, I consider pushing her away. It could be amusing to watch her desperation unravel in front of me before I send her back to her room to fret for the next six days.

That's the sadistic part of me, but it's not the part that's controlling me tonight. No, tonight need has gotten the better of rage, and I want to know how good it will feel to be balls deep inside Lily.

So I don't push her away, and I take her answer, even though it's a lie. It's enough that I'm going to make her mine tonight. I don't need the truth from her, too.

My mouth crushes hers in a kiss meant to show her what's coming when I take her. And that's what it will be. Taking. If she has any illusions about what I'm after, she needs to forget them right now.

I am who I am, and whether that's a killer or a monster, I'm always one thing. Merciless.

Her hands clutch the back of my neck, surprising me with how much she returns my kiss. I expected her to recoil at its hardness because she's so small and so defenseless, but here she is standing on her tiptoes to meet my need with her own, pressing her lips to mine with the same intensity before sliding her tongue into my mouth to tease me.

Backing away, I smile at her efforts. "Be careful, little girl. I'm not one of those boys you play with."

But she doesn't cower at my warning. Instead, she steps forward, pressing her body to mine, and nips my bottom lip playfully with her teeth.

"I don't play with boys. You're not even the oldest man I've ever been with, Cason. And I'm not a little girl."

Every word drips with defiance I want to rip from her body, but at the same time, her strength arouses me like nothing or no one has ever done before. I want her more than I can explain, and the thought of her being with a man even older than me burrows into my brain like some infection. Within seconds, it's all I can think of.

"Really? So you're not as innocent or sweet as you look?" I ask, my mind consumed with questions about that detail she dropped into our time together.

Her dark eyes grow wide, making her look utterly angelic, but her smile is nothing less than wicked. "I never said I was innocent or sweet. I'm simply me. What you see in that is more about you than anything I am."

Fuck. The unknowing girl I thought I had standing in front of me suddenly seems to be more seductress than she let on all day. That's okay, though. It doesn't change who I am either.

Or what I'm going to take from her.

I slide my arm around her waist and pull her hard into my body, loving the look of surprise that fills those eyes. "Enough talking, Lily. You wanted to be in here, so now you are. What do you plan to do for me?"

Left unspoken at the end of my question is the part I know she'll fill in for herself. To ensure I don't kill you. But that's all in her mind and has nothing to do with me. Sex is sex, and work is work.

And never the two shall meet.

She doesn't answer with a single word, but I watch her slowly lower to the floor so she's kneeling in front of me. Definitely not a bad start.

Her fingers shake as they fumble with my zipper, but she gets it open and a second later, her hand palms my hard cock. The feel of her skin on mine sends a jolt of need racing through me, and for the briefest second, I consider pulling her up off the floor and skipping this to get to fucking her.

I don't, though, because a moment later she takes the head of my cock into her mouth and I can't think of a fucking thing other than how goddamned incredible her lips and tongue feel around me. A woman who knows how to suck cock well is one of the few distractions in this world I've never been able to overcome.

Not that I've tried very hard.

Lily goes to town on my dick like she's an expert, her tongue flicking along the vein that travels up the underside of it and making my eyes roll back into my fucking head. She can't take the whole length into her mouth, so she wraps her fingers around the base and pumps gently as her blond head bobs up and down.

I stuff my hand in that pretty hair and tighten my fist to set the pace. Speeding her up a notch, I push my hips so she has to take just a little more of me each time. She doesn't make a sound or complain, which makes me wonder how often she's done this before.

Why the fuck I should care is beyond me. Who fucking cares how many guys she's blown?

Those questions sound off in my mind, but others drown them out. How old was that guy she was with? When the hell was that? She's only eighteen, so when did that happen?

Distracted with all that, I don't notice when she stops. Only when she speaks do I realize I've completely let myself get lost with shit that doesn't matter when I could have been enjoying getting a first-rate cock sucking.

"Cason, is something wrong?"

Shaking my head, I look down at her. "No. Don't stop."

I expect her to keep talking, but to my surprise, she doesn't say another word and takes my cock into her mouth once more. I watch, mesmerized by how erotic she looks as she slowly slides her lips over me until they reach the side of her hand at the base of my dick. Her eyes closed, she is focused on entirely one thing.

Pleasing me.

To keep myself from thinking about anything else,

I tilt her head back and say, "Look at me while you suck my cock."

She doesn't fight or even try to speak. She just immediately turns her eyes up toward me so she's watching me as I watch her. It doesn't take long for me to realize this is a mistake. Something about those big brown eyes staring up at me makes those fucking questions pop back into my head. I don't want to think about who else she's been with because it doesn't matter. Why my goddamned brain doesn't get that escapes me.

I can't stop myself, though, so another minute of what might be the best blowjob I've ever had and I push her away. She looks up at me with something that appears to be hurt and fear in her eyes, but before she can say a word, I lift her off the floor to stand her up on her feet.

"Did I do something wrong?" she quietly asks, her gaze still fixed on my face even as I wish she'd look away. I don't want to look at that innocence right now.

"Not in the mood for that. Take the underwear off or I'll rip them off myself. Your choice."

The change in me startles her, but she does as she's told just as she has since the minute she walked into this room. That makes my inability to focus on what's right in front of me even more confusing. She's doing what I want. No useless chatter. No complaining. No fighting me.

So what the fuck is my problem?

My cock aches it's so goddamned hard. She gives head better than I've ever had before. Yet, here I am watching her carefully toss her underwear aside instead of fucking her mouth like I rightly should be doing.

I need to focus and stop letting my curiosity about this girl get the best of me. She's a female I can have. I want to have. Nothing more.

"Cason…"

Lily begins to ask me something, but I stop her with a kiss as I undo my pants and push them down to the middle of my thighs. Lifting her to waist-height, I push what's left of her shredded T-shirt up over her stomach and back her up against the wall.

The head of my cock teases the wet opening of her cunt, and I barely get stable on my feet before I lower her in a rush down onto me. I fill her completely in one quick motion, and she exhales a deep sigh into my mouth, followed by a moan that I swear goes straight to my balls.

We stay perfectly still for a long moment before she rolls her hips and sends a feeling through me that makes my head swim. That's all it takes, and I pound into her, loving the feel of her cunt around my cock.

Lily scratches her nails across the back of my neck, and I rear back in pain to see her staring up in terror at me. Her fear feeds me. I want it and need it like I need all she is right now.

I pull out until there's nothing but the last inch of me inside her. For a moment, she looks dazed, like she doesn't understand why I'm stopping.

Shaking my head, I smile. "Don't worry. This I'm in the mood for."

A second later, I tilt my hips and fill her again until I hear that little moan that does something to me I can't explain. It's like a mixture of desire and pain that I swear makes me want to fuck her even harder.

We get into a rhythm of me slamming into her followed by her moaning next to my ear, and with each thrust into her body, she sounds less like I'm hurting her and more like she's enjoying this as much as I am. For as small as she is, Lily takes everything I force on her and still doesn't cry out.

By the time I feel the first twitch of my cock telling me I'm about to come, I'm tired of trying to hurt her. I slow my pace so I'm practically motionless and let my head fall against her shoulder. I've given her all the rage I have and still she's right here with me, her hands clinging to my shoulders as she whimpers softly with every push into her.

Then just as I feel myself beginning to lose control, her cunt tightens around my cock and she comes hard on me. She presses her heels into the bottom of my spine and moans louder before sinking her teeth into my shoulder.

It feels fucking incredible, her body milking me to my own release, and I explode inside her. We fall still when we both finally finish, and as I hold her against me, our bodies both covered in sweat from our fucking, I can't help but admire her strength.

She took everything I forced on her and never gave in. I don't know how, but she did it.

Finally, in the silence of that room, a heavy sigh

escapes from her. It's the sound of someone who finally believes she's safe.

I should correct her about that. She isn't safe. No safer than she was before I fucked her. No safer than she was before she walked into this room.

I don't say anything, though. For a moment in this day, I don't want to be that man.

For the first time in my life, I don't want to be the cause of someone's pain. That feeling will go away soon, but for now, I let it be just as I let her be with her hope that I won't kill her if I'm ordered to.

CHAPTER TEN

*L*ily
　　My eyelids slowly flutter open, and I realize immediately I'm not in my room when I focus on the blue-green walls surrounding me. I'm in Cason's room.

The next moment, the warmth from his body registers in my brain, and I look to my right to see his chest slowly rising and falling while he sleeps. A tattoo of what looks like a skull moves with each breath, up and down as I watch it.

My gaze roams over his skin covered in tattoos, some shaded in grey and others with colors. A woman's face on his chest above the skull. What may be a dragon with green eyes on his right shoulder. Dozens of others I can't make out in the dim light of his room.

A thin stream of sunlight reflects off his nipple piercing when his chest fills with air, and then the glint of light disappears when he exhales. I stare at the silver barbell through his skin and wish I could touch it. In the whole time we were together last night, I didn't even see it.

The hours in this room are a blur, even now as I try to remember all we did. His arm around me says I fell asleep in his arms, but I don't remember that. My memories are filled with little else other than sex.

Violent, passionate, unforgiving sex that began with me on my knees on the floor and ended with me on my hands and knees on the bed. An ache in my thighs and my shoulders reminds me of all the other positions too.

I would have said yes to anything he demanded to make sure he doesn't follow through on orders from his boss to kill me at the end of this week. Not that I didn't enjoy fucking him. He's beautiful and built and has a cock that makes me moan and beg for more. Even more, he's not like those boys he kept referring to. They treat me like I'm a dainty little flower who might break if they thrust too hard.

Little do they know that I like it hard. A little pain adds to my pleasure. So while they worry they might hurt me, I spend my time wishing they'd do just that.

Cason either doesn't worry about inflicting pain on me, or as I suspect, enjoys doing that with everything in his life. The more he tugged my hair, I wetter I became. The harder he fucked me, the more I squealed for more.

We were a match made in heaven. Well, maybe a

few feet below that. If it wasn't for the fact that he's my captor and possibly will be my killer in a few days, we'd be perfect together.

As it was, we were perfect for a few hours.

I can't forget who he is, though. No matter how good he felt inside me. No matter how much he knew just what I needed to get off. No matter how sweet he looks sleeping there beside me.

He's a killer, and he'll kill me if I don't give him a reason not to.

Last night was my first attempt to convince him not to be that person with me. But it doesn't end with that.

A fleeting thought about running away as he sleeps rushes through my mind, but between the guards and that electrified fence, I'd never make it away alive. Better to take my chances on changing Cason's mind.

He moves against my arm and then turns away from me, taking my arm with him as he rolls over. Still asleep, he shifts around before getting settled and holding my hand against his chest. Is he worried I'll try to escape, or does he simply like the feel of me against him?

I don't know, and it doesn't matter. All that matters is by the end of this week he likes the feel of me alive more than he wants to obey an order. I don't pretend to think this will be easy. He's worked for that boss for a long time and only known me for a day.

That doesn't matter either. Men are men, and even the hardest of them want to feel like they aren't despicable pieces of shit with one person in the world. I need to do that with Cason.

I repeat the same mantra over and over when I begin to doubt myself. *I have a body, and I can use it. I don't have a weapon or strength, but I have my body.*

When all you have is your body, then that's what you have to use. Purity and goodness exist only in safety. I don't have that, so they'll have to be patient. For now, whatever he demands of me he'll get, and in return, I hope on day eight I can say it was worth it.

I lay my head on the pillow and close my eyes, ever aware of how tightly he holds my hand to his body. As I drift back to sleep, I say my mantra once more, not even finishing the ending words.

"Wakey wakey. Time to get up."

Cason's deep voice sounds like it's a million miles away, and for a few seconds, I think I'm dreaming. Then I feel his hand on my shoulder pushing hard against me, and I know none of this is a dream.

Opening my eyes, I see him standing next to the bed looking down at me. He's dressed in a white T-shirt and jeans and looks oddly refreshed after the night we spent together.

"What time is it?" I ask as I push my hair back off my face.

"Time to get up. You don't listen well, do you?" he says in a ragged voice that doesn't match his appearance at all.

"Not when I just wake up, no," I mumble and push myself up.

He doesn't continue our sad attempt at a conversation, so I do what I always do. I talk more. Fill the dead space. Maybe he'll jump in with something to say.

"Well, if you won't tell me what time it is, can I at least know what I'm supposed to wear? You ripped that T-shirt and my clothes are dirty. I don't have any others either."

Cason's eyes narrow to slits, and I can't decide if he's angry or confused by what I've said. Slowly, he shakes his head and sighs. "Why do you ask me questions I have no fucking answers for?"

Without missing a beat, I respond, "Because I don't have anyone else to ask. You are the person holding me hostage. That sort of forces me to deal with you."

I want to mention that hours of dealing with him has left me feeling like I need a massage or at least a hot bath, but there's no hint of him being interested in even talking to me, much less about the sex we had last night. The only thing coming off him right now is irritation at my very simple question.

He thinks about what I have to say, and then in a flash, his face is in front of mine, his eyes full of that same rage that so often marks them. "Maybe I should just tie you up in here so the issue of clothes isn't something I have to fucking think about."

The words come out in a hiss, like every ounce of

anger inside him rides out on the back of each syllable. Each one terrifies me, but all of them together make me want to cry. After all we did just hours earlier and now he's threatening to tie me up again?

"No, Cason. Please. Don't do that. I'll do whatever you want. Just don't tie me up again. Please."

My words are nothing short of pure begging, and I don't care. I mean every one of them. I'll do whatever he wants. I just don't want to be tied up again.

He looks into my eyes, and staring into his, I see a hint of humanity in them. He doesn't want to tie me up again. I have to believe he doesn't.

"Then don't ask me about what clothes you should wear. Put the ones on from yesterday and don't talk about them again."

Relief rushes through me, and I eagerly nod, happy to wear yesterday's outfit if it keeps me free. "Okay, I'll do that. Are you hungry? Do you want me to make you breakfast?"

Cason leans back and shakes his head. "You sound like my boss with the playing house shit. Don't get confused about what this is, Lily. In six days, if your father is too stupid to pay up, you get to pay the price."

God, why does every word out of his mouth right now have to be so cruel? Like I could ever forget that I may only have six more days to live.

"I just thought I'd be nice and ask since I need to make myself something to eat. If you don't want anything, okay. I won't make any for you."

He doesn't say anything in response, so I move

across the bed and stand up to go into the bathroom. My legs ache and my shoulders feel the sting from him holding my hands behind my back while he fucked me, and all I want to do is sit in a hot bath until my body doesn't hurt anymore.

I barely get two steps toward the bathroom before he grabs my arm to stop me. His fingers press into my skin, instantly hurting me.

Turning back to look at him, I see him glaring at me. "I just have to go to the bathroom. What did I do wrong now?" I ask, unsure if in my frustration I've pushed too far.

"Don't be too long in there, Lily. And don't even think about climbing out the window and escaping. I'd hate to see that pretty little head of yours get hurt."

His warning comes through loud and clear, but something in the way he says those words make me wonder if he actually would hate to see any part of me get hurt. Not that he isn't in total control of that. He could let me go anytime he wants, and then my pretty little everything would be just fine.

I know there's no point in saying any of that to him, so I just paste a smile on my face and nod. When he lets me go, I head toward the bathroom, but when I take a quick look back, I see him watching me as I walk away.

Closing the door, I have to admit that maybe even though he's just as callous and unkind as before we slept together, perhaps it did have an effect on him after all. Step one in my plan to stay alive might have worked, even if only a little bit.

Now onto step two.

I CLOSE MY EYES AND LET THE HOT WATER COVER MY body as it fills up the bathtub. The only thing missing are the bubbles, but even those wouldn't help my muscles this morning. I point my feet out in front of me and touch the tips of my big toes against the other end of the tub, stretching every inch of my legs from my hips to my ankles. Pain gives way to relief, and for the first time this morning, I feel like a normal human being.

Congratulating myself on what I've accomplished with Cason so far, I plot out what I'll do next. He doesn't have to want me to cook for him to be pleased by it. Twice already, I've seen him genuinely happy because of the food I've made, so I need to continue to offer that to him.

How does that old saying go? The way to a man's heart is through his stomach? I'm not interested in Cason's heart. Just his conscience. But whatever works.

After that, whatever he wants is what he'll get. Sex, however he likes it, followed by food.

Feed him and fuck him so he'll free me. Maybe that will be my new mantra, I think to myself.

A hard knock on the bathroom door tears me from my thoughts, and I open my eyes to see Cason standing over me staring at me for the second time this morning. His gaze zeroes in on my breasts, so I arch my back ever so slightly so my nipples peek out of the bathwater.

"I'm almost done. I promise. I just needed to have a hot bath after last night."

"Do you always just lay there when men barge in on you in the bathtub?" he asks like he's disappointed by my show.

I quickly sit up and push my wet hair off my face. "I figured after what we did last night that I didn't have to pretend to be chaste and cover up like some virgin."

"Time to get moving. I'm hungry, so get out of there and get dressed," he says just as irritated as before, but this time I know better.

He's getting used to the idea of me feeding him. Good. The more he thinks of me as someone who can give him something he wants and needs, the better my chances of staying alive are.

"Okay. I'll be out in a minute. My clothes are back in my room, so I'll have to run down the hall to get dressed. That Nate guy isn't here, is he?"

Cason's expression turns instantly darker, and he spins on his heels out into the bedroom. "Move it or I'll tie you up again, Lily. Understand me?" he barks just before he slams the door and walks out.

I don't answer, but I do understand. I understand far more than he realizes, in fact. I understand that he's getting used to me cooking for him, and I understand he's got some issue with that Nate guy around me.

Whatever his issue is with him, if the opportunity

presents itself, I need to use it to my advantage. That I understand all too well, Cason.

As I dry myself off and knot the towel above my chest, I take a deep breath and look in the mirror. "You aren't some little girl who can't handle herself. Never forget that."

When I walk into the bedroom, I see my black yoga pants and my green T-shirt from yesterday on the bed. They aren't laid out and they were clearly tossed onto the sheets with little care, but they're here and not in my room, as I mentioned to Cason.

I dress alone by the side of the bed where we slept together, and I can't help but wonder what kind of captor and killer gives a damn about who sees their hostage in a towel. Even more, what killer bothers to do anything thoughtful at all for their hostage?

Maybe last night had more effect on him than I thought.

Or maybe he's not as cruel as he wants me to think.

As I walk downstairs, I tell myself I can't get lured into believing he's some guy who's deep down not the person he is on the outside. He is. I remember back in school when the teacher talked about that famous person who said something like don't disbelieve when people show you who they really are. They aren't lying to you. You're lying to yourself.

I can't afford to lie to myself here in this beautiful place that's one big lie. A beautiful cage is still a cage. A prison with lovely furniture and decorations is still a prison.

And Cason is still a killer, no matter how he makes me feel when we're naked in each other's arms or how many little gestures he does that seem like nice things. A killer is still a killer, no matter how beautiful his face may be.

No matter how much I may wish he wasn't.

CHAPTER ELEVEN

*L*ily

Although he said he wasn't hungry, Cason eats yet another meal I make him, this time bacon and scrambled eggs. Not exactly my finest culinary creation, but the satisfied look on his face when he finally sets his fork down on his empty plate says it's enough.

"You enjoyed your food?"

He slowly nods. "It was fine. I have work to do today, so you'll have to stay in your room so you don't get in the way."

I don't say anything, but my expression doesn't hide how much I don't want to be stuck inside on such a gorgeous day. The sun's shining, and I'm going to be trapped in my room like a real prisoner, just like that first day at his apartment.

Standing up, he shoves his stool back, sending it skittering across the tile until it tips over and crashes to the floor. This sudden explosion of anger stuns me, and it seems to enrage him.

"Do you want me to tie you up? I can do that and be perfectly happy, Lily. Your choice. You either get to spend the day in your room, or I tie you up. What's it going to be?" he barks in my direction.

I don't know why he's so angry all of a sudden, but I frantically shake my head at his mention of tying me up again. "No, please don't do that, Cason. I'll stay in my room. I'm fine."

But even my answer doesn't make the darkness that's come over him disappear.

Leaning toward me from the other side of the kitchen island, he glares at me full of more rage than I've seen before in him. In a low voice, he says just an inch away from my face, "This isn't a fucking vacation, little girl. You seem to be confused. You don't get to be fine this week. You're not out here to have a good time. We aren't playing house."

His words echo off the walls around us as I stare up in horror at how enraged he is. About what, I have no idea. The bar stool tipping over? My asking how his breakfast was? I don't know.

All I do know is whatever I thought might have improved between us after last night doesn't exist. I'm still just some stranger he's holding hostage, someone he doesn't give a damn about and will tie up if he wants to.

I nod my understanding of his threat, but he barely sees it before he storms out of the kitchen. A few seconds later, I hear the front door slam, and I exhale the breath I've held inside me from the moment he began yelling.

This episode is no worse than anything else in the time since he took me from my home, but as I stand at the island looking down at his empty plate, I can't stop my hands from shaking.

It's stupid, really. I should have known better than to think one night would have changed anything or a few home cooked meals could change how he sees me.

Shuddering, I take a deep breath in and remind myself of what my father always says. "Rome wasn't built in a day." I can't give up on my plan. He needs to see me as a human being whose life is worth something, as opposed to someone he doesn't know and doesn't need to consider before he kills them.

Before he kills me.

My hands trembling, the silverware and plates clank off one another as I move them to the sink. His plate slips out of my hand and crashes into the stainless steel basin, breaking into pieces. It's nothing, but suddenly, it's too much. I back away from the mess, shaking my head as tears begin to run down my cheeks.

Burying my face in my hands, I let out every ounce of emotion cooped up inside me right there in that kitchen in someone else's house, a home that's my prison and may be the last place I'm seen alive. I feel foolish crying like this, but what the hell does it matter anyway? I'm alone, so who cares if I spend the whole day crying?

A noise from the hallway startles me, and I turn

around to see a man I've never seen before standing in the doorway. He's tall and ominous, much like Cason, but he seems just as confused to see me as I am to see him there.

"Sorry. I didn't know anyone was up here. I came to check the place and found the door unlocked," he says in a deep voice.

I shake my head as I wipe the tears from my cheeks. "No, I'm here. I have to stay here, and I just finished breakfast. I was just going to wash the dishes, but one broke and…"

Even though he doesn't seem annoyed by my longwinded explanation, I let my words fade to nothingness, leaving the two of us staring at one another once more. I don't know what to say to this person. Is he like Nate, or is he like Cason? He's dressed like them in a dark blue T-shirt and jeans.

Unlike both men, though, he seems older. Wrinkles around his eyes make me want to put him in his mid-thirties. Or maybe he just likes to smile a lot. That can cause crow's feet to appear early. He hasn't shaved today, and his stubble looks almost grey next to his tan skin and dark hair. More evidence he's older than the two men I've been around here so far.

After a few seconds, he extends his hand and walks toward me. "Excuse my manners. I'm Doc."

I can't stop myself from instantly thinking he has a name that matches one of the seven dwarfs. I don't say that, but it's impossible not to make the connection. Even if it's a nickname, he's chosen one from a cartoon character.

As if he can read my mind, he smiles at me. "Yes, like the dwarf. Who are you?"

Pressing my hand into his, I feel calluses on his palms rub roughly against my skin. "I'm Lily."

Nodding, he smiles as he releases his hold on my hand. "Nobody told me we'd be having anyone at the house today. You must be a guest of the boss's."

Disappointed to hear him mention the same person I know may give the order to end my life, I shake my head sadly. "I'm not his guest. I'm here with Cason."

A flash of something appears in his eyes, instantly making me uneasy. Does he know Cason? That would mean he knows he's a killer and likely thinks I'm his next victim.

"Oh, Cason. Not a guest of his either, I'm guessing, though."

Doc's words sound kind, like he doesn't approve of who Cason is and what he does. Is it possible he might help me?

I force a smile and nod. "Not really. What do you do here?"

"Security. I've been off for the past few days," he says before noticing the bar stool tipped over on the floor. As he stands it upright and slides it under the island countertop, he adds, "When did you get here?"

"Yesterday." I hesitate to tell him the truth, but if he's to help me, I have nothing to lose now. "I'm here for another six days — no five, after today — and then I either get to go home or I die."

Doc doesn't even blink a single eyelash after I drop that bomb into our conversation. I watch to see any reaction, but nothing changes in his expression. It remains as calm and pleasant as before I mentioned dying at the end of the week.

"It's not like Cason to take prisoners. He's more of a shoot-first-ask-questions-later kind of guy. You must have been very convincing for him to let you live an extra week."

My hopes fall through the floor, and I sigh in utter disappointment. Turning away from Doc, I go back to the sink to clean up the mess. "I didn't convince him of anything. He took me to make sure my father paid back some money he owes your boss. If he doesn't pay, I get to go live with the angels. If he does, I get to go back to my life."

"Well, whatever you did, I can tell you he's not the type to let people live," he says with more than a hint of amazement in his voice.

How nice to find yet another person who has no interest in helping an innocent woman escape from her captor. I can't wait to meet all the useless pieces of shit working here so they can all be as unhelpful as this one and Nate.

"Thanks for that piece of information. I'll keep it in mind as I'm held here like a fucking prisoner," I mumble under my breath and then turn on the water to drown out any other useless tidbits of information this guy has to offer.

When I finish washing my breakfast dish and the silverware, I toss the broken pieces of plate into the garbage. Doc is nowhere to be found, so I walk back to my room where I've been told to stay.

The room that had seemed so welcoming now feels like my own personal jail. Exhausted after only being awake for an hour, I sit down on the edge of my bed and try to tell myself this will all be over in a few days. My father will pay Cason's boss the money he owes, and I'll be able to return to my life.

Assuming he doesn't go back on his word and kill me just for shits and giggles.

I don't want to believe that will happen, but everything around him makes no sense, so why should he? Grown men see me here and know I'm being held against my will, and yet they do nothing. This place looks like the perfect setting for a vacation, but in truth, I'm serving a sentence courtesy of Cason.

So much for chivalry not being dead. Here, at this house, it's dead and every one of these men probably took turns killing it.

With nothing to do, I lay back and close my eyes, imagining what prisoners in jail do with their days. I honestly have no idea since I've never even known anyone who saw the inside of a police station, much less a cell. Everyone I know lives a boring life like I do.

Or at least like I used to.

As I drift off to sleep, I think about what I'd be doing right now if I were home. For as boring as calling my friend Kat and making plans to meet up with her for lunch used to sound, now as I imagine that very commonplace thing, it sounds like heaven.

. . .

"DID YOU STAY IN HERE ALL DAY?" CASON ASKS IN his usual brusque way.

I look up at him, still hazy from sleep, and nod. "What time is it?"

"Five o'clock. Answer the question."

My eyes focus on him standing over the bed staring down at me. His expression tells me he's upset about something. Frowning, his narrowed eyes hide just how angry he is, but I've learned in the short time around him what his rage looks like.

"Yes," I answer, rolling over onto my side as fear of him takes hold of me once again.

"Then how did you get to meet Doc? Didn't figure I'd find out, did you?"

Now Cason's eyes are wide and flashing that fury I knew was simmering inside him. I'm not sure what he's so angry about, but I'm unfortunately on the receiving end of it.

I slowly sit up and look at him as the last remnants of sleep sadly fade from my brain and I have to deal with the reality that is my life. At least for the next few days.

"He came into the kitchen right after you left. I didn't leave. I stayed in the house, like you told me I had to."

Cason shakes his head, and once more, his eyes narrow. "I told you to stay in this room all day, not to stay in the house. Those are two different things entirely."

"You don't have to worry about that Doc guy or anyone else helping me. They're all just like you."

In a flash, Cason's hand shoots out to grab my neck, and he lifts me off the bed. I hang in the air from his fingers that press hard into my flesh, threatening to cut off my air supply. Frantic, I flail my arms and pull at his to release me, but he stands perfectly still just staring into my eyes.

"Don't concern yourself with Doc. You're the problem, Lily. You seem to think this is some week-long spa vacation for you where you lounge around in the bathtub and chit chat with the help to pass the time."

His voice is eerily calm, like nothing he's sounded like before. I can feel myself getting lightheaded as he speaks and pull hard at his arms to free myself, scraping my fingernails across his skin.

But he doesn't flinch. He simply holds me at the end of his arm like some fish he's caught that he doesn't enjoy.

"Do you understand, Lily?"

I rasp out, "Yes," as I desperately scramble to pry his fingers from my neck.

My answer is all it takes to be freed, and as quickly as he shot out his hand to grab me, he opens his hand and releases me. I fall to the floor gasping for air while pain in my throat makes me feel like I've swallowed a red-hot coal.

I hear him breathing above me, but I'm too afraid to turn around. I know I should. I don't want to be surprised by the next move he makes, but I can't force myself to look up at him. The hate in his eyes is too much for me to bear at this moment when all I can do is struggle to get air into my lungs.

"Get up, Lily."

Every fiber of my being silently screams, "No! Fuck you! I don't want to get up. I don't want to look at you or do anything for you. Fuck off and die!"

I know even a moment's hesitation might worsen any punishment he has in store for me, so while those words echo in my brain, I do as I'm told and push myself up to my feet. I don't look at him, though, unable to make certain what appears in my eyes won't tell him the truth of how I feel.

He has to think I'm the same person as always. Helpful. Compliant. Obedient. I have to make him think I'm still that.

But as if he knows better, he grabs my jaw and forces me to face him. "Look at me."

Tears prick at the back of my eyes, but I stop them from escaping, unwilling to look as weak as I feel at this moment. I want to spit in his face to show him how much I hate him for what he's done. My plan to placate him and convince him that I'm a person is supplanted by my desire to make him see what I truly think of him, but I can't let that rule me.

So instead, I repeat my mantra over and over as he stares into my eyes. *I have a body, and I can use it. I don't have a weapon or strength, but I have my body.*

And then I add two new lines to my mantra. *Let him do what he will. I won't break.*

"You are not to speak to Nate or Doc again. Next time, I won't be so understanding."

It's a Herculean struggle to not show in my expression how utterly ridiculous I think his words are, but I silently fight against the urge to let my face show that. Understanding? He has no concept of the word. It's a completely foreign concept to someone like him.

But I know he requires me to answer, so I do as I must and give him what he wants to hear. "I won't."

"Good. Trust me, you'll thank me someday."

His statements just keep getting more and more ridiculous. I'll thank him someday? For what? Not talking to two men who wouldn't lift a finger to help me get away from this fucking place and him?

I say nothing to that because I have no response that won't get me choked again. The only thing I'll ever be thankful for concerning Cason is when I hear someone has rid the world of him.

"Now, go downstairs and cook us a nice dinner," he says with a smile that seems wholly out of place at this moment. "I brought some groceries back, so use them to make something good. You can find the rest of what you need in the cabinets."

He acts like some doting husband who's done me a favor by bringing food home for me to make him. Just the way he stands there smiling makes me want to reach out and smack that stupid grin off his face.

I move to leave, but he stops me. "When we finish with dinner, I have a surprise for you. I got you something I thought you'd like," he says in a voice far softer than just a minute before.

Instantly, a thought flashes through my mind.

Something I'll like? My freedom, you fuck? Or maybe some dignity to replace the utter fear you want to fill me with.

He's gotten me something I'll like while he was out working, which in his world means killing someone. I can't imagine what he could offer me that I'd want, but once more, I need to pretend his words don't utterly disgust me.

I force yet another smile and push out of my mouth the words I need to say so he doesn't hurt me again. "Thank you."

His fingers release my arm, and I hurry out of my room into the hallway. Nothing he could give me will ever make me feel anything but revulsion for him. I don't care what it is or how nice whatever this thing may be.

But I'll pretend to love it because I've figured him out. Feed him. Fuck him. Flatter him. So he'll free me. I didn't realize how important that third F was, but now I do.

He's bothered by me talking to those two men because even though they have no intention at all to help me escape from him, just having them be nice to me hurts his ego. So flatter him I will.

And if I'm ever able to, I'll include a fourth F.

Fucking kill him.

CHAPTER TWELVE

*C*ason

For a change, Lily talks very little while she's making dinner. I could stay in my room and just join her when it's time to eat, but I want to keep an eye on her since it seems every goddamned security asshole working at this house feels the need to just fucking pop in whenever they want to. This is supposed to be a week off for me. Well, except for having to watch over Lily until her father does the right thing. Instead, it's turned into a hassle because of Nate and Doc.

Fucking dwarf asshole.

She probably likes talking to him just like she's into talking to that jackass Nate. Doc probably told her one of his stupid stories about his exciting life as a security guard for an estate in the middle of goddamned nowhere. She probably laughed at his stupid jokes, too.

I watch her at the stove as she stirs the vegetables

in the pot. She just stands there and stares at it like some zombie. Probably wishing Doc or his buddy Nate were here to join us so she could return to her chatty self.

No wonder my father rarely comes out here. There's no peace to be had in this place with his security staff wandering in and out whenever they damn well feel like it. Although they most likely don't do that to him when he's around. He gets peace and quiet.

Meanwhile, I get a fucking conga line of assholes parading in and out when I'm not watching. You'd swear they don't know what my job is, for Christ's sake. It's not like I'd bring a girl out here just for the freaking scenery. This isn't a romantic getaway for Lily and me. We aren't playing house like Victor suggested either. She's my fucking captive, so why are these shitheads acting like they should be coming up here and talking her up to pass the damn time?

"Is it almost ready?" I ask, needing to talk so my mind doesn't get fixated on her talking to them again.

I haven't been able to think of anything else since Doc caught me driving back onto the property and told me about meeting Lily this morning. He had a smug look on his face as he leaned down into the driver's side window to tell me. Like strolling up to the house to check her out would ever be okay.

Then he mentioned how Nate said she's sweet. I wanted to pull my gun out and blast his fucking head off right out the damn window. What Lily is or isn't is none of their concern.

She turns around as all of this runs through my head and forces herself to smile back at me. "Almost."

I've already figured out when her smiles aren't genuine. They don't go all the way up to her eyes and make them light up. Her eyes light up when she's truly happy and truly angry. I admit, I've seen most of the second type, but when she looked at her father back at their house, those dark eyes of hers lit up with happiness for him.

Not that I give a fuck about how genuine or not her smiles are when she's dealing with me. It doesn't matter. Smile. Don't smile. I don't care. Just don't talk constantly and give me a headache.

"Is it just the two of us tonight? I don't know if I've made enough for anyone else."

I hear the hope in her voice. She wants one or both of those security guard assholes to come up to eat with us. Like we should all sit down around the dining room table and eat a meal together as if we love having guests.

Rage courses through me like someone just injected me with pure anger. "I just told you not to ever speak to them again, and now you ask me if anyone else is joining us for goddamned dinner? I swear to God you have a death wish, Lily."

Her smile instantly disappears, replaced by a deep frown that pulls her eyebrows in toward her nose and makes her look like the saddest goddamned person I've ever seen. I swear the girl has no filter on her emotions.

"I didn't mean them. I just figured I should ask if

you were going to have anyone else here when we eat. I didn't mean to upset you."

Ignoring her apology, I point at the jar of sauce on the counter to her right. "Is that the jar of sauce with meat in it from last night?"

She nods, still sad looking. "Yes. I didn't cook pasta, though. You didn't say you wanted that again."

This whole conversation makes me want to kill someone. I don't give a fuck about sauce or pasta. I don't give a fuck about any of this. All I want is to eat dinner and then give Lily what I bought her today. Is that so much to ask?

"Do you want me to cook up some pasta too? I can make that in a few minutes," she says sweetly, but I've already moved on from the sauce and pasta topic and back to Doc and his stupid face in my window telling me how right Nate was about her being sweet.

"How long was Doc up here today?" I ask, and then a thought occurs to me.

Was he with Lily all morning? Is that why she was sleeping when I got back here? Did he fuck her while I was out on a job?

I'm out of my seat and standing next to her at the counter before she can get the words out of her mouth. "Answer me! How long was he here?" I bark, frightening her.

She shakes her head and backs away from me, but I follow her. "Just a few minutes. It's not like he was here to help me or anything. I told you he didn't give a damn about me."

"Is that why you were asleep when I got back?

Did you spend all morning in bed fucking him?" I ask as I scan her body for any hint that he touched her.

Her eyes grow wide, and in them I see the shock register at my question. But is it shock because I found out about what they did together or shock because it never happened?

"No! Did he say that? Because it didn't happen. He was only here for a few minutes, and then he left. I swear, Cason," she says in a panic, her head continually shaking the basic answer of no to my question.

I walk toward her as the vegetables begin to boil over onto the stove, but I don't care. At this moment, all I care about is knowing what happened between Lily and Doc.

"What did he say to you? Tell me now, Lily," I demand before stopping just inches away from her, trapping her in the corner of the room.

For a second, she doesn't say a word, and then her answer spills out of her mouth. "He thought I must have convinced you to let me live an extra week, but I told him that wasn't true. I didn't do anything. Then he said you aren't the type to let people live, so I must have done something to make you want to let me live. That's it. I swear."

Her voice hitches on the last words, so I lean in close and say in a low voice, "Are you sure you two didn't talk about anything else?"

She shakes her head no but then stops as her eyes flash the truth. They did talk about something else. What was it?

"I asked him what he did here at the estate and he told me he works in security. He said he was gone on vacation or something for the past few days and asked me how long I'd been here. That was it. I swear."

"If I find out you did anything with him or Nate…"

My threat hangs in the air between us, unfinished for a long moment, before she shakes her head again. "I didn't. I wouldn't."

Before I can stop myself, the question rattling around in my head comes out. "Why not?"

And with that, tears begin to roll down her cheeks. Between sobs, she answers, "Why not? I'm being held hostage here. I'm not here to be having sex with every guy who shows his face in this house."

Behind me, the water from the pot splashes onto the hot burner, and Lily pokes her head around me. "Cason, the beans are going to burn. I need to go over and take them off the heat."

I step aside, and she hurries over to the stove. Grabbing the pot with her bare hand, she releases it a second later, and it crashes to the floor. Scalding hot water splashes everywhere, and she collapses onto the floor clutching her right hand and crying.

She looks like a broken bird some animal has left for dead sitting there like that in a heap on the ground, and I can't help but feel bad for her as she sobs. I walk through the water all over the floor and lift her up into my arms.

Holding her hand up in front of her, she cries, "I didn't mean to drop the pot. It's just that I was in such a hurry that I forgot to grab an oven mitt, and my hand got burned."

Her explanation drifts in one ear and out the other as I carry her to the guest bathroom nearby. I set her down on her feet and search through the vanity, but there's nothing to help her burned hand.

I turn back to look at her staring at her red palm. "There's nothing here for first aid. You're going to have to run your hand under the cold water and hope that helps."

The look she gives me seems strange, like she doesn't understand why I'm saying that. I guide her over to the sink and turn on the cold water before pushing her hand under the stream.

"Let it sit under there for a minute. I'll be right back."

"Where are you going?" she asks in a voice that verges on panic once again.

"To clean things up. Keep your hand under there until I get back."

She starts to ask another question, but I leave the bathroom and head back to the kitchen. In the time we've been gone, the potatoes have overcooked and splattered all over the stovetop and counter next to the pot. Carefully leaning over the still hot burner where the beans had been, I turn all of them off.

As I scoop up the vegetables off the floor and toss them into the garbage, I can't help but wonder if taking Lily was a mistake. She's done nothing but irritate me, and now I'm stuck cleaning up her messes.

Not that she's been a total disaster. Fucking her

wasn't bad. And her cooking usually tastes better than the food that ended up on the floor. And that talking of hers has settled down so she isn't filling up every goddamned moment we're around each other with words.

By the time I get everything cleaned up and return to the bathroom, she's still standing at the sink with her hand under the cold water. Surprised she hasn't moved, I turn it off and grab a towel from the shelf behind me.

"Why did you leave it under the water for so long? You're practically waterlogged," I say as I pat her palm with the towel.

Lily doesn't answer, so I look up to see her staring at me. Fear fills her eyes, although I don't know why.

"What?"

"You told me to keep my hand under the water until you got back. That's why I kept it there so long," she finally says in a shaky voice that barely contains the tears ready to begin again.

As I dry her hand, holding it in my own, I have to admit sometimes she does listen to what I tell her to do. She still cries too much, but maybe I can understand that.

"Well, you'll be fine. It's just a little burn. So you won't be able to do anything for a few days. You'll be back to normal soon enough."

Tossing the towel onto the vanity, I catch a glimpse of the two of us in the mirror. She looks so helpless standing there, and even stranger to my eye is how helpful I look.

Lily gives a smile that barely lifts the corners of her mouth. "I'm left-handed, so I'll be fine. It just hurts a lot right now."

"So no dinner tonight. Guess I'm going to have to run for something," I say as I let go of her hand and walk back toward the kitchen.

"Can I come with you? I've been stuck in your apartment or this house for two days."

I look back at her and shake my head. "No. You have to stay here."

And just like that, whatever kindness that exists inside me retreats to its usual hiding place. She doesn't respond, remaining silent as I head toward the front door to leave. It's hard not to notice that in just two days, while she's been held she's also learned not to ask twice for things she can't have.

I'm impressed with how quickly she's picked up on that. A far more stubborn girl her age would still be fighting me tooth and nail. Maybe I underestimated Lily.

SHE EATS THE FAST FOOD I BRING BACK WITHOUT A single complaint, even though it's nearly ice cold by the time I drive the twenty-five miles back from the restaurant. I watch her baby her right hand, laying it on the island countertop as she eats only with her left hand. She's a crier, for sure, but there's strength inside her, too.

When we finish eating, I ask her, "Did you go up to your room while I was gone?"

"No. I sat here with my throbbing hand."

"Aren't you going to ask me why I wanted to know if you went upstairs?" I ask, a little thrown off my game by her sudden lack of questions.

Lily sadly shakes her head. "There's no point. You don't like me talking so much, and you aren't going to tell me anything unless you want to, so why bother asking?"

The defeat in her expression also fills her voice. Two days and she's given up. I thought she was stronger than that.

For a few minutes, we sit silently across from one another, but her gaze is fixed on her hand. Mine, though, focuses on her. Dressed in the same clothes she was wearing when I took her from her home, she looks different than she did yesterday. Maybe it's the lack of makeup, although she looks identical to when she wore it. I'm not sure what's different, but she doesn't look the same.

Then I remember the surprise I brought back for her. Standing from the stool, I toss the wrappers from our dinner into the garbage as she continues to stare down at her red hand.

"Come upstairs with me, Lily."

She stands up without a word and not a single question leaves her lips, even though at this moment I'd like her to ask why or where we're going. She simply walks next to me, letting out a single sigh as we climb the stairs together toward my room.

Finally, as we walk past her bedroom door, she asks, "Why are we going to your room?"

I know what she's thinking, but that's not what's on my mind at the moment. Maybe later, though.

Turning to look down at her upturned face, her eyes staring up at me with that curiosity I knew couldn't have been completely extinguished in merely two days, I answer her question. "Because I have something for you. Remember?"

Her response is less than thrilling. She doesn't say anything or even smile. Lily simply nods and sighs a second time, and I can't help but decide I don't like this quiet version of her.

I open my door for her and guide her into the room where clothes lay on the bed. Two pair of yoga pants just like the ones she wears, four T-shirts in pink, black, light blue, and white that I thought would look nice on her, and five pair of underwear I had to get the person at the store to help me with because women's underwear are sized completely differently than their pants, although I have no idea why.

When Lily doesn't say anything, I explain, "They're for you. So you don't have to wear the same clothes all week."

Still, she remains silent, so I add, "With the clothes you have now being washed once downstairs in the washer, you won't have to wear anything more than for one day."

She stares at the bed for a long moment before turning to look at me with utter confusion in her expression. "You bought me clothes to wear while I'm here?"

"Yes. You were going to start to smell, and I didn't want to have to deal with that."

It's not the truth, but she doesn't need to know that.

Lily opens her mouth to speak, but nothing comes out. After the second time she tries to say something, she finally asks, "You bought your captive clothes? Is that how this usually goes?"

That question she can have the truth to.

"No," I say flatly. "I usually just kill people and don't bother taking anyone captive."

What I get in return for the clothes and my answer is another sigh. I don't know if she's happy or not by what I've done.

Well, at least she won't start to stink the place up. I hadn't bought the clothes for that reason, but it will have to do for the time being.

$\mathcal{L}$ily

    I stare at the clothes Cason's bought for me, still not understanding why he'd do this for someone he's holding hostage. First, Doc tells me the guy doesn't let people live, and now he buys me clothes so I don't have to wear the same ones all week?

None of this sounds like how someone's supposed to act when they keep someone captive. Also, none of it meshes with how he's acted toward me every other moment of the time I've been with him. Not including when I burned my hand, which I don't understand either.

He's a violent killer, yet he's worried about my comfort. Even more, he's a jealous killer. Is he worried Doc or Nate might put a bullet in my brain before he gets the chance to?

None of this makes any sense.

I see by the hint of hurt in his expression that he expected me to react differently to his gesture, so I quickly regroup, pushing aside the pain in my hand to give him a smile. "This is so kind of you, Cason. I'm going to change into a new outfit right now."

He focuses his attention on my face, as if he's searching for some answer to a question he's silently asking himself, so I make sure my smile is as genuine as possible. When I see his eyes lift to meet mine, I know he's convinced by my acting.

"Wear the pink shirt. I want to see you in that first," he says as I gather up the clothes to take to my room.

The killer likes pink. Okay. I can give him that. Anything to keep him from barking at me, or worse, threatening me with being tied up again.

I do as he commands and dress in the new pink shirt with my new yoga pants and underwear. Every pair is white, which seems strange. I haven't worn white panties since I was a little girl, but the killer likes white underwear. Anything to make him happy.

When I return to his room wearing what he wants, he's standing there in the middle of the floor waiting for me. His gaze travels down my body, like he's examining his purchases, and then up again until it reaches my face. I make sure I'm smiling so he thinks I'm happy with what he's done.

In truth, I'm a mixture of baffled and terrified. I don't understand why a man holding me hostage would give a single damn what I'm wearing or if I'm wearing any clothes at all. Beneath that, though, is the real fear that his kindness is merely a prelude to some horrible thing he's planning to do to me.

That's how he seems to work. One minute he's kind — or at least not awful — and then the next minute he does something that makes me think he's grown tired of waiting to kill me and will put his gun to my head at any second. I hold my breath and wonder if this is my last moment in this life.

"Are they the right sizes?" he asks almost innocently, like he isn't sure of what he's done or if it's the right thing.

"Yes, thank you," I answer honestly.

He likely looked at the sizes inside my clothes, but I have no idea how he figured out what size underwear to get me. Half the time I don't know what size to get since each brand seems different from all the others.

"Would you like to go outside and get some fresh air before it gets too cool out?" he asks in that same tone that reminds me of those boys he likes to reference every time he's close to me.

My heart leaps at the idea of finally getting to go outside again, so I quickly nod my head. "Yes, I'd love that. Thank you!"

I don't try to conceal the excitement in my voice, even as I hold my breath and wait for him to pull the rug out underneath me and bark that I can't go out for some reason only he understands. But he doesn't do that this time.

A rare smile forms on his lips, and he walks over toward where I stand near the door. "Then we'll go outside for a little while."

There's something surreal about his behavior, but I

don't want to ruin my only chance at getting some fresh air today by second-guessing why he's being so nice. He'll stop, like he always does, but until then, I want to enjoy the tiny taste of freedom he allows me, even if it's only getting to walk outside in the grass and getting to feel its coolness on my feet.

When we make our way out onto the porch, he sits down on the top step and waves me off, as if to say I have permission to go play. It reminds me of when my father would sit outside on our steps and watch me run around the yard when I was a little girl right after my mother died. All day, we'd stay inside as long-lost family and friends of my parents came to visit to pay their respects, but as the sun set and the two of us finally got to be alone, he'd brush my hair and make sure I was clean before taking my hand and walking me out to the porch.

"Time to play, Lily. Don't worry. I'll be right here, but you run around and tire yourself out so you can sleep tonight."

He said the same thing every time. I never had trouble sleeping, even in those weeks after she died. Losing my mother exhausted me more than he could ever know. He couldn't rest, though. Every morning he'd show up to the kitchen table looking like he hadn't slept for even a few minutes, the dark circles and bags under his eyes evidence of how impossible sleep had become now that my mother wasn't by his side each night. I was only a little girl, but I knew he looked tired.

I didn't find out until years later that he never slept a whole night through again after she died.

Lost in memories about that time long ago, I don't hear the footsteps of someone walking up the front sidewalk until out of the corner of my eye I see Cason jump up and begin walking toward me. Startled, I look around for any hint why he suddenly wants to be with me in the yard, and I see Doc standing there smiling.

"You finally got to come out, huh? Good for you," he says with a broad grin that would make me want to smile in return at him if Cason hadn't told me never to speak to him or Nate again.

I give him a slight nod and look away, directly into Cason's eyes. Dark and angry, they look right past me to Doc.

"Why are you up here at the house again for the second time today? Some silent alarm we can't hear keep going off, so you need to come scurrying up here to check it out?" he asks, his voice edged with a flintiness I've never heard him use before now.

Behind me, I hear Doc chuckle. "Actually, our boss wanted me to check on things every night, so here I am."

Cason's expression grows dark. Narrowing his eyes to squints, he practically growls as he listens to Doc's explanation. "Well, you've already been up here today and you can see everything is fine, so get lost."

I sense the tension between the two men and hold my breath, hoping Doc just goes away quickly, but then he speaks again and I know he's ruined everything I'd hoped to enjoy with just one question.

"You okay, Lily? You don't seem as talkative as this morning. You're not still upset about that dish breaking, are you?"

I don't turn around and answer him with as few words as possible. "I'm fine."

But those two words are enough to make Cason's eyes flash with rage.

He grabs my arm and tugs me toward the front door as he snaps, "Thanks for checking, Doc. We're all fine here, so blow."

I stumble up the front stairs he pulls me up them so fast. Flinging the door open, he nearly tears it off the hinges before shoving me inside the house and slamming the door behind him.

As much as I want to run away because I know what's coming next, I stand perfectly still where I land, cowering next to the doorway that leads to the kitchen. All I wanted to do was get to enjoy the nice weather and feel the grass under my feet, but now that's all ruined.

I don't know who I blame more. Doc for asking his stupid question or Cason for taking out his dislike of him on me.

Cason marches over to where I stand and leans down so his face is level with mine. The rage in his eyes terrifies me like it always does, and I recoil in horror even before he starts to speak.

This time, though, he doesn't yell. He doesn't even

raise his voice. In fact, it's barely above a whisper but more frightening that way.

"So you broke a dish and Doc was kind enough to help you this morning? You neglected to tell me about that."

Barely able to form words, I stutter out, "I—I did br—break a dish, but he didn't help me with anything. He came in after it happened, and I cleaned it up all by my—my—myself, Cason."

Grabbing my upper arm, he squeezes tightly, hurting me as he yanks me into the kitchen. He points at the garbage, and again in a voice barely above a whisper, he says, "I didn't see any broken dish in there when I cleaned up the mess you made with dinner. Where is this dish, Lily?"

My heart skips a beat as I try to imagine why he didn't see the pieces of that broken dish in the garbage. I set them all right on top. Where could they have gone?

"I don't know. Maybe the pieces slipped to the bottom?" I suggest half-heartedly, too afraid to think of any other reason they wouldn't be there.

In a flash, he has the garbage can above his head, and he tips it over, dumping all the food and everything else. The broken pieces of the white dish hit the tile floor, each one clanging when it lands.

But something snaps inside me, and as he's staring at that disgusting pile of garbage in front of him, I rush over to the countertop and yank a knife from the wooden block sitting under the cabinet. Cason spins around to look at me, and I point the knife at him, my left hand shaking uncontrollably.

"Stay away from me! I didn't lie about anything with that asshole! I broke the dish and cleaned it up myself. I don't know what your problem is with him, but I did nothing wrong!" I scream, tears clinging to every word.

Cason watches me silently, saying nothing to my outburst but never taking his eyes off my hand with the knife in it. The two of us stand like statues with only our eyes and my trembling hand moving for so long it feels like I'm frozen to the spot on that tile floor.

When he does finally speak, his voice isn't that icy whisper from just a few minutes before but soft, like he's placating me just as I've been doing with him. "Lily, put down the knife. Put it back where it belongs."

"No!"

"Don't make things harder on yourself than they have to be."

I want to throw that knife straight into his chest for that comment. As tears well in my eyes, making focusing on him more difficult by the second, I calm my shaking hand and scream, "Harder on me than they have to be? They don't have to be hard at all! You took me because my father needs to pay your boss. I shouldn't even be here! Harder? How much fucking harder do you think this could be on me? You keep me tied up or threaten to, and when I'm not stuck in that fucking chair in front of your TV, you force me to stay in this gilded cage all day. When people come to the house, you blame me, not that either one of those assholes would ever help me get away from you! Then when you finally let me out to get a breath of fresh air, you blame me when Doc shows me a shred of kindness by asking if I'm okay. What exactly is harder, Cason?"

He stands in front of me stunned by my words, but by the time I'm finished, my emotional outburst has sapped all my strength. My hand begins shaking again, and the knife drops to the floor, skidding over the tile until it comes to rest right in front of his feet.

Cason looks down at the knife and bends over to pick it up, but I won't stand there and let him punish me. I run out of the kitchen, bouncing off the walls because my tear-filled eyes make seeing where I'm going nearly impossible.

I reach the front door feeling bruised from all the times I've hit my arms and reach for the doorknob. I don't know where I'm going since that damn fence he warned me about is electrified, but I can't stay in this house with him anymore. I have to try to get away.

But he reaches me just as I grab for the doorknob, wrapping his arms around my waist and yanking me away from freedom. We stumble backwards, and he throws me onto the floor with such force that it knocks the wind out of my lungs.

Wiping the tears from my eyes, I try to get away, but it's no use. He's on me in a second, pressing the tip of the knife to my throat and straddling my hips so I can't move.

He stares at me like he's in disbelief that I could do all of this. Like because he bought me some clothes and underwear that I'd want to stay with him and not try to get free the first chance I got.

Cason tightens his thighs against me, crushing my body between his legs, and presses the knife into my skin. His eyes flash that usual rage that seems to nearly always exist in him, but I'm strangely calm now. He doesn't terrify me anymore.

Either he's going to kill me now or in a few days. Somehow, my failed attempt at escape has made that crystal clear, and I'm not afraid of dying.

"You might only have days to live, and still you insist on making me hurt you."

"I don't insist on you hurting me ever. That's all you. You like hurting me. That's who you are."

My words stun him for a moment, and then he throws the knife away near the stairs. Knives aren't his weapon of choice, so why would he need that anyway?

Seconds pass while I wait for him to take out his gun and shoot me. I think about my father and my mother and how happy I am that they can't see me when I die like this. I try not to cry, but as much as I want to believe I'm not afraid to die, that's a lie.

I don't want to die. I just want to go home and try to forget this all ever happened.

Unable to face what's about to happen, I close my eyes and take a deep breath. I want the last one I ever enjoy to be as full and pure as possible.

I feel Cason's hands press against my shoulders,

and then the pressure on the outsides of my legs disappears. Am I dead? Is that what this is?

A second later, he lifts me up, and without a word, he carries me up the stairs. I don't open my eyes, too afraid if I do that I'll realize this is all a dream, or worse, all in my head as I lay there dying on the hardwood floor in the entryway to his boss's home.

When he sets me down on the bed, I don't know if I'm still alive. All I know is I didn't hear his gun go off. But that's not possible. There's no way I could threaten him with a knife, try to escape, and then get to live.

Doc's words echo in my brain. "He's not the type to let people live."

I open my eyes and see him standing over me, just staring down at me like he doesn't understand what I am. The look in his eyes isn't that rage-filled one like usual. Now his eyes study me intensely, like he can't believe he didn't kill me for what I did downstairs.

Cason's a killer, so why am I alive?

CHAPTER FOURTEEN

*C*ason

Any other person would be dead now.

I don't know why I haven't pulled my gun and shot her in the fucking head for that shit downstairs. I can't, though. But I have no idea why I can't.

It's not that the idea hasn't occurred to me. More than once, my hand has twitched, needing to reach for my gun, but I stopped myself every time. I make excuses for her to keep myself from doing what I would do to any other person who's done what she has.

Her father's wrongs aren't hers.

She's innocent. That one isn't really working much anymore, to be honest.

This whole thing is only going to last for a few more days.

I wasn't even supposed to take her to get her father to pay up, so killing her would probably be a step too far, even for Victor.

The excuses rotate like a carousel of justifications for going against my nature. I've never done this for another soul in this world. Look at Creighton. I made no excuses for him. I just killed him without a second thought.

I can't do that with Lily.

She looks up at me and I see those tears that always seem to be in her eyes. "Please don't kill me."

Shaking my head, I climb onto the bed next to her and let out a deep breath that feels like I've been holding it in since she pulled that knife on me. I'm not going to kill her, so if I'm going to keep her here for the rest of the seven days, I have to accept who she is.

Lily moves her body next to me, brushing her thigh against mine, and it's almost as if it's the only natural thing to pull her close. I feel her trembling as I wrap my arm around her shoulders, her terrified body melding with mine. She's warm and smells new, like the clothes I bought her today.

I should be enraged that she tried to run away after I did that for her, but somehow that's not what I feel. I don't know why, but as I lay here holding her to me, I'm more relaxed than I can ever remember feeling.

Leaning forward, I drag her up with me as I reposition myself to remove my gun. I set it down on the nightstand next to the bed and turn to see her staring at it, her eyes wide and filled with fear again.

"Don't worry. I'm not going to kill you," I say matter-of-factly before gently pulling her back down onto the bed next to me.

Still shaking, she doesn't say a word but tentatively rests her head on my shoulder. Her warm breath brushes my cheek when she sighs a minute later, and slowly, she relaxes against my side.

She's so small in my arms. I could crush her with little effort, if I wanted to. It would take next to nothing and the breath would be squeezed right out of her slight body. But that decision's already been made, so the thought of that quickly passes from my mind. It's replaced by another far more pleasing idea.

My cock stiffens, and I pull her on top of me. Lifting my hips from the bed, I press against the front of her yoga pants. Lily watches with wide eyes, probably unsure what to do. One minute I act like I'm going to end her life, and the next minute I'm rock hard and craving to be buried balls deep in her tight cunt.

But she can't hide what her body wants either. I watch her nipples tighten under the pink T-shirt I knew would look fucking incredible on her, and that was without imagining seeing her tits through it.

"You should be afraid of me, Lily. But you're not. Why's that?" I ask while my hands burrow under that T-shirt to get to what's beneath it.

She arches her back, jutting out her chest for me, and closes her eyes just as my fingers reach her hard nipples. Cupping her soft flesh in my palms, I squeeze them roughly and hear a tiny moan come from her.

"I am afraid of you. Just not at this exact moment," she answers softly as I continue to pinch her tender skin.

I sit up and pull her shirt over her head to expose those beautiful tits all for me. Leaning in toward her body, I suck a hardened nipple into my mouth and crudely tug on it with my teeth. I'm not gentle and I'm not careful, yet she moans her pleasure, giving me the green light to do as I desire.

My front teeth sink into her deep pink flesh around her nipple, and Lily slides her hands over my head to hold me there. The harder I bite and suck, the tighter her hold becomes. All the while my cock feels like it's going to explode in my pants if I don't get inside her cunt now, and Lily rocks her hips, grinding her pussy against me.

Releasing her from my mouth, I push her off my lap and rip my jeans down my legs while she wriggles out of her yoga pants. A willing participant, she's naked before I am and reaches over to lift my shirt over my head, the two of us frantically trying to shed the clothes that keep us from what we both want.

My mind races with how I want to take her first, and memories from the last time we fucked flash through my head. I don't understand why, but I need to see the look in her eyes this time, so I pull her back on top of me. She straddles my hips and lifts herself up over my cock that's standing at attention.

As much as I want to be inside her, I pull her head down to me and kiss her. My tongue snakes into her mouth, and she sucks on the tip of it, teasing me even more than the mere thought of feeling her tight cunt around me.

She stares down at me, and I see a hint of fear still in her eyes. Holding her to me, I move my lips to her ear and kiss her softly before whispering, "I'm not going to kill you, Lily. I promise."

Those are words I've never said before in my life. Not to any man or woman. But I mean them, and even though she likely thinks I won't kill her at this very moment right before we sleep together, that's not what I mean.

Lily lifts herself off my chest and looks down at me for a brief second before everything between us begins to move in a flash, but for that single moment, I see the fear is gone now. It's been replaced by that softness that hope brings to her dark eyes.

I can't offer her that. Only that I won't kill her, even if her father is stupid enough not to pay off his debt to my father. But right now, none of that matters. All that I care about is being inside her and what she makes me feel when I fuck her.

My hands hold her where I need her to stay, and with one hard thrust of my hips, my cock sinks deep into her cunt. She's warm and wet and perfect, and I need this more than I can explain right now.

Neither of us make a sound as we move in unison, two people surrounded by madness searching for a few precious seconds of peace. Lily rolls her hips, taking every inch of me, and I push into her body craving that sense of losing myself only it provides.

She bites her lower lip when I slam into her, and a second later, I roll the two of us over on the bed so I'm on top. I want to look down into her eyes as I fuck her. That hope that shines in them makes me want more of it, even if I'm destined to never have that like she does.

I watch that glimmer mix with an innocence that seems wrong at the same time I fill her with my cock. She's tight and sweet around me, and still it's not innocence that rocks against me and sends waves of need racing through my body.

The memory of her telling me she'd been with someone older than me marches through my mind, leaving behind a feeling of wanting to protect her when it disappears into nothingness. I shouldn't care who she's been with. She has no idea who's been in my bed before her.

Yet, still I wonder about what her world was like before I threw her over my shoulder and kidnapped her.

"Cason..." she says before moaning something I can't make out.

The last thing on my mind now is talking. I don't want to think about what will happen when we leave this room. I don't want to think about what I'll have to do when this week is up. I don't want to think about anything but how fucking good it feels to get lost in her.

Her fingernails rake across my back, leaving stinging trails from my spine out to my sides. I rear back at the pain and plunge into her body with all the force in mine. She doesn't cry out or even whimper. She simply takes every bit of me I give her.

The good. The bad. The cruel. The need to forget everything else but this and her.

The first hint of her release comes with a tightening around my cock and her heels pressing hard into my back. I don't stop pumping into her, and go even faster, eager to feel and see her come for me. Her body arches and her head tilts back, and then it rushes through her. Her legs tighten around my waist, but I keep going, desperate to feel the ecstasy that makes her look like an angel beneath me.

A whimper breaks the silence, and then all I hear are the grunts and groans coming from me as I explode. Her legs quiver against my hips, and I still my body to revel in the feeling of coming inside her.

She's perfect and nearly innocent, and whatever goodness she possesses now mixes with the bad that takes up so much space in me. Part of me feels like I should apologize for corrupting her like this, but one look at her expression filled with pure pleasure stops me.

I don't care where she's been before or where I've been. All that matters at this very second is where we are now and what we've given to one another.

Collapsing onto the bed, I pull Lily to me and close my eyes. Another round can happen later. For now, I want to lay here and enjoy the peace that's settled into me.

THE FEEL OF LILY DRAGGING HER FINGERTIPS OVER my collarbone wakes me, and I open my eyes to see her lying with my arm around her just as she was when I drifted off. Pleased but not surprised, oddly enough, I give her a sleepy smile.

"What are you doing?" I ask as she continues to almost pet me.

My question makes her stop, and she moves her hand away from my neck. "I was looking at your tattoos and felt like touching them. I've never known anyone who has so many tattoos."

As if I need to look down to know what she's talking about, I lower my head and scan my chest. "I can't remember not having them."

"Did you get them all around the same time or did it take a long time to fill up all the empty space?" she asks, her question sounding so naïve.

"That's not exactly the goal for getting tattoos. At least not for me. I didn't need to fill up any empty space on me."

She reaches over and touches just above my chest on my right side, lightly poking her fingertip against my skin. "What is this one? I think I figured out what all the other ones are, but I can't make this one out."

I don't need to look to know which one she means. It's the oldest tattoo I have, and after twelve years, it's faded against my tanned skin to look like a random series of lines.

"The wheel of fortune, like the tarot card. I got it a long time ago, but it wasn't done very well, so it's all faded and broken looking," I explain.

Lily leans over and puts her face just an inch away

from my chest to study the image for a long moment. When she finishes, she looks up and shakes her head.

"I don't see it, but I'll take your word for it."

"Have I ever lied to you yet?" I ask with a chuckle, knowing how ridiculous that question is since we've only known each other for a few days.

Her smile fades as a darkness comes over her expression. She tries to move away from me, but I stop her with my arm behind her back so she has to stay right where she is.

I know what she's wondering. Am I lying about not killing her, or was that just something I said because I wanted to fuck her.

"You're safe, Lily. I promised not to kill you, and I won't."

"Ever?" she asks in a way that sounds like a child would say the word.

"Ever. I won't kill you no matter what."

She searches my face for what the real truth is because she doesn't believe my promise. Her gaze fixes on mine and won't let go.

"What about if my father doesn't pay the money?" she asks in a small voice.

"No. I won't kill you then either."

Still, her focus doesn't waver. I don't blame her for not believing me. I can barely believe it myself.

"What if your boss tells you to kill me? What will you do then?"

I shake my head. Victor was never going to order me to kill Lily. He just wants his damn money paid back. Even he isn't in the business of killing people's children for that.

"He won't."

"But what if my father doesn't get the money by the end of the seven days?" she asks, her voice hitching on the word end.

"Nope. I can't say what will happen to him if he doesn't pay my boss, but you won't be hurt."

She frowns at the mention of her father's possible future. That I can't help. He knew what he was doing when he took the money. If he's not stupid, he'll cash in some of those fucking plates he's got hanging on his walls and save himself and his daughter.

"I'm worried he won't pay up in time, Cason. Please tell me you won't be the one who's ordered to do it."

Again, I shake my head. "I don't know who it will be."

"I won't let you kill him. I can't. You'll have to kill me to get to him."

Her bravado amuses me, even as I know it would be nothing to get past her to him if I'm the one who's ordered to do the job. I can't help but admire her strength, though. It will do her no good, no matter who has to get to her father, but it makes me hope her father does the right thing.

"I just told you I won't kill you, Lily. As for your father, I have no control over that. Maybe he'll sell some of those plates he loves and end this whole thing."

My mention of those ridiculous blue and white

plates makes her hang her head, and in a tiny voice, she says, "He won't. They mean too much to him."

"Why? They're just plates. What's the big deal about them that he can't sell even a couple to get himself and you out of this jam?" I ask, finally hoping she can explain the importance of those damn things.

Lifting her head, she forces a smile I know isn't genuine, and with tears in her eyes, she answers, "They were my mother's. He couldn't part with a single one. It would be like giving away the only things left he has of her. He'd rather die."

When I don't say anything, she says, "I bet you think that's stupid, don't you? Like my father's a sentimental fool. I bet your father isn't like that, is he?"

I think about my father and how he got this house and shake my head. "No. He's a fucking monster. Definitely not a sentimental bone in his body."

"Well, my father is. Those plates are all he has left of my mother, except for memories and me. I know it sounds silly, but they mean the world to him."

I don't know what to say to Lily about her father and those plates. All I can hope for is he finds the money somehow and pays his loan before the seven days are up.

If he doesn't, Lily won't die but he might. That I can't do a damn thing about.

She falls silent and lays her head on my tattoo of that faded wheel of fortune tarot design on my chest. Whatever his fate turns out to be, she can't change it. No matter how much she may want to.

Nobody can. Our fates may not be carved in stone, but every choice we make, every action we take, makes them harder and harder to change.

I've protected Lily's in all of this. Now it's up to her father to do his part.

Even if that means trading a sliver of his past to secure his future with his only child.

CHAPTER FIFTEEN

*L*ily

Next to me, Cason makes a low noise and then moves to roll over onto his side. It sounds like a small growl from a contented animal, but I can't let myself get lulled into a false sense of security. He is still very much the man who's repeatedly threatened to kill me, no matter what he promised last night.

I have no reason to believe he isn't the same killer he proudly claims to be, no matter what he said after we slept together. He is that man, and I'm still in as much danger as I was when he tied me up in that chair in his apartment.

So I have to find a way to escape.

His chest expands and contracts as I watch to see if he's truly sleeping. Every inch of my body is on edge as I slowly back away from him. Instantly, I miss his warmth.

I can't think like that. A moment's comfort can

easily turn into an hour's pain. I just have to get away from this place and then everything will be okay. Of course, that's assuming the fence isn't electrified.

No. I can't think about that either. The fear of being fried like a mosquito on a bug zapper can't be the reason I stay here. Somehow, I'll get around the fence. It might not even be electrified. Maybe Cason only said that to scare me into not even trying to get away. That would make sense.

He stops breathing for a moment, and I hold my breath while I wait for him to say something. Is he awake? I watch for a second and then another and then finally he exhales as relief washes over me.

I can't wait forever. I have to take a chance. The worst that happens if he wakes up is he thinks I'm going to the bathroom and I have to wait for a little while longer.

But no matter what, I have to try to get away tonight.

Cason rolls over onto his back, so I quickly drop my head onto the pillow and shut my eyes. I hear him breathing, in and out and in and out, and gradually I open my right eye to check if he's asleep.

He looks like he's out. Slowly, I sit up next to him, letting my gaze roam over his naked torso down to where the white bedsheet drapes across his hips. While his chest expands, the muscles in his abdomen gently ripple under his skin, and then the whole thing repeats when he lets out the air from his lungs.

Asleep, he looks like a warrior lying there covered in tattoos, his body tight and toned. I imagine more than one woman has watched him sleep like this and thought how lucky they were to get to be with him.

But he's no warrior. There's no nobility in him. He's just a killer, and I can't forget that. Even though I can't forget how he's made my body come alive.

That doesn't matter. It can't. Bodies lie, or at least mine does. What he makes me feel is a physical reaction. It doesn't mean anything. It doesn't reflect what kind of man he is or what he does without a hint of guilt.

Cason is a killer. Now I need to get away from that killer.

I take a deep breath and hold it in as I crawl down to the bottom of the bed and gingerly step off. The bed moves, and I quickly look back to check he's still asleep. My heart races by the second, but he seems like he's out cold.

Praying to God I'll be able to get away, I lift my other leg and stand up. The bed moves again, and I glance back to check Cason one more time.

Still asleep.

My heart slams into my chest, but I take a step toward the door and then another, careful to walk as lightly as I can. With every one, I twist my head to look back to see if he's awake, but I think I'm going to make it.

All I have to do is open the door and hope against hope it doesn't make a sound. The problem is I don't know if it usually creaks when I open or close his bedroom door. I've never paid attention.

I stop in front of the door and close my eyes,

silently praying I don't wake him up on this last hurdle to my freedom. My palms are drenched, and when I reach out to grab the doorknob, my hand shakes. I twist it and slowly pull the door open, listening for any hint of noise.

But there is none. The door silently swings toward me, and then with one last look back at Cason, I step out into the hallway and close it behind me.

I'm free!

I hurry to my room and dress in another new pair of black yoga pants and the white T-shirt he bought for me yesterday. It takes me only seconds before I'm ready to make my escape down the stairs and out the front door. Slowly, I open my bedroom door and look down the hall toward Cason's room to see if he's realized I'm gone yet.

Nothing. Not a sound. Hopefully, he's still asleep.

With no idea what time it is and only a sense that it must be the middle of the night because it's dark outside, I tiptoe down the stairs and make my way to the front door. I twist the lock, and then just like with his bedroom door, I open it slowly, desperate to make not even the tiniest sound. I swing it open, eager to finally be free, and step outside into the cool night air.

I almost can't believe I've made it to the outdoors. Closing the front door behind me, I take a deep breath of air into my lungs and hold it there for a moment. It feels different outside now than it did when he brought me out here yesterday.

No one is letting me out now. I'm here because I want to be. I'm free.

The moment passes, and I run as fast as I can toward the front of the property. Clouds mask the moon, thankfully, making my escape harder to see, I hope. I just need to get to where the road turns onto the driveway that travels up to the house, and then the time to see if he lied about the electrified fence will come.

My bare feet glide over the wet grass, and when I begin to run on the pavement, they make a slapping sound with each time they hit the ground. It's the sound of freedom, the sound of me getting away to safety the only chance I have.

And just as I congratulate myself on escaping, I see up ahead the silhouette of a person standing near the road. In seconds, he turns to face me as I quickly turn and run away. If he yells, Cason will hear him and realize I'm gone, but if I stop to approach him, I'll be caught anyway.

I have no good choices, so I keep running. Away from the man. Away from the house. I don't know where to, but I have to find a way to get away from everything and everyone here.

Behind me, a noise that sounds like someone running makes my heart nearly explode out of my chest. I turn around to see the man coming after me. Much larger, his legs are faster than mine. In no time, he'll catch up to me.

I have to think of something to make sure he doesn't catch me and take me back to the house. But what? If I climb a tree, he'll have me trapped. If I try to hide, it will only be a matter of time before he finds me. My plan to get free will be ruined.

There are no choices, good or otherwise, but I keep running, pushing my legs and lungs to perform better than my body is capable of delivering. Pain stabs through my chest, and with every second that passes, the burning in my thighs makes me question if I can go on. I can't get a full breath of air into my body, and my head is pounding.

I glance back and in horror see he's catching up. A second later, the clouds clear away from the moon, and in the dim light, I see it's Doc chasing me.

Should I stop and gamble on him taking me back to Cason? My mind flashes back to the three of us outside on the front lawn. There's no love lost between those two, and he did ask how I was doing. Maybe he will help me get away?

It's a stupid idea, but I don't have any others. I can't outrun him. He's just too big and too fast. I can only hope he won't force me to go back to the house.

Gradually, I slow to a walk and wait for him to catch up. With each second that passes, I pray to God for him to be a good man who will help me now. If I can just get off this estate, I can get back to my father and the two of us can go into hiding. That way he won't get hurt if he can't pay the money back, and I'll be safe from Cason. We can pack up those plates of his and drive away to a place nobody will ever be able to find us.

I just have to get home to him.

"Lily? What are you doing out here?" Doc asks just as his face comes into full view.

"Doc, I need your help. I need to get away from here. Please help me."

Those weren't the words I'd planned to say. I wanted to sound strong and powerful, but suddenly when I looked into his eyes, I saw a glimmer of kindness I hope wasn't my imagination.

He doesn't answer for what feels like forever, and my heart sinks at the realization that I've made a mistake. Doc won't help me any more than Nate would. They're just like Cason.

Waving his hand, he beckons me toward him. I don't have a choice. If I run again, he'll catch up to me, so why even try?

I take a step in his direction and hear him whisper, "Come with me. Don't say a word or you'll be stuck here, so keep your mouth shut."

What? Does that mean he's going to help me get off this estate and to freedom?

"Where are we going?" I ask as he takes my hand in his.

Doc flashes me an angry stare and lowers his head to whisper in my face, "Didn't I just tell you to be quiet?"

Nodding, I try not to think of the heavy smell of coffee that coats every word that comes out of his mouth. It's pungent compared to the fresh late summer night air and turns my stomach when his breath hits me. He pulls me toward where I first saw him, walking much faster than I can and making me run to keep up.

When we make it to the guard shed at the edge of the property, he turns to look back at me and whispers angrily, "Don't move."

Again, I nod my understanding and watch him fling open the shed's door. A few seconds later, he returns to where I'm waiting and tugs on my arm to follow him.

"Did you have to turn off the electric fence?" I whisper as quietly as possible but still loud enough so he might hear me.

The expression on his face when he turns to look at me makes me feel stupid. There never was an electric fence like Cason said. That lie was just another one he used to control me.

"Nobody uses electrified fences anymore. We have cameras that do the job without frying people. Why would you think we had one of those?"

I hang my head and continue walking with him. "Cason told me it was an electric fence," I say quietly, not out of a need to be discreet but out of shame for being so stupid.

Doc chuckles at my foolishness. "You really are young, aren't you?"

He says that like it's an indictment of not only my age but my intelligence, which only serves to make me feel worse. But even if I could explain to him why I believed it when Cason told me that lie, I wouldn't. There's no point.

Looking up, I see a car and my heart leaps in my chest. Doc is going to drive me away from here!

"Get in the back and keep your head down until I tell you otherwise. And this time, do as I say," he orders before folding the upholstered driver's side seat forward so I can climb into the back seat.

It's a small car, which seems strange for someone his size to drive, but I fit easily into the dark area behind him. I press my head against the cloth seat and close my eyes as he starts the car and quickly drives away.

I have no idea how long it will take and even if he intends to drive me all the way to my house. I don't care. As long as I'm away from that estate and the man I still believe plans to kill me if my father doesn't pay up, I'm much better off than I was an hour ago.

The car careens left and then right, turning onto roads I don't know and can't remember from when I was brought to that house just days ago, my head bouncing against the seat whenever the tires hit a pothole or bump. Doc drives faster than Cason did when we came here, but that's a good thing.

The sooner I'm far enough away from Cason that he can't reach me, the better.

Finally, after we ride along those winding roads with me lurching from one side of the car to the other with each turn, the car comes to a skidding stop. I know Doc told me to keep my head down, but I can't stop myself from popping up to look out the back window.

It's pitch black outside, so I can't see where we are,

but I know it's not a city or even a small town because there isn't a streetlight anywhere nearby. He turns the car off and quickly pushes his door open before poking his head back to look at me.

"We need to stop here for a little while. I think I saw him coming out the front door as we drove away. He won't find you here, though, so don't worry."

Panic rises inside me, and I shake my head in disbelief. "He can't find me! He'll take me back there and kill me. Please don't let him find me!"

Doc reaches into the car and tugs me out of the backseat, but I fight him every inch of the way. In that car, I'm safe. Or at least I feel safe.

"Come on. We'll go inside and you'll be fine. I won't let him get you," he promises as I stick my head out of the car to see nothing but blackness. "Trust me. It's a good thing I got to you before he did."

"Where are we?" I ask and step out onto the gravel dirt road.

He closes the car door and grabs my hand, tightening his fingers around my wrist. "Just a house we can use to hide out for a little bit. Cason doesn't know about this place. It's somewhere the security guys use to sleep when they don't want to drive all the way home after a long shift."

As he explains about the house I'm about to walk into, it makes sense that Cason wouldn't know anything about it. He doesn't seem to have anything good to say about either of the security guards who came to the house while I was there, so naturally, they wouldn't be close enough to let him in on their secret place to crash.

My heartbeat calms from that thought. Doc's right. This is a good thing just like him finding me before Cason could was a good thing.

"Okay. If you think it's going to be safe."

Doc smiles and tightens his grip on me as we walk through the front door. It's dark inside, but he continues to guide me into the first room while he mumbles something about not remembering where the light switch is.

That sounds odd, and I wonder about it since he just told me this was a place he and the other security guys use, but maybe he doesn't use it often himself. I start to ask him about it, but a second later, fluorescent lights flicker on above my head.

I turn to look at Doc to thank him for helping me, but the words never make it out of my mouth. His arm swings around, and his meaty fist hits my cheek like a brick to my face. Pain explodes into my right eye, and I collapse to the ground clutching my head as the agony spikes across my scalp.

Stunned, I try to stand, not understanding what's happening, but he shoves me back onto the floor with an angry grunt. "Get down, you stupid fucking girl!"

My head pounds from the shot to my cheekbone, but I see out of my left eye Doc glaring down at me with more anger than I ever saw in Cason. How could I have been so naïve? Instead of helping me get away, he's been working with my captor this whole time.

"Why are you doing this? I thought you were going to help me."

Doc lets out a low chuckle and shakes his head even as he continues to angrily glare down at me on the floor. "I never said I'd help you. I want to see what's making that asshole Cason so crazy about you. What do you have that makes you so fucking tempting to a man like him? No point in trying to say nothing because if that was true, he would have killed you already. I'm guessing it's between your legs, and I plan to have a taste of that myself."

I try to push myself away from him, but he's on me in a matter of seconds. His clawing hands grab at my new clothes, ripping the white T-shirt off my shoulders to grope my breasts. He's not even as rough as Cason, yet it's far more violating. I cry out, but he doesn't care. His fingers squeeze my tender flesh, leaving painful wounds on my skin.

"Stop! You're hurting me!"

For a moment, he leans away from me and shakes his head, like he can't believe I want him to stop pawing at me. But then he grabs the top of my yoga pants and tugs them hard down my legs, leaving me open to him.

I fight back, but it's no use. He's stronger and crueler than I can handle, and it takes no time for me to be naked and cowering on the wood floor. He looms over me, unzipping his pants, and grins when he flops his hard cock out.

"Now we'll see what's so special about you that a fucking killer can't bring himself to get rid of you."

Shaking my head, all I can do is push him away with my hands and kick my legs to slow him down. I can't stop what's about to happen, though, even as regret fills me for the choice I made to trust this person.

CHAPTER SIXTEEN

Eason

At least I can rely on Lily being exactly what she is. Not that I blame her, to be honest. I'm not sure I'd believe me either. I'm a killer, so why wouldn't I kill her?

She's crafty. I have to give her that. But I'm craftier. Hers is tinged with desperation and inexperience, and that will always be her downfall until she becomes more jaded and distrusting.

Then again, I can't deny I like how naïve she is, and not only because it makes my job easier. It's refreshing to be around someone who still believes in good. I don't think I ever can again after all I've seen and done, but Lily still does, and I like how that looks on her.

Reaching across the bed, I grab my phone to see how far she's gotten. I'm guessing maybe out toward the edge of the estate where she went that first day I brought her here. Will she dare to touch the fence I told her was electrified?

See, that right there is fucking charming in its naiveté. It's like everything she knows about bad guys has come from old TV shows. Nobody's used electrified fences in over a decade. Hell, maybe even longer. I'm not even sure my father has a goddamned fence up anymore. With cameras and drones, in addition to those asshole guards of his, who needs to fry people who trespass?

I tap on my phone's screen to get a sense of where she is and where I'm going to have to hike to get her. As I wait for the map, I smile. She really did think I just bought those clothes for her because I'm a nice guy. It's almost like this was too easy.

But my amusement quickly evaporates when I see she's at the edge of the estate and still moving. Fuck. Maybe she's cleverer than I thought.

Jumping out of bed, I throw on my pants and shirt before slipping on my shoes to go get her. It's the middle of the goddamned night, and I'm forced to spend my time chasing down some girl.

A girl I just promised not to kill.

By the time I get outside, I see that asshole Doc's car speeding away out the front gate. A quick check of the tracker on my phone shows me she's in that car with him.

Fuck! I told her not to speak to him. Why the fuck can't she listen when she's told something? Doc gets his kicks fucking with women. I expressly forbade her from even talking to him ever again. Now he's got her and only God knows where the hell he's taking her.

After running upstairs to get my gun, I get to the car and tear off, hoping to catch them before he does something to her. Stupid girl! Why would she trust him?

It's that ridiculous fucking name of his. Doc. Like he's some cartoon character and couldn't hurt a fly. Except he isn't and hurting people is what he loves to do.

Adrenaline courses through my body as I floor the gas. They're only a few minutes ahead of me, but what he likes doesn't take long, especially if you're a clumsy fuck like Doc and just want to inflict pain.

I shouldn't care what the hell he does to her. After all, she's been nothing but a hassle. I should just leave her to Doc and let him handle her. If he fucks her up, so be it.

Even as I say that to myself, I push my foot down on the gas even harder to catch up with them. Yes, she's been a pain in the ass, but she's my pain in the ass. Not his. That fuck will just rip her apart for kicks because he gets off on hurting women and then bragging about it to other guys in the organization.

The memory of him grinning like a fucking cat who swallowed a canary that one time he sat in Victor's office talking about cutting up that girl just to hear her cry while he fucked her races through my head and makes my stomach turn. He laughed his ass off as he gave the details about how all her blood and his cum mixed to get him off the best of his life.

Fucking animal. I kill people for a living and I'm not even that bad. Killing is killing, and fucking is fucking. Only a goddamned savage would combine the two.

I wanted to punch the asshole in his smiling face that day, but Jaxon beat me to it and broke Doc's jaw. He should have put a bullet in his fucking head. Tearing up girls for no reason is the surest way to get us all thrown in jail, and that son of a bitch is probably up to it again with Lily.

Rage makes paying attention to the road in front of me next to impossible, but I have to watch for any sign of his car. Grabbing my phone, I take another look at the tracker map and see the car has stopped up ahead.

Probably at that super-secret hideout he and the other security assholes use when they're too tired to drive home after a long shift at the estate. They like to act like it's their clubhouse, the fucking jackasses, like it's some exclusive place only the cool security guards can use. None of them think we know about it, but the truth is the rest of us who aren't ten year olds don't care about their stupid little hideout.

I take each turn on the winding road leading to the cabin like a bat out of hell. Every second he's with her is another chance for him to hurt her.

When I see the cabin and his car parked out front, I tighten my grip on the steering wheel and floor it as I mumble to myself, "Doc, you better hope you didn't do something stupid because I swear to fucking God I'll blow your head off if I see one drop of blood on her, asshole."

I can't even let myself think about the idea that there might be his cum mixed with her blood like with that poor girl he was bragging about that night. If he touched her like that, I swear to God I'm going to kill him.

The car barely stops rolling before I'm out with my gun in my hand. I press my palm to the hood of his car and feel it's still warm. They haven't been here very long. He better hope it wasn't long enough for him to make a mistake he won't live to brag about with his buddies.

My foot hits the front porch when I hear a bloodcurdling scream come from the inside of the cabin. It's Lily's voice. I'd know it anywhere.

The sound makes my heart skip a beat. She's in there with him and he's hurting her. Fucking asshole! One sign of blood—one fucking drop—and I'm going to blow his fucking head clear off his shoulders.

A single kick sends the front door flying open, and what I see when I take that first step inside makes me nearly blind with rage. Naked on the floor, Lily's fighting to get him off her while Doc hovers over her with his dick out and a knife in his right hand while he holds her down with the other. I can't hear anything but her screaming my name over and over like some horrible, desperate plea she hopes will save her.

"Cason! Help me!"

I rip him off her and shove him across the floor into the wall. He's stunned for a few seconds, but he's not knocked out. Lily scrambles to grab her clothes, curling up in a ball on the other side of the room as she gets dressed.

"Go out to the car and wait for me. I'll be out in a minute."

Her eyes wide and full of pure fear, she still bothers to ask me a goddamned question. "What are you going to do to him?"

It draws my attention away for a second, and I look over at her in disbelief. "Go! Now!"

Before she can run away, Doc gets up on his feet, his stiff dick still poking out of his fucking pants. It's not every day I interrupt an attempted rape, and as much as it's against everything I am as a man, I want to shoot that fucker's prick right off with one clear shot.

He takes a step toward her, and I point my gun straight at the center of his forehead. "Don't move one more inch from that spot, or I'm going to blow your head off."

Lily makes a whimpering sound as she stands up to walk to the door, but my attention is firmly on Doc. One move. That's all he has to make and I'll pull the trigger. Just one twitch of any part of his body and he gets what he deserves.

"Are you fucking kidding me? You're going to threaten me while the cunt you're supposed to kill gets to walk out of here? What is it that makes this girl so fucking special? Tell me since you stopped me before I got to figure it the fuck out. What is it, Cason, that makes you want to kill me over her?"

Every word out of his mouth makes me more eager

to blow him away. I'm not supposed to kill her. Not yet. What I do with Lily is none of his goddamned business anyway. It's nobody's business but mine.

"Shut the fuck up. You took something of mine. Now you get to see how I feel when someone does that, Doc."

His name comes out of my mouth in a hiss I hate it so much. One move is all I want him to make. Not that I can't just shoot him without it. He's a fucking security guard who watches a house my father doesn't even like to visit, for fuck's sake. This time, even my father would have to agree a son beats some easily replaced security asshole.

Behind me, Lily lets out another piercing scream like the one before, and a second later, Doc makes that move toward me I knew he would. He barely gets two steps closer to me before I do what I've wanted to do for a while. The gun goes off, the bullet exploding out of the chamber, and a second later, he drops to the floor like a bag of wet shit.

I walk over and look down at him in disgust. Stupid fuck. I watch him for a moment to make sure he's dead, but it's not necessary. I aimed to kill, so that's just what I did. The proof is his brains splattered all over the wall behind him.

Instantly, I know what I have to do. Turning around, I see Lily staring at me in horror. No wonder she didn't believe me when I said I wouldn't kill her. Now she's gotten to see what I am in full view.

"We need to go."

"What are you going to do? Bury him?"

Again, with the old TV shows shit.

"No. I'm not going to bury him," I answer while I walk over to see if he cut her anywhere.

Lily looks up at me far too innocently for what she's just been through and seen. I can feel those dark eyes of hers focus on me as I scan her body for what he did to her.

"So what happens now?"

The truth is I don't know what happens now. I just shot one of my father's employees, so I'll have to deal with that when the time comes. At this moment, all I can process is the utter relief that Lily's not bleeding, as far as I can see.

"You come with me. That's what happens now," I say when I finally let my gaze move back to her face.

"Back to the house?" she asks sheepishly.

I shake my head. "No. We need to go somewhere else now."

Turning to walk out the door, I feel her touch my arm and look back to see her eyes filling with tears. I've never seen the aftermath of a kill. There's nobody left standing when I do my job. Nobody to cry over the people I've killed.

"I'm sorry I ran away, Cason," she says before she covers her face and begins to cry. "I didn't know."

Her tears anger me. Is she crying over that fuck I just shot to protect her?

"Yes, you did. I told you not to ever speak to him again, and you went ahead and did it anyway. Why did you think I said that?"

Lowering her hands, she sniffles. "I thought you might be jealous because he was so nice to me."

I can't decide if her innocence is something I still like or if she's just plain stupid. Either way, she wasn't entirely wrong. I knew about Doc's penchant for hurting women, but I also didn't like the way he talked to her because it made me jealous.

She doesn't need to know that, though.

"What I was doing was trying to make sure he didn't get a hold of you and cut you up. That's his thing. He likes to cut girls while he fucks them. Cum and blood get him off. But then, I guess you know that."

I don't know why I say that. It makes no sense, and it's intentionally cruel. At least at this very moment, I shouldn't be that way to her. Still, the words come out before I can stop them, and they have the exact effect they're supposed to.

"I'm sorry," she sobs and covers her face again.

Part of me wants to ask if she's okay, but another part of me hates how easily she read my jealousy over that asshole. The shitty part wins out, and I say nothing before pushing her out the door of the cabin onto the porch.

"You must think I'm really stupid, don't you?" she says as I guide her to the passenger side of the car.

Whatever a decent man would say to that, I have no idea. I want to tell her I think she's incredibly stupid at times, but that will only bring about more crying and then more questions. I don't want to deal with either.

So I say nothing and slam the car door behind me before walking around the car and getting in. I need to figure out where to take her now that the house is no good. I need time to get my answer straight in my head for why I killed Doc because my father is going to be asking as soon as they find the son of a bitch sprawled out in that cabin with his brains all over the place.

Most of all, I need some peace and quiet, but with Lily around, that's not going to happen.

I drive about a mile before she starts talking again, and I silently remind myself I could just tape her mouth closed for the rest of the time she's around. I won't, though. As much as she practically drives me insane with all her questions, I think I might miss them if she stopped now.

"Are you angry with me because of what I did?"

That wasn't a question I'd expected to hear, and as I slow down to drive onto another dark country road, I turn to look at her. "I told you I wouldn't kill you. I don't think good old Doc would have made you the same promise."

A sound like a tiny whimper escapes from her, and I wait for the tears to come once more. But they don't. Instead, she says in a voice barely above a whisper, "Please don't be angry. I thought he was going to be nice to me."

And that, right there, makes me angrier than I can even explain.

$\mathcal{L}$ily

Cason's expression hardens when I say I thought Doc would be nice to me. I guess I deserve that. It was stupid to believe he'd help me escape and expect nothing in return. I just didn't realize rape would be the payment he demanded.

The car falls silent, so I keep talking, hoping Cason's mood will soften soon. "Thank you for saving me. I know I made it necessary for you to do it, but thank you anyway."

In the moonlight, I watch him shift his gaze to give me the side-eye, but he says nothing in response. He probably wants to tell me how my stupidity nearly got me killed, and not by him, by the way. I'd deserve anything he says since I made the mistake of running away in the first place.

"Cason, are you going to be in trouble because of what happened to Doc?" I ask just as a shiver races down my back at the memory of the terrifying sound of his gun and bullet sending Doc to the floor.

"No. He took something that was mine. I had every right to do what I did to him for that."

"Your boss isn't going to be mad at you?"

That makes him look over at me, but in the darkness, I can't see his expression now. I know how foolish my questions can sound, and that one did seem particularly ignorant of what Cason's world is. The problem is that I don't know much about what it's like or what kind of relationship he and his boss have. He did let him use his house this week to hold me, so maybe he likes him enough to understand why he had to kill Doc.

Not that I truly understand, though.

"Am I that thing he took?" I quietly ask, unsure if that's what he meant when he said Doc took something of his since I'm a someone, not a something.

"Yes," he answers flatly, a clear sign he doesn't want to talk about that anymore.

But the way he said it earlier—he took something that was mine—makes me wonder even more about what he meant. Am I his? Why does he consider me that?

"Cason, can I ask you a question?"

Suddenly, he lurches the steering wheel to the right, sending us careening off the road to the shoulder, and slams on the brakes. Jamming the car into park, he turns in his seat to face me, and I sit there frozen in fear that I've pushed him too far.

"Did you just ask me if you could ask me a question?" he says in utter disbelief.

"Yes," I answer in a voice barely above a whisper.

I don't know what to expect as we sit there in the dark, silence surrounding us and the seconds ticking by while he says nothing more. Will he reach out and grab me by the throat to take out his anger at what I've done? Will he hit me for causing such a problem for him? Will he lean over me and open the car door to push me out because he can't deal with the hassle of having me as his hostage not another minute longer?

His breath sounds heavy in the darkness, and when he moves closer to me, I feel the warmth of it brush across the top of my head. My muscles in my neck tighten as I await whatever he plans to do. Tears well in my eyes, but I'm thankful he can't see them because I don't want to be even more difficult to deal with, in case he isn't planning to do something terrible.

Then just as I'm sure he's about to yell at me for all that's happened, I feel his lips press against my forehead. The breath I've been holding in since I answered his question comes out in a shudder of pure relief.

"You're mine to decide what to do with, Lily."

I can't see him in the pitch blackness, but his voice sounds different, gentler than usual. He sounds kind, like he did when he promised he wouldn't kill me as we lay in each other's arms just hours ago.

Lowering my head, I press my cheek against the spot at the base of his throat and let the tears come that had been threatening this whole time. "I just wanted to get to my father and take him away before one of us gets hurt because of what he's done. I'm sorry I made the mistake of going with Doc."

Cason's arms slide around my shoulders, and then as he holds me to him, he whispers, "Did he do anything to you?"

I know what he's asking. Did he hurt me? Did he rape me?

Shaking my head, I reply against his skin that smells like it did when my head was on his chest in bed before I ran away. "No. He almost did, but then you showed up and stopped him."

His body expands when he takes a deep breath in. Letting it out slowly, he quietly says, "Good."

"I'm sorry. I should have believed you when you said you wouldn't kill me. I'm sorry I didn't."

And then in the time it takes for my heart to beat just once, he changes back to that man he usually is.

"I gave you my word, Lily. Believe it or not," he says icily as he pushes me off him and turns back in his seat to face the road.

I want to believe him. More than he can possibly ever imagine I want to believe he won't kill me if my father makes the mistake of not paying his boss back. He likely doesn't understand how much believing him would make me happy. He's got all the power and the gun. All I have is the body I agreed to use in a deal between the devil and myself.

And after all that I've done, I don't know if I've ruined everything now.

But maybe if he thinks I do believe him, he'll want to live up to his promise.

"I do believe you. I do."

As he shifts the car into drive, he sighs. "Then no more stupid stunts from you. I agree to not kill you, and you agree not to run away and nearly get yourself hurt. Or worse."

Nodding, even though he can't see me agreeing to his deal, I notice he doesn't use the word for what Doc planned to do. Is the reason because he thinks of me as his that way? Why does he care if another man fucks me? I'm just his prisoner, although we have slept together, too.

If he was any other man, I'd ask him these questions. Maybe if I hadn't made the mistake of running away and having to be rescued from that asshole, I'd ask those questions.

But he's Cason, a man who I worry might lose his mind on the next one I ask, and I did make the mistake with Doc, so I don't ask what I so desperately want to know.

Closing my eyes, I let those thoughts dance around in my brain as I drift off to sleep and give Cason the peace and quiet he so desperately wants. Maybe when I wake up I can ask him then.

THE CAR JERKS TO A STOP, AND MY EYELIDS FLY open in surprise. In front of the car I see motel doors. I turn my head to the right and look out the window to see a neon red sign that says REST INN.

Cason shuts the car off and looks over at me. "Don't do anything stupid when we go inside and talk to the clerk. Understand?"

"Okay."

He hasn't threatened to tie me up since he took me out of that cabin, so I have no intention of making him want to do that again now. I watch him walk around the car to my side and open the door. It's an oddly kind gesture that I don't know how to interpret.

As I get out and he slams the door behind me, I ask, "Are you doing that to make it look like we're a couple for anyone who's seeing us here? Are we pretending to be a happy couple or are you a man cheating on his wife with me and we're supposed to look like we're sneaking around?"

Cason narrows his eyes and stares down at me like he doesn't know what to say. "How do you come up with these ideas? Who thinks that way?"

"Me."

"Since I don't know how to look like I'm sneaking around on someone, just go with the quiet but happy couple that doesn't talk much to the desk clerk. Can you do that?"

"Yes."

"Good. Now let's go."

When he takes my hand in his, I look down, surprised he wants to take the charade that far. "So you're really into this happy couple thing?"

"You know what would make me really happy?" he asks as we walk toward the front office.

I smile for the first time since I stood outside the

house and took my first breath of fresh air as a free woman. "Me pretending to be your mute wife?"

And for the first time since he found me in that cabin, he smiles too. "That's the nicest thing you've ever said. Mute wife. Perfect. Now let me do all the talking."

We walk into where the desk clerk sits behind a wood counter cracking his gum and watching something on his phone. He appears to be about my age or maybe a year or two older, and when he looks up at us standing there, his face shows how annoyed he is at being interrupted.

"What's up?" he asks in a far squeakier voice than I've ever heard on a man, even a young one.

Cason sets his black leather wallet on the countertop. "We want a room for the night."

I watch as the kid types in the information he's given into a desktop computer that's nearly a gold color it's so old. Standing at Cason's side, I say nothing and avoid looking the clerk in the eye. The thought of trying to get him to help me crosses my mind, but I discount that idea immediately and remind myself that Cason promised he wouldn't hurt me.

Plus, I doubt this guy would help anyway, and the last person I thought would help me escape nearly raped me, so my belief in my fellow mankind isn't exactly unshakeable at the moment. Better to stay with the one who at least claims he won't kill me than make another bad mistake and end up in an even worse situation.

Ten minutes later, Cason and I walk to room 33 at

the end of the line of white motel doors. Immediately, I notice someone scratched the word liar into the paint near the doorknob.

"Seems this has been the scene of some cheaters who got caught in the past."

Looking down at where I point my finger, Cason smiles again. "That's what you get for screwing around. Someone calls you out on the door where you're fucking someone else."

As I follow him inside the dark room, I wonder if he's the cheating type. Something tells me he isn't, but not because he's a moral man or even a loving one. I get the sense he just can't be bothered with creating the lies that cheaters are forced to. He freely admits to being a killer. I can't imagine he wouldn't be as willing to admit he doesn't care about someone and wants to leave them.

When he turns on the light, the terrible change in our circumstances becomes instantly obvious. My eyes fill with the vision of faded tan walls around us, a threadbare dark brown carpet beneath our feet, and dated furniture that looks like something from a sixties sitcom. On the bed, a dark brown and salmon pink swirl patterned bedspread completes the horrible décor.

Hanging my head, I look down at the floor and see a pale stain that looks like someone in the past drew a chalk outline right where I'm standing. "Oh, Cason. I'm so sorry."

"Close the door. No point in complaining. This is where we're staying, at least for the next few hours."

I quickly make a beeline for the bed so my feet don't have to be stuck on that filthy carpet. "I'm going to have to boil my entire body when we leave here."

Cason flashes me a look before he sits down next to me. "So much for the silent Lily the desk clerk got."

Sulking, I fall back onto the bed. "I'm sorry. I thought I could talk again."

He turns around to glare at me, and I remember all too well that whatever kindness he has in him can be replaced by the very man who took me and threatened my life before rescuing me from that cabin. My captor is a killer, as he's told me repeatedly.

"I just realized your T-shirt is ripped," he says, pointing at my collar.

My fingers trace the tear that goes clear to my shoulder as the memory of Doc shredding my new shirt comes rushing back. I shrug, like it doesn't matter.

"It's just a T-shirt."

Cason shakes his head. "No, I mean the desk clerk guy saw you standing there in ripped clothes. He probably thinks I've been roughing you up."

"What do you care what he thinks? He's just some kid working the overnight at a seedy motel in the middle of nowhere. Who cares if he thinks you're not some charming date?"

"I don't care. I just noticed it." He stands up and heads toward the door. "Stay here. I'll be right back. Don't do anything stupid, Lily."

Under my breath just as he leaves, I mumble,

"That's my thing. Doing stupid stuff. That's how I ended up in this place with a man like you."

I don't know why his noticing my ripped shirt bothers me, but it does and I don't have the ability to do anything other than lash out that way. I doubt he even heard what I said, so it isn't like it matters.

Still, his callous attitude after mentioning something about what happened with Doc stings.

I lay there staring up at what I hope is a water stain on the ceiling and not the result of someone's ass exploding upwards at some point. We're stuck in this place because of me. God, I'm so stupid. Why did I have to run away, even after he said he wouldn't kill me?

"Because I didn't believe him," I say under my breath. "Because once someone tells me they're going to kill me, it's hard to get that out of my goddamned head."

God, is it possible my father has paid his debt to Cason's boss and this can all be over? Maybe that's what he's hearing right now if he's out there talking to him on the phone. If that's the case, we can leave this shitty motel room and I can be home by dawn.

With only that tiny bit of hope, my mood improves and I jump off the bed to go check out the bathroom. As I make my way across the disgusting carpet toward the bathroom door, I silently pray to God it doesn't look or smell like someone died in there.

Opening the door, I flick on the light switch and see pink tiles on the wall and floor that aren't seriously dirty. The grout looks like it needs a good bleaching, much like the rest of the motel room, but the sink isn't filthy from hard water stains and the pink toilet is actually clean inside. I pull back the white shower curtain that looks sort of new and see not pink tiles with grimy grout lines, thankfully, but a shower enclosure without a hint of mold. It's nothing like the bathroom in my room at the estate, but for a rundown old motel, it's a pleasant surprise.

"Wow. I guess this comes under the heading of thank God for small favors."

Behind me, I hear Cason return to the room and slam the door behind him. I peek my head out and see he looks even more miserable than before he left.

"Just to let you know, the bathroom isn't terrible, believe it or not. It's actually sort of clean."

He sits down hard on the bed and sighs. Without looking at me, he nods and says, "That's good. We're going to be here for at least tonight, so it's nice to have a bathroom that isn't roach infested."

Roach infested? Holy mother of God! Even the thought of that makes my skin feel like bugs are crawling up and down my body.

"What's wrong? You don't look like you're thrilled about the semi-clean bathroom."

I walk over to the bed and sit down next to him. Waves of anger come off him, frightening me. He doesn't answer my question, so I ask again, hoping his mood isn't due to anything I've done.

Tilting my head, I lean down in front of him to meet his gaze. "What's wrong? You seem upset. Did something happen outside?"

He doesn't answer at first, but simply shakes his head and frowns. With every second that passes, I grow more and more frightened. Has something bad happened? Did he call his boss?

Suddenly, fear rushes through me, and I jump up from the bed. "Did something happen to my father? Cason, please tell me. Did your boss do something to him because he hasn't paid yet?"

I can barely control my emotions while I wait to hear his answer. His expression doesn't change, but he shakes his head as he reaches out for my hands. Taking hold of them, he stills my movement and then looks up at me.

"No, your father is fine. He still has a couple more days to pay. Victor hasn't done anything to him because I have you as collateral."

Collateral. And right there is the truth of all I am in this nightmarish game. Just something to make sure my father pays his debts. Not a person who's scared and worried she won't make it out of this.

Just a thing.

CHAPTER EIGHTEEN

*C*ason

As soon as the word comes out of my mouth, I see Lily's face grow sad. To everyone else in my life, the word collateral simply means those people who aren't the targets for me or anyone else I know. But to her, I see she doesn't understand it's not meant to hurt her. It's just the fact of who she is in all of this.

"Collateral," she squeaks out around a sob that chokes the word into her throat. "That's all I am."

I stare up at her not knowing what to say. I'm not unfeeling. I've just never felt anything for someone like this before.

When I don't respond, she walks away to the bathroom, closing the door behind her. I watch her and wish I knew something that would help. I just don't.

For a few minutes, I stare at the bathroom door as I wait for her to come out. She doesn't. After a while, I begin to wonder if there's some way she can escape out of the bathroom, so I hurry over to the door and put my ear to it to listen.

The sound of water running in the shower calms me, but only for a second or two until I wonder if she turned it on to make it seem like she's still in there. Flinging the door open, I walk into a room full of steam so thick I can barely see through it.

A quick glance at the bathroom window doesn't tell me if she's slipped out through there or not.

"Lily?"

I hear the panic in my voice coming through loud and clear. I shouldn't care if she leaves. She'll just go back to her house to be with her father, so it wouldn't be like I couldn't find her.

Not that I should want to find her either. She's collateral, pure and simple. A means to an end. The method I decided to use to get her father to pay his debt. Nothing more. Nothing less.

She pokes her head out from behind the white shower curtain and scowls at me. Her hair is soaking wet and pushed off her face, sort of like when I'm on top of her and fucking her hard. Still, even as she glares at seeing me, her eyes are wide and innocent like usual.

"What? Why are you in here?" she asks in a hurt tone that's as unmistakable as my panicked one a moment ago when I thought she'd left through the bathroom window.

I don't answer her and simply stand in the middle of all that steam as it makes my skin damp. She doesn't need to know I thought she left or that I cared if she did.

But she's too smart to not realize what I'm up to and shakes her head. "Come to check on me to make sure I didn't squeeze through that tiny bathroom window? I guess it would be a problem if your collateral slipped away, wouldn't it?"

Before I can think of something to say, she yanks the curtain closed, leaving me standing there with nothing to do but not wanting to leave. I can't explain why her being hurt about that collateral comment bothers me. It shouldn't. It's what she is.

Yet, I hate how it makes me feel.

"I'm sorry for that collateral thing. I didn't mean it that way, Lily."

The words come out like foreign objects my body doesn't know what to do with. I've never apologized to a single person in my life. At least not since I was eleven years old and I stood watching my mother take the last breath of her life.

I don't say I'm sorry because I'm not. I am what I am, and for that, I'm not sorry. Still, something about Lily makes me need to let her know I didn't mean to hurt her.

When she doesn't say anything, I wait for a minute and then pull the shower curtain open. My eyes fill with the sight of her body covered in bruises, and rage bubbles up inside me at what Doc did. Lily pushes her hair off her forehead and simply stares at me in surprise as my gaze catalogues the harm he caused her.

"You told me he didn't hurt you."

Water runs down over her head in streams that trail over her tits and onto her stomach. Every place it touches has purple bruises. I feel my hate and rage grow by the second as the water makes each of them glisten, highlighting them for me to see.

"Why are you staring at me like I'm some broken thing? I don't need to see that in your eyes, so close the curtain and go away."

I don't want to look at those marks on her body anymore. The evidence of what he did gnaws at me, and I'm not sure I'll ever be able to think of anything else with her.

That's not how I want to remember her, though.

Stripping out of my clothes and shoes, I leave them in a pile on the bathroom floor and pull the curtain back one more time. Lily stands with her eyes closed letting the shower drench her and doesn't see me step inside with her.

I shouldn't want her now. I've hurt her and let her be hurt by someone else, but something in my brain pushes me toward her, needing to soothe her pain. I want to touch her and cover those purple marks with my hands and my mouth, making what he did disappear and what I do all she thinks of when she looks down at her skin.

Drops of water hit my face and turn into streams pouring down on my head as I lean in to kiss her. She opens her eyes and looks up at me at the first brush of my lips against hers, and it's all I can do to control my need for her when I see the hurt in them.

My tongue slides over her lips and into her mouth to mingle with her tongue. At first, the kiss is tentative and unsure, like neither one of us knows how to handle what we feel at this moment. Every second that she doesn't pull away ratchets up my need to have her again.

Lily pulls my hands up to cradle her face and tilts her head back to look up into my eyes. Jesus, I can't hold back for much longer when she shows me the pain in them, like she blames me.

She has every right to. If it weren't for me, she'd be safely in her home living her life and not recovering from nearly being raped in this shitty motel with a man who's done little more than threaten to kill her.

So again, the words in my head come out like ragged thoughts I don't know how to express, torn from my throat by the need to show her how I feel. "I'm sorry, Lily. I'm sorry about all of this. What he did. What I've done. All of it."

They're the most honest words I've uttered in more years than I want to admit. Once they're out, I stand there with the water rolling over me down onto Lily as she stares up at me like she can't believe any of them.

Like with my promise not to kill her, I don't blame her for not believing me now either. My life has been a long series of acts that make believing anything good from me next to impossible.

She takes a step closer to me and presses her hand over my heart. "Tell me I'm more than just a thing that means nothing to you. Tell me that when this is all over that you won't just think of me as collateral."

Every syllable cuts me like a knife through my skin, slicing through years of cruelty I've used to justify not feeling anything for anyone. She is not a thing. That my actions have made her think I see her as nothing more is something I'll carry long after she's back home and has forgotten me.

"You are not a thing, Lily."

She kisses me in response, and I taste the forgiveness in her. It's utterly foreign to me, but I instantly love it. I don't know if I deserve it, but I could spend the rest of time reveling in it.

My hands slide from her face down her body to cup her ass. Pulling her into my body, I lift her to just above my hard cock and ease her down onto it. Her cunt is wet and warm, and with each inch I push into her, I feel some of the rage inside me ebb away.

When I'm completely inside her, she slides her lips along my jawline to my ear and whispers, "I want to be someone to you, if only for this very moment."

Need for her consumes me, and I shove my hand into her hair to tug hard. My body aches for her, like being balls deep inside her cunt isn't enough. I want to taste her, hear her cry out, feel her body surrender to mine.

I sink my teeth into her shoulder, biting into her tender flesh as I push her back against the wall and begin fucking her. She pulls me in, her legs wrapped tightly around my waist and her heels pressed hard into the base of my spine, and I plunge my cock into her cunt as deeply as she'll take me.

It's raw and ragged, but so are we. I need to feel

that forgiveness she offers, and she needs to feel that I need her for just what she is.

The water turns much hotter, scalding my back and legs as Lily and I get lost in one another. My skin stings, and when she rakes her nails across my shoulders, I rear back like an animal in pain.

Still, I can't stop fucking her. I'd willingly let the skin on my back be flayed off to feel that moment when her body begins to milk my cock and she becomes mine completely.

She's mine to do with as I want. She's mine to keep. She's mine.

Those thoughts march through my brain with every time she moans in to my ear, begging me not to stop and saying my name like it's some promise or prayer she needs to make her whole. I don't know if the thoughts are true or not, but in these last moments when she cries out my name and clings to me like I'm the only thing that can save her from all the bad in the world, I believe them.

I have to.

With one last thrust into her, I fill her body with everything inside me. Her thighs quiver against my sides, a feeling I don't think I'll ever be able to forget because it's such a pure example of her surrender. She can't control it, so her legs shake from her release, and as she holds on to my neck, I hear her let out a sigh full of contentment.

I don't know how long we stand there, but when she rests her head on my shoulder, I can't imagine another place in the world I'd rather be at that moment. She is not just a thing. Not now. Not ever.

Not to me.

"I feel you slipping away already, Cason. It happens every time. I hold on, but you back away."

She's not wrong about the other times. I barely finished coming before I needed to put that distance between us. Even a few inches let me remain far enough from her. Killers don't let themselves get close to anyone.

Not even beautiful girls they want to hold on to forever.

But this time, I don't want that distance. I don't need it. I want her next to me, her skin pressed against my skin so there's no end or beginning for her or me.

There's just us.

Pressing my lips to her forehead in a kiss, I whisper, "No, not this time. I'm right here, and I'm not going anywhere."

I'm rewarded with a gentle smile that lights up her face, and for a moment in time, I'm not a killer and she's not my captive. We're just Cason and Lily, two people surrounded by circumstances that make the two of us being together impossible, and yet, somehow we're there in that motel bathroom with me still inside her and hating the moment I won't be.

CHAPTER NINETEEN

*C*ason

My leg brushes against Lily's, and a second later, her eyes open. I've been up for hours just watching her sleep. I didn't want to wake her, but now that I have, I pull her close to me. She curls up against my chest, tucking her head under my chin.

"Do we have to go?" she asks.

So many questions in one person. From the moment I took her from her house, it's been question after question. At first, I hated them. Then I simply didn't understand her need for asking them. After that, they began to grow on me.

Now as I lay there holding her in my arms, I wonder what life will be like without all of Lily's questions.

I shake my head and press a kiss against her hair. "Not yet."

My answer is met with a sigh, and she crawls up

my body so my face and hers sit next to one another on the pillow. "I thought this was the most disgusting place when I walked into this room two nights ago. Now I don't want to leave it," she says in a sad voice.

"Not yet. A few more hours."

We haven't left this bed for more than a few minutes each since that night. We sleep and then wake up and then she asks me the same question about having to go every time. For the first few, I answered her with a kiss that led to us getting lost in one another again. Then these last couple times, I held her as she drifted back to sleep, all the while knowing I wouldn't be able to do the same because our time was quickly coming to an end.

I haven't answered my phone since that night we stopped here. I know my father has called, but I don't want to hear what happened with her father. If he paid, then she gets to go home and I get to return to my life.

If he hasn't and his week is up, then I may be ordered to kill her after what I did with Doc. I've already promised her that won't happen, but what will instead I have no idea.

That hasn't been something I've let myself think about yet. For now, she's here and safe with the one person who has sworn to not let anything hurt her. Not even me.

"Cason, what's going to happen?"

When she says things like that in that innocent voice so full of fear, I know I have to lie. I have to tell her I will take care of everything because that's what I promised. She's probably figured out I'm not telling the truth when I say that, but she doesn't want to know what's really going to happen when we finally leave this motel room either.

I want to say that she'll be safe with a father who makes friends with the wrong kind of people and I'll stop being the killer I've always been. Neither one will be true, though.

"Your father will pay back the money, so you'll go home and go back to your life," I say quietly, hating that I'll play no part in her world after today.

"What if he didn't?" she asks, lifting her head to level her gaze on my face.

"Then he's going to have to part with some of those plates of his," I say with a chuckle, forcing myself to make a joke, even as I look at the black eye that asshole Doc gave her.

Lily falls silent for a few minutes, and I close my eyes, thankful I don't have to continue with the charade of being happy about anything that's about to happen. The only thing I know is she won't be hurt. I won't let Victor or anyone harm her.

Other than that, I don't know.

My brain lost in the fog of how these are the last few hours for us, I hear her say, "Tell me about your parents. I told you about mine, so now you tell me about yours."

"No. The story of my parents isn't one of love or memories in keepsakes hung on walls."

It's one more suited to our fate, though.

Opening my eyes, I see hers practically begging me to give her this. "Please?"

Maybe if I tell her she'll understand why I am like I am. Why there's nothing but hardness in me. Why I can't feel like I want to for her.

"There's not much to say. My mother's dead," I whisper as she curls up closer to me.

I close my eyes again and the memory of the last time I saw my mother alive flashes through my mind as clearly as if it just happened a moment ago. Taking a deep breath in, I let it out in a rush and tell her the truth of my parents and their story.

"My father is a monster, like I told you," I say, staring up at the water-stained ceiling above us. "He used her up, and then when he was done with her, he sent her away."

Lily shakes her head, like she doesn't want to hear any more, but I can't stop now.

"He got a new wife when I was a little boy, so he didn't have any use for her or me. When I was eleven, I don't know why, but he decided he didn't want her in the world anymore, so he had her killed. That house we were at was hers. I lived there with her until that night he sent someone like me in to get rid of her."

I hear Lily take a sharp breath in and shudder. I told her this wasn't like her parents' story.

"He came in and walked right past my bedroom to hers and shot her in her bed. I'll never forget the sound of his footsteps that night. I don't know how she didn't hear him coming because he practically stomped all the way down the hallway. Maybe she did hear it. Maybe she decided she couldn't live worrying when my father would finally get rid of her. I heard the shot, and when he left, I ran to her room to see what happened. I got there just as she was taking her last breath."

"I'm so sorry. Don't tell me any more. It's too terrible."

It's been so long since I told this story that I need to get it out. Something about Lily makes me need to confess my family's sins.

Stroking my hand up and down her back, I continue. "He's never denied he was the one who had her killed. He had a new family, and we were in the way. It was as simple as that. It didn't matter that he never saw either of us. His new wife couldn't stand the idea that we were out at that house still in the world. So he got rid of the old one for the new one, even if he didn't want to get rid of me."

I look down at Lily to see tears rolling down her cheeks. Gently wiping them away with the pads of my thumbs, I take a deep breath to finish the last part of my story.

"He killed my mother, and then I had to go live with him and his new family. I hated every minute of my life until I could move away from there. The only happiness I had was when I got to go live at my cousin's once it was decided by my father's new wife that they had their own son to take care of and didn't need another one hanging around."

"I don't think I'd ever want to meet your father," Lily says softly against my chest.

"You already have," I say before pressing a kiss to the top of her head. "My father's the man your father owes money to. Victor Varens, my boss. The head of the Varens family."

Lily looks up at me in horror. "You work for your father after all he did to you? After he murdered your mother?"

"I never had a choice. I'm his son. My future was set in stone from the moment I was born a male. Males in my family work for the family. That's how it goes."

Choking back the emotion I didn't expect to come over me, I smile at how good it feels to admit the truth for the first time. "I guess you can say I'm a killer who comes from a killer. So that's my story."

Just like my father. Or maybe not. Maybe he's a better man than me because he only ordered her death and didn't do it himself. Or maybe having your son's mother killed is worse than what I am.

"I'm sorry, Cason."

"You don't have to be sorry. I am what I am."

Lily kisses me softly, letting her lips linger on mine for a moment before she asks, "Why did you promise not to kill me then? Doesn't that show you aren't just a killer?"

"You're an exception I'm willing to make."

It's a lie, and she knows it as well as I do. Then again, maybe it's not. The truth is I won't kill Lily because unlike my father I don't kill women I care about.

I've killed enough people to know when it isn't something that needs to be done.

She lays her head on my chest and wraps her arms around me. "Cason, we aren't just what others make us. You're not a killer with me. Maybe you don't have to be a killer with anyone else either."

"Oh yeah? What would I do with my life? Maybe find a place in the country and live out my days with a nice girl and a dog? Maybe I could find a nice nine-to-five job too."

Lifting her head, she smiles up at me. "It doesn't sound like an awful life, if you ask me."

Even as I try to brush off her idea, I can't help but think that's what Lily's life will probably end up like. She'll find some guy who's nice and likes Labrador Retrievers, and they'll find a little house in the country where he leaves early five days a week for a job he doesn't care about but needs to keep to pay for the house she loves. They'll end up with a bunch of kids, and she'll be the most beautiful mother at the playground.

He won't know how lucky he is to have her love him, and she'll be sweeter than he deserves. But she won't leave him, even if things go bad. She'll stay because he's nice more often than not and they have the kids and she doesn't want to move to a different house.

"I guess you would never want to live like that?" she asks in that hopeful tone I'm going to miss when she's not around anymore.

"I don't think it's for me," I lie.

It sounds a little boring, but I have a feeling anywhere she is would be better than not being around her. But there's not much of a calling for hitmen in the suburbs, and in the end, that's what I am.

A killer.

Or after Lily, a killer every time but once.

AFTER LETTING ALL MY CALLS GO TO VOICEMAIL, I finally answer one late that afternoon. I paid for another night in this seedy motel, as Lily calls it, but I have a feeling we won't be staying until tomorrow.

The moment I put the phone to my ear, I hear my father say, "Twenty-five fucking calls later he answers the phone. You better have been underwater or under the fucking ground to not answer me all those goddamned times."

I look down my body to see Lily's head resting on my stomach and smile. "I was under something. What's up?"

My father stutters out a few sounds I don't understand and then repeats my question. "What's up? What the hell is wrong with you? I've been trying to get in touch with you for two days. What the fuck is up? I better hear something more than that, Cason."

It dawns on me that at this point in the conversation with him, I should be up out of the bed and getting dressed in a hurry to get back to his office since he's obviously pissed at me. Ordinarily, I would be like that, but today, I don't feel like moving. Lily looks comfortable right where she is, and I feel perfect with her head resting on me.

Moving can happen some other time.

"I've been doing what you told me to do for the past week."

My answer only frustrates him more. "What I told you to do? Two days ago, I left you a message to bring the girl back because that father of hers paid the money. I have another job that's being held up because you can't seem to find your fucking way home. Should you have left a trail of breadcrumbs on your way out to the house?"

His joke makes me chuckle, even though I know he didn't intend it to be funny. He gets downright comical when he's really pissed, but the fact that he hasn't brought up anything about his missing security guard tells me I still need to stay away for a little while longer.

"I'll be doing that later today, probably. Maybe early tomorrow, depending on how things go."

"Well, fuck, I hope I'm not hurrying you," he says, clearly exasperated.

"You said to take the week off. That's what I'm doing."

He's silent for a few moments before sighing. "Be sure to lock the house up when you leave. I haven't heard from anyone out there after the first couple days, so I'm assuming everything went fine. No problems with the girl?"

Lily lifts her head and pushes her blond hair off her face before smiling up at me. I don't need to bother telling him about the problems she and I had out there. That's all in the past. Now when I look down at her groggy face, I don't have a problem in the world.

"Everything is fine," I answer, leaving his question basically hanging with my vague response.

"Fine. I'm going to be heading out there this afternoon to handle some business, so I'm happy I'm not walking into a goddamned mess. You cleaned up after yourself, didn't you?" he asks in an odd voice.

Something's wrong. He never goes out to the house.

"Yeah. But I did break a plate, so I wanted to make sure I told you that," I answer as casually as I can as my heart begins to race.

"Whatever. Why would I give a fuck about a single plate?"

I shrug as Lily stares up at me with a confused look on her face. "I don't know. It seemed like something I should tell you. I can pay for it, if you want. I just wanted you to know."

My father huffs in disgust. "Who fucking cares about a single plate? It's not like you killed someone against my direct orders, Cason. I'll just get another plate. You know what, on second thought, stay at the house until I get there. Then you can take the girl home."

Red flags go up all over the place in my mind. He knows about Doc. He wouldn't say that part about me killing against his orders if he didn't. Even more, Victor hates that house. He hated it when my mother begged him to buy it. He's hated it ever since, even after killing her. It sits empty ninety percent of the time, so why does he now have to go there on some random day in September?

I need to make him think I don't know something's changed, so as calmly as I can, I say, "Okay. I'll see you in a little while then."

"Fine."

The call ends, and I set my phone back on the nightstand as my mind races with what to do next. My father knows about Doc and he plans to punish me for doing that. I've seen him do that to others, and I know what it means.

He plans on today being my last day working for him. And breathing. So much for being his son meaning a goddamned thing.

"Why did you tell him you broke the plate? Isn't he going to be angry with you now?" Lily asks as she crawls up my body to give me a kiss.

"It'll be fine. Everything will be fine," I say, avoiding yet another set of questions as I wrap her in my arms and hold her to me.

Snuggling against me, she kisses my neck sweetly. "Did he say anything about my father paying the money? Today's the last day."

Thoughts tumble around in my head. I don't know how long he's known about Doc. Did he tell me Lily's father paid him just so I would take her back to her house where he would be waiting for us?

But no, he said he was going out to the estate later today, so maybe he told the truth when he said he got the money two days ago. If I take her home, though, he might be waiting and ambush us there.

Whatever the truth is, it isn't good for me, and by extension, for Lily.

Staring up at the ceiling, I close my eyes and lie to her. "Not yet, but I'm sure he'll pay it today and this will all be over soon."

For a few minutes, Lily says nothing. The mood in the room has changed, but I don't know if it's because of me or her. Did she hear my father on the phone tell me Harry already paid and she knows I lied? Is that why she's uncharacteristically quiet now?

As I replay every word of my call with him, she sits up next to me and nudges my arm. "I know I'm not supposed to think this, and to be honest, it sounds a little crazy even saying the words in my head, but I'm going to miss you, Cason. I know that's insane, right? You took me hostage, and if I'm being entirely truthful, I only slept with you that first night because I wanted you to see me as a person and not just a thing you could easily kill at the end of this week, but I want you to know that wasn't how I felt by the time we got here."

Her honesty makes my lying all the worse.

In her eyes, I see she means every word she's saying. I don't know what I thought she felt, if anything, the first time we slept together. I didn't think about that at the time.

But she's right. By the time we got here, things weren't the same as they were back at the estate. Now

I can't imagine putting a gun to her head like I did with Creighton.

None of that matters now. I need to keep her safe, and not only from the likes of my father. I'm not good for her either. All this playing house may have convinced me that I might be, but the truth of who I am hasn't changed.

I might not be as bad as my father—I don't know —but I'm still a killer, and the sooner she gets away from me the better.

"You were smart to use everything you had to make me not want to kill you, Lily," I say with a smile at how proud I am that she's far more intelligent than most women her age. "You were strong and smart when you had to be. Never forget that because you'll have to be that again a million times in this life."

"It wasn't like that the whole while, Cason. You know that, right?"

That she's worried I feel bad because she did the best thing she could is so Lily. I'm a killer and never let her forget that, yet the look on her face says she's upset that I might think she tricked me into not killing her.

I pull her to me and kiss her mouth with as much sweetness as I can muster now that I feel the end coming for us. "All I know is you were strong and took everything I put on you. No matter what happens, be proud of that."

We have to leave this place before they find us, but I have no idea where to take her to make sure she's safe. I don't know if my father plans to kill both of us or just me for Doc's death. I don't know what will happen to her if he gets to me and she's left unprotected.

All I know is until my dying breath, I won't let her get hurt.

CHAPTER TWENTY

*L*ily

Worry comes off Cason in waves, like the anger I felt in those first days with him. I thought that rage was bad, but this is worse. This makes me think I might not get out of this alive.

Will he kill me after all?

I want to believe what I see in his eyes. That kindness that shows itself when he looks at me in quiet moments. The softness I doubt he even knows exists inside him but I see so clearly when he holds me in his arms.

But if it isn't that he's afraid he'll have to kill me after all, what is it? I don't want to believe my father wouldn't pay the money he owes to get me back safe and sound.

I could ask Cason what's wrong, but he won't tell me. Of all the questions he's had to deal with from me, that's the one he'll answer with a lie. I just wish I knew why.

"Time to get ready, Lily," he says and then presses a kiss to the top of my head.

Ready for what? I want to believe it's time for me to go home, but something about his call felt wrong. Does his father know that Cason killed Doc and plans to punish him? Surely when he explains he was trying to rape me he'll will understand.

Cason walks toward the bathroom but doesn't suggest I join him in the shower. Something's very wrong.

"No interest in some morning shower sex today?" I ask with a nervous giggle.

Looking back at me, he smiles. "Not this time. I won't be long."

When he closes the door, I slump back on the bed and wonder what's changed. Maybe it's because our week is over. I shake my head in disbelief at that idea. Just because he's not going to kill me doesn't mean he cares. I may have meant what I said about things being different since we got to this motel room, but I'm not naïve enough to think he feels like I do.

Letting me live isn't the same as caring for me.

I listen to the water in the shower and can't help but wish we weren't two people who could never be together. I know he's a killer. He's practically pounded it into my head. But with me he's more. So why couldn't he be more with me after today?

Maybe we wouldn't be that happy couple in the country living in a little house with a dog, but isn't it possible for us to be happy somewhere else where we could start over fresh? It's not so impossible, is it?

A knock at the door startles me out of my fantasies, and I hurry to the bathroom. "Cason, someone's at the door. Should I answer it?"

The water stops a second later, and he rips the curtain open to reveal his wet and muscular body. Shaking his head no, droplets of water fly everywhere as he points at a white towel sitting on the sink.

"No. Give me my towel. I'll get the door in a minute, but I need you to stay in here and don't come out."

Fear fills his eyes like I've never seen in him. Who could be outside the door?

A minute later, Cason's dressed, and just before he walks out into the motel room, he turns around to face me. Cradling my face in his hands, he leans down and kisses me on the lips like I'm the most important thing in the world to him.

"Don't worry. Just make sure you don't come out of this bathroom. Lock the door behind me and stay quiet."

Now I'm afraid. "Who's outside the door that I have to stay in here?" I whisper as he pulls away from me.

But he doesn't answer that question.

I do as he told me to and press my ear to the bathroom door to listen to him speak to someone. His voice and another person's are muffled, so I can't make out what's being said. I want to believe everything's okay because they aren't yelling, but I don't know.

Holding back tears, I strain to hear at least what Cason's saying, but I can't. Who knocked at the door?

A few moments later, the door flies open and I stare out in surprise. Cason looks back at me, and suddenly, all my fear dissolves into tears. Covering my face, I sob, "I thought you were someone here to kill me."

He takes me into his arms and smooths my hair down my back. "No, it's okay. It was only the desk clerk. She thought the room was empty because that kid from the nightshift didn't fill out some form right. It's okay. Don't cry. I won't let anyone hurt you. They'd have to get through me first, and that's not an easy job."

I tilt my head back and look up at him smiling down at me. Drying tears off my cheeks, I sniffle. "Is this how you have to live all the time?"

Cason's smile fades at my question. "Not really. I'm the person people are afraid to see when they open the door. Not the other way around."

For the first time, the reality of his life hits me squarely in the chest. All this time, he's repeatedly told me he's a killer, but all I've seen of actual killing is when he protected me from Doc. Now, suddenly, I understand what someone who he targets goes through. The terror. The panic. The emotional whirlwind every time they hear a knock at the door.

It fills me with more sadness than I thought possible, and I pull away from him to walk out into the room.

"I better get dressed."

He doesn't say a word but watches me put on the ripped white T-shirt and black yoga pants he bought me. When I finish, I hang my head, still filled with all that sadness that doesn't seem to go away, no matter how much I try to remind myself he saved my life.

Cason is what he always claimed to be. A killer. I can't change that.

I turn around and try to fake a smile, but the corners of my mouth barely move. "I'm ready."

He nods, and I see he doesn't understand what's wrong with me now. A hint of hurt tinges his dark eyes, but still he doesn't ask me what's wrong or what's changed. Maybe he doesn't care.

I have no idea where we're going since my father hasn't paid the money yet, but as uncharacteristic it is of me, I don't ask Cason about it. I don't dare because my emotions threaten to force out all the other words inside me, words that will show how much I care and wish I didn't for a man I shouldn't want.

Pointing at the phone on the nightstand, he says, "I want you to call your father first."

I look over at it and then back at him. "Why? Is there something I should know?"

"Just call him."

I pick up the old black phone and put it to my ear as I press the number in and begin to hear his phone ring. When my father answers, relief washes over me that he's still alive and hasn't been hurt.

"Daddy, it's Lily. Are you okay?"

He lets out a heavy sigh and says, "I'm fine. I've been so worried about you. I paid the money I owed, so why haven't they brought you back home yet? It's been two days."

I whip my head around to look at Cason standing across the room. Did he know all along that my father had paid his debt? Why not tell me?

"Two days?" I ask, the question as much for Cason as my father.

My father explains that he got the money early, so he made sure to get it over to Victor as soon as he could, but all the while I stare at Cason looking for his explanation. He never looks away, but I can't discern any answer in his eyes and his expression that remain emotionless.

"Are you safe, Lily? Did he harm you?" my father asks in fear at what I'll say back to him.

"I'm fine, Daddy. Nothing happened to me. You don't have to worry. I've been thinking a lot about you and Mom this week."

"Honey, so have I," he says with a smile in his voice. "That's why I sold some of my plates to pay off the debt. Your mother would never forgive me if I didn't do all I could to make sure her little girl is safe."

Hearing my father sold even one of his beloved collection breaks my heart. Shaking my head in disbelief, I tremble, barely holding the phone in my hand. "Oh, Daddy, you love those plates. They remind you of Mom. I hate that you had to sell any of them."

"Those plates aren't half as valuable as you are to me, Lily. They were put to good use. I was the one who made the mistake of getting involved with a mobster who told me upfront what would happen if I didn't pay him in time. It's my fault you were taken at all. The least I could do to save my own daughter is use my plates to get you back. Now, I just want you to come home."

"I will. Don't worry about me. I'm fine. You'll see me in a little while. I love you, Daddy."

"I love you too, honey."

After I say goodbye, I hang up the phone and look over at Cason. "My father says he paid the money to your father two days ago. Did you know?"

He shakes his head and frowns. "No. I just found out when I talked to him today. I was avoiding his phone calls while we've been here."

Disappointment at his answer fills me with even more sadness. I wanted to think he knew but stayed here in this motel room because he wanted to be with me for just a little while longer. But that's foolish. Being with me was merely a by-product of ignoring the world in favor of enjoying the last few days away from work. It had nothing to do with me.

"Are you going to take me home now?"

Cason walks across the room toward the door and opens it up just a crack to look outside. "I don't know."

"Why? My father paid the money he owed your father. You don't have to keep me as collateral now."

That word tastes like ash in my mouth, and Cason jerks his head around when he hears me say that. It's the truth, though. Maybe not to him, but to his father I've always been just that.

Collateral.

"Let's go. Where I'll figure out in a bit," he says

angrily, returning to the man I first met seven days ago.

His transformation makes me change back to who I was then too, so I snap, "I'm not going anywhere with you, unless it's back to my house."

I watch his eyes open wide in what I imagine must be shock at my outburst. For days, I've been sweet and kind because that's how I felt. Now I just feel betrayed, even though that's probably the stupidest thing I've thought in all my life. Still, I believed for the last couple days that he cared like I did, no matter how dumb that belief was.

Slamming the door behind him, he storms over to where I stand next to the bed and grabs my wrist. "I'm doing my best to keep you alive, Lily. Now let's go, or do I have to carry you out of this room?"

I tug my arm to get away, but it's no use. He's too strong and his hold on my arm is too tight. "What do you mean doing your best to keep me alive? Why would anyone want to kill me now? My father paid the money back, so let me go and take me home."

Cason leans down close to my face so I think he's going to kiss me but says in a low, terrifying voice, "I killed a man for you. My father is either going to only kill me for that or he's going to kill both of us. I told you the truth about what he did to my mother and me, so it's no surprise that he would kill me for what I've done. That phone call I had with him before let me know he found out about Doc, so now it's just a matter of time before he comes looking for us. I'm not even sure your father was telling you the truth when he said he paid the money two days ago. He may have had a gun to his head and someone forcing him to tell that lie because that's what my father told me. I don't know. All I know is the two of us are in danger, and I'm going to do everything in my power to protect you. So let's go."

Panicked by what he's just said, I clamp my free hand down on his arm. "They won't kill him, will they? He'll give them the money. He said he sold some of his plates."

"I don't know what they'll do, but my guess is they won't kill him before they get their money," he says flatly, like it's all the usual business for him.

But it's not for me.

"Cason, I can't let my father die. Please don't let that happen!"

"Lily, I can't do much about that. At the very least, there's a target on my back right now, so we need to get the hell out of here before we're found. If I can help your father, I will, but first I have to save us."

I hold on tightly to his forearm as he leads me out into the late afternoon sun. His body stiffens before we take two steps toward the car, and I follow his gaze to the check-in office at the end of the sidewalk. Inside, a dark-haired man who reminds me of Cason talks to the woman behind the desk, and I watch her point out the window in our direction.

Cason turns to look at me and tries to smile. "Lily, I want you to go back inside the room and stay there. I know this guy, and it's going to be okay. I just need you to go to the room, okay?"

"That's the first time you've ever asked me if something you want me to do is okay. That tells me nothing about this is going to okay. I don't want to leave you, Cason. Just let's get in the car and go. I don't care where we go. I just want to go now."

Taking my face in his hands, he presses a kiss to my forehead and then whispers in my ear, "I promise everything will be okay. Believe me."

I want to believe him. I want to think that just like he told me he wouldn't kill me that he's telling the truth now and everything will be okay. But every fiber of my being screams it won't be.

He pushes me away and orders me back to the room as the man walks out the door of the motel lobby. "Don't worry. It'll be okay."

With one last look into his eyes, I hurry back to the room and slam the door behind me. Like before, I try to listen to what's happening outside, but the room door is even thicker. There's no peephole, so I can't see outside either.

All I can do is believe everything's going to be okay and wait for Cason to return.

Five minutes later, I hear a noise outside and jump back away from the door. Terrified, I stare at it as I wait to hear Cason's voice, my heart pounding in my chest as the seconds tick by. A few moments later, it slowly opens, and the man I saw in the motel office appears in the doorway.

"Come with me. I'll take you home."

"Where's Cason? What did you do to him? Where is he?" I ask as tears stream down my face.

Did he kill him?

"We don't have time for this," the man answers, waving me toward him. "You can trust me. Cason wants you to come with me."

Looking around the motel room, I glance at the bed where I've spent the last two days with Cason. He promised me everything would be okay. How can that be true now that he's gone?

My crying morphs into hysterics as the truth settles into my brain. Cason's dead, and he can't protect me anymore.

Cason's dead.

The man marches over toward me and lifts his hand above his head. In the sunlight coming in through the doorway, I see the gun and turn away to hide my face in my hands. Something hard hits me, and then everything disappears into darkness.

CHAPTER TWENTY-ONE

*C*ason

My uncle's office reminds me a lot of my father's with its bookcases filled with books, but unlike my father, Ryker runs his part of the family so different that it's like he and Victor couldn't possibly be related. As he jokes with Kane about some job he sent one of us on, I can't imagine how the two brothers could come from the same parents.

It's likely because Ryker is so much younger than my father. Just a few years older than me, my uncle seems to have gotten all the happiness his mother and father had and less of the cruelty so ingrained in the Varens line.

"Everything okay, Cason?"

I shake my head to get rid of my thoughts about my family and smile. "All good. Just waiting for your command."

Kane laughs at my soldierly way, as he likes to call it, and shakes his head. "Your brother obviously runs a much tighter ship than you do, Ryker. This one is so serious I wonder if I'd survive a minute there."

From behind his skull mask, my uncle chuckles. "You and Victor would knock heads from the second you got there. My brother thinks running this family should be done like a dictatorship. I'm more about benevolent despotism, myself."

"Like Catherine the Great?" I ask, remembering a documentary I watched a few nights ago.

Before Ryker can answer, Kane throws his head back and laughs. "Isn't she the one who fucked a horse?"

My uncle rolls his eyes and shakes his head at me. "I'd say more like Frederick the Great, but you're on the right track. Your father, on the other hand, thinks that's too generous and likes to rule with an iron hand. I guess it suits his personality more."

I don't answer, even though I have the sense that after all these months working for Ryker that I could and not suffer any punishment. He's not wrong, so I wouldn't try to disagree with him. My father is a dictator in every way. From the way he got rid of my mother and forced me to work for him to the way he treats everyone around him, he rules with that iron hand Ryker mentioned.

Kane walks out after making another joke about Catherine the Great fucking a horse, leaving just the two of us in the office. Neither of us say a word for a long time, which allows me to let my mind drift off again but not to my father.

Like I do every night, I think about Lily.

From that day at the seedy motel until now, I've never seen her again. Jaxon promised to watch over her and let me know if my father ever made a move toward her, but every time I've asked, all he's told me is she's fine.

"You know, Cason, none of us approved of what your father did with your mother or you," Ryker says in a low voice, tearing me from my thoughts again.

I don't know what to say to that. Ever since her death, I've wondered if anyone tried to stop Victor from murdering her. Did even one of my uncles ever say a word to let him know it wasn't right to kill her while I lay in my bed in the room right down the hall from hers?

My silence seems to encourage him to go on, so he continues, "I think in some ways Jaxon was luckier than you, Cason. I would never say I wished my brother Maxim dead, but when he was killed, his son became a son to all of us. That didn't happen with you. I'm sorry for that."

What he says makes me angry and sad, threatening to make my emotions overwhelm me. This is the first time anyone in my family has ever said a word about what my father did to my mother and me. I've waited all these years to hear this, and now that Ryker has said it, it's almost too much to bear.

Looking away, I clear my throat. "You didn't do anything wrong. It was my father who's to blame. Not anyone else."

"I think I benefited from the distance I got from having this home left to me," Ryker says with a sigh.

"What happened with my brothers stayed far enough away that I felt like I didn't have to deal with it. When you showed up here that day last year, I thought maybe I finally had the chance to make up for what I never did for you."

I force a smile and pretend what he's saying isn't affecting me. "I appreciate what you've done for me, Ryker. All of it. I couldn't go back there. I don't think I ever can. He won't forgive, so I can't return. It's probably for the best, though."

What I leave unsaid is that my father has his favorite son, so he'll be fine. As long as Michael lives, Victor Varens will be happy.

"Do you ever wonder what life would be like if we didn't live in our family and didn't do the things we do?" I ask, almost like thinking aloud something I've thought of so many times over the past year.

I glance over at Ryker to see him nodding. "Yes. More since Kaia came into my life, but even before I thought about it."

Just hearing that he has thought about what life would be like away from the family and all that entails makes me feel better. I've never told him about Lily, but I think like Kaia, it's because of her that I wonder about living a different life away from all the Varens family business and my part in it.

"You know, your father never thinks anything we do limits him. Wives, girlfriends, whatever he wants, he has. I get the feeling you're more like me, though, Cason. This life of ours puts limits we aren't sure we want."

I nod my agreement to that. So much of this life feels like it's trapped me forever now.

"You finally gave up being a bachelor, though," I say to him with a smile. "Maybe we've been thinking about this stuff all wrong?"

His eyes show he smiles at the reference to Kaia, but that disappears after only a few seconds and he sighs heavily. "I wish that was the case, but it isn't. I can't have everything I wish I could with her. And she gave up a lot to be with me. I still don't know if that's fair."

My momentary happiness is dashed by his answer to my question. So much for being able to live as a Varens and still have a normal life.

Ryker leans back in his chair and folds his arms behind his head. "Jaxon told me something about a girl a few months ago. Is this about her?"

I take a deep breath in and let it out slowly as I try to figure out the honest truth about that. I'd thought about wanting to leave the life of a killer before I met Lily, so maybe I've always felt like I wanted something else. It's just that being with her made it all feel so much more urgent, as if the universe had finally sent me a real life answer to my questions.

"Yes and no. It's all for nothing anyway since the minute I leave here my father is going to put that target on my back again, so it's not like I can just go off and live happily ever after with her or anyone else."

And that right there is the truth neither Ryker nor I can deny. While I've been here, Victor has let me live in peace, but the moment I'm not working for his brother, I'll return to being public enemy number one. Fuck the fact that I'm his flesh and fucking blood. Nope. I'll just be a man with a huge fucking target on his back courtesy of his own father.

"He wouldn't do that to you, Cason. I wouldn't let him, and your Uncle Joseph wouldn't let him either. I know he likes to rant and rave, but Victor Varens believes in one thing above all else. Family. We were brought up to believe that family is the most important thing in the world."

I can't stop the chuckle from escaping on that one. "Even if it's a son he doesn't give a fuck about anymore?"

"Even if it's a son who reminds him every day of what he did. Your father is a lot of things, but we're all sons of Dmitri Varens, and I swear to you your grandfather would come back and haunt Victor if he followed through on his threats with you."

"So it's perfectly okay to kill an ex-wife you have no use for anymore but not a son?"

Ryker shrugs at my sharp question. "Believe it or not, yes. Your great-grandfather was that type of man, even if your grandfather wasn't, and Victor's the same way. Most women mean nothing to them, but family, especially sons, well, that's a different story entirely."

At least there's one good thing to being born a male in the Varens family.

A KNOCK ON MY DOOR RIPS ME OUT OF MY thoughts about Lily, irritating me that whoever it is has interrupted me. I fling open the door to see Jaxon standing in front of me wearing a shit-eating grin like he's some damn Cheshire cat.

"Busy? Mind if I come in?" he asks as he marches past me without waiting for my answer.

I slam the door and follow him in to see he's already begun to make himself comfortable in my favorite chair. "Make yourself at home, Jax. It's not like I was doing anything."

He rolls his eyes and puts his feet up on my coffee table. "You weren't doing anything, so don't bother fucking lying to me. You were just sitting here doing your best vegetable impression while you watch some stupid documentary."

"I guess the fact that I felt like being alone tonight means nothing to you," I mumble as I kick his feet off my table.

Jaxon shrugs in his usual whatever way. "Hey, you live your life as you see fit. Who am I to say you should do more than hide out here every night?"

"Don't you have a girlfriend or something to occupy your time? Or did she end it with you finally?" I snap at him, knowing my words will hurt.

He winces and then shakes his head like he hopes that will make the thought of her disappear. "Why do you have to bring Tia into this? And for your information, she didn't end anything, thank you. Anyway, who's to say I won't be driving down there later tonight to see her? You, on the other hand, choose to live your life like a fucking monk and sit in your room alone night after night."

"I'm not alone. You're here," I say with a smile, pleased with how pissed I've made him. Misery does love company.

He rolls his eyes again. "Nice way to treat your favorite cousin."

"Why are you here again?"

"Business, Cason. Unfortunately, business."

I shake my head at the sound of that word. "Whose business?"

"Family business."

"Ryker would have called if he needed something. He wouldn't have sent you up here to tell me he needs me."

Jaxon's face turns stony. "Not Ryker. Your father."

"I have nothing to do with his business anymore. Whatever's going on, I'm not part of that, and you know it."

He holds his hand up like he wants me to stop, but he needs to understand that world isn't my world anymore.

"I get that you're staying in with him, and that's fine, Jaxon. I'm not, though."

My cousin nods and gives me a sheepish look. "I know. Things have changed, though. Something's happened."

"What? What could have happened that I'm suddenly so fucking important to my father? I lived ninety-percent of my life being looked at like I'm some goddamned red-headed stepchild, and now all of a sudden, the world can't do without me? Why?"

"There are enemies, Cason. Our enemies. You

know that as well as I do. And when they strike, we have to strike back."

What the fuck is he talking about? Who struck at us? No, it's not us anymore. I need to stop thinking of the world like that. There is no us. I may still be a Varens, but I'm not part of that side of the family business anymore.

"It can't be anything life threatening if you're able to sit here and get in my face about what the fuck I do with myself every night" I say, already wishing Jaxon would leave and not involve me in family business, no matter what it is.

Leaning forward, he levels his gaze on my face and frowns. "Duke and your father have been at war for months now. He pops one of us. We get one of them. He pinches something of ours. We grab something of theirs. Victor thinks we need to strike hard and end this shit once and for all. He wants you with us when we do that."

I shake my head, hating every word he utters. "No. I can't help him or you or anyone with this strike. That's not my life anymore. I get to work for the other brother. You know, the sane one."

Jaxon nods, but I know what he's thinking. You can't separate our family. Maybe that's true, but I'm damn well going to try.

"I get what you're saying, Cason, but this is about family."

The way he says that, like I'm not understanding how important family is, makes something inside me go off. Barely able to contain my rage, I storm over to him.

"Family? Is this the same fucking family that watched as my father had my mother killed because he didn't want to have to bother with his ex-wife anymore? A woman who simply wanted to live in peace out at the house she loved and wasn't even allowed to do that because it upset my father's new wife. You know, the same family that stood by as he fucking discarded me because he liked her and their son better? You got to be taken care of because your father died for the family. I got shit because my father did the killing and no one dared to fucking say a word to him about it. I worked for that family since you and I were teenagers, and what the fuck did I get for it? A target on my goddamned back when I killed a useless security guard because he was trying to rape Lily. Fuck the family! And you can tell Victor that for me. Fuck him and fuck all of you who think I owe our family anything."

My outburst doesn't surprise him, but then again, it shouldn't since I've said much of this before to him. The closest thing I have to a real brother since that fuck Michael is nothing to me, Jaxon knows all too well what I've had to endure because of Victor. I don't know why he thought he should come here tonight and lay all that family bullshit on me, but he knows better.

"Your father thinks you came here to Ryker because of her, you know."

He says those words so calmly, but beneath each

one is the thinly veiled belief that if it wasn't for Lily that I'd still want to be my father's killer and henchman. How can I be related to these people and be so different from them?

"You tell him to leave her out of this. She has nothing to do with why I don't want to be back in his part of the world again, and he knows that."

Once more, Jaxon nods. "So is that your final word on all of this?"

My heartbeat pounds in my ears as rage courses through me. There are a million other things I want to say to my father, but they will have to wait for another time.

"That and don't send one of the few members of the Varens family I like here with that shit again. You know you're like my brother, Jaxon, but there's nothing you can say to change my mind. I'm out of his life. You either accept that or you don't. That's your choice, but it doesn't change mine."

He sighs and then stands up so we're eye-to-eye. "I get it. All of it. I just had a job to do, and now I've done it. Stay safe, Cason, and stop sitting here in this room getting stuck in your damn head, man."

"Yeah, yeah. Go find your girlfriend and let me be. And next time you come by, leave my father's business nonsense somewhere else."

"Got it."

Jaxon chucks me on the shoulder and pushes past me on his way to the door, yelling back, "Remember what I said. Get out sometime. Don't be a jackass all your life."

Just before he leaves, I ask the question I always ask when he comes to see me. "How is she? Is she okay?"

But unlike all the other times, he hesitates before answering, "She's fine, Cason. Now that her father's dead, she moved out to the country to a nice house. There's no guy, though, so don't sit here and torture yourself that she got married or anything like that. Her father must have left her some money because she doesn't work. She just stays in that house. You two are like two fucking peas in a pod, now that I think of it."

I watch him slam the door behind him and smile. Lily's okay and there's no one in her life. Even better, her father finally did the right thing with those damn plates.

Two lonely peas in a pod.

CHAPTER TWENTY-TWO

*L*ily
    I watch him for hours, focused on every tiny move he makes. His very existence enchants me. Out of something very dark came someone purely good.

Touching his hand, I smile when his fingers wrap around my pinky and tighten to a firm grip, even as he sleeps. He instinctively knows he can cling to me.

It's been just over a year since I last saw Cason, but every day for the past four months, I've gotten to see the child we created who looks like the spitting image of his father with his dark hair and deep brown eyes. I fantasize that he's out there somewhere and keeps an eye on us, but out here in the country, there isn't much to worry about.

My father passed away just a month after my son was born. He never had any more run-ins with men he owed money to after I came home, but the stress of what happened to me made him an old man overnight.

I think he only lived as long as he did to see his grandson come into the world. He never asked who his father was, and I never told him.

But one look at Lukas and he knew the truth.

It's not that I'm ashamed of who his father is. Never once have I felt anything but pride that my son grew out of something that most people would think was the worst part of my life. It wasn't. The bad parts of that week have faded away, leaving only the good, and my son is the best thing I have to remember his father by.

Not that I ever mention the circumstances around how he came to be to anyone. We live quietly in the house my father's plates helped pay for out here in the country where no one bothers us. I have enough money that we're comfortable and I can stay home with Lukas until he goes to school. Then our lives will change, but until that day comes, it's just the two of us living that life I described to Cason that morning in that dingy motel room.

Is he still alive, or did his father kill him for what he did to Doc to protect me? I wonder if I'll ever learn the truth. Until then, he remains only a memory that lives through our son.

I lay my head on the pillow as Lukas holds my finger and whisper, "Never doubt that you are loved. Whatever your father was to everyone else, he protected me so you could come into the world."

Pressing my lips to his forehead, I kiss him goodnight and smile at the feel of his soft skin. He's so new and so pure that I wish I could keep him this way forever. Cason's words that day as he told me how he was destined to work for his father never leave my mind, but I won't let Victor Varens do the same to my little boy.

"I promise you won't ever have to do that, Lukas."

As I close my eyes, I repeat that pledge to myself over and over until I drift off to sleep. I will never let that happen to my son.

JOLTED FROM A DEEP SLEEP, MY EYELIDS FLY OPEN at the sound of a door closing. I quickly look across the room toward the TV and see it isn't on, and a second later my brain understands that sound means someone is in the house with us. I scoop up Lukas into my arms and tightly clutch him to me before hurrying over to the closet door.

I freeze as my hand grips the doorknob, straining to hear where the intruder is in the house but unable to as my heartbeat pounds in my ears. I've feared this moment every day since Lukas was born. When nothing happened in the past few months, I convinced myself that I was just being paranoid.

Now I'm sure I wasn't.

A tiny cry escapes from Lukas, and I stare down at him in terror. Holding him against my chest, I kiss the top of his head and silently pray to God the person outside my bedroom didn't hear him.

Slowly, I open the closet door, wishing I had oiled that damn hinge like I planned to weeks ago. The creaking sound slices through my body, paralyzing me. I can't move or cry out. I'm trapped.

Now I hear heavy footsteps coming toward the room. Clomp. Clomp. Clomp. Whoever it is, they walk slowly and confidently, not afraid that I know they're here. They know I have no defense against them.

My imagination runs wild as my heart races in terror.

A man.

Twice my size.

With a gun.

He's here to kill me and take Lukas.

The intruder heard the door like I feared they would and knows exactly where we are. My gaze frantically darts around the room as I desperately search for a way out. The door won't work, but what about the windows?

My bedroom is on the second floor. I chose this room because of the beautiful view of the sunrise I get every morning through those windows that now serve no good purpose to me. Even if I could get down to the ground, I can't do it safely with Lukas.

One footstep followed by another and another down the hallway, each one closer to where I stand with my infant son in my arms. Then they stop. I hold my breath and listen for the next sound. Will it be another footstep or will it be someone's hand twisting the doorknob before they find us?

"I know you're here, Lily," a man's ominous voice calls out from the other side of the door. "Don't make this difficult. Come with me and you won't get hurt."

The voice sounds familiar in some way, but I don't recognize it. The man knows who I am, though, and one terrible thought races through my mind.

Victor Varens has finally decided to come for my son.

Against Lukas's cheek, I whisper, "I promise we'll be okay, honey. Just hold on to mommy and don't cry."

I don't have a choice now. I have to go out the window.

Rushing across the room, I push up the screen and stick my head out into the October morning air. An unusually warm fall day, the air feels heavy, like a water-logged sponge, and it makes filling my lungs difficult. I struggle to inhale fully, but I need to so I can calm myself as I quickly scan the size of the jump I'm going to have to make in mere seconds.

God, what if I don't make it? Or what if Lukas is hurt in the fall?

The bedroom door begins to open, so I don't have time to think about the answers to those questions. Pulling my head back inside, I hold my son tightly to me and put one leg out the window. It dangles against the side of the house as I desperately work up the nerve to send the rest of me out after it.

I crouch down, my cheek pressed against my baby's head, and start to ease myself out the window until only my left leg still remains inside. Just one more thing to do and then I hope God protects us when we fall two stories.

"What the... get the fuck back in here!" the man

barks before charging toward where I hang halfway out the window.

"Leave us alone! I won't go with you!" I scream as Lukas begins to cry, startled by all the yelling.

The man is the definition of burly, at least twice my size and easily able to grab hold of my body. He pulls me inside with a single yank and a deep grunt, setting me on my feet with a look of disgust.

"You're on the second floor, for Christ's sake! Did you want to kill yourself? What the fuck are you thinking, little girl?" he asks, scrunching up his fat face.

"I don't know what you want with us, but I won't go. I'm not afraid of you," I say, not bothering to answer any of his idiotic questions.

"You will go, and if you had any sense, you'd know that I'm not here to hurt you. If I was, I would have pushed you right out that window myself."

As much as I don't want to admit it, that makes sense. Even coming from him.

Grabbing my arm, he tugs me toward the door as Lukas cries even louder. I rub his back to soothe him, but it does no good.

"My son is just an infant. Please don't hurt him."

"I'm not here to hurt either one of you," the man says in frustration. "Now just come with me and nobody will get hurt. You know how this works. Don't make it hard on yourself."

I don't know him, but I do know how this works. I know all too well.

"Why does Victor Varens want to see me? I'm

nobody to him," I say quietly as I'm lead down the stairs toward the front door.

But suddenly the man who was so chatty just a minute ago now has nothing to say. All the better. I know the answer to my question, so I don't need this guy to tell me why.

Lukas had the bad luck of being born a male, and just like his father, he's worth more because of that.

THE MONSTER'S OFFICE LOOKS JUST LIKE IT DID THE last time I was brought there. Anyone who doesn't know the man would think all those books would make him more civilized, not less, but somehow they don't. They're probably all for show.

"Little girl, Scotch here says you tried to jump out a second story window with my grandson," he says in a voice that makes it sound like he gives a damn about Lukas or me. His tone changes to one far more menacing when he continues, "That makes me wonder about your fitness to be his mother, to be honest."

I squirm in the leather chair I'm forced to sit in at the mere mention of my not being the best person to take care of my child. "I am the only person in the world fit to be his mother," I say defiantly.

My attitude goes unnoticed, however. Likely, the rebellious tone of a nobody to him doesn't faze Victor Varens in the least.

"I'm curious why this child has never met his father," he says as he turns to look over at Lukas as he sleeps in the bassinette on the side of his desk where he placed him when we arrived. "It's obvious he's my son's child. Doesn't take a rocket scientist to figure that out."

The truth is Lukas looks like his grandfather too. Victor and Cason's dark hair and deep brown eyes have made their way to the next generation. But that's where the similarities end.

When I don't answer him, he gets up from his chair and walks over to stand next to the bassinette. Without saying a word, he leans down and stares at my son. It's a look that reminds me of how animals gaze at their prey before sinking their teeth into their flesh and ripping them apart.

Quickly, I try to force his attention back on me. "I've never seen Cason again. I don't even know if he's alive, so there was no one to inform about his birth."

Victor lifts his head and smiles. "I bet you thought I'd never find out, didn't you? A single week you two spent together, so why would anyone think anything came of it?"

I have a sense he doesn't want answers to those questions, and because I have no answers, I stay silent. I never thought I'd be able to avoid having him find out about my son. I've dreaded that fact since the moment Lukas came into the world after hearing Cason tell me what his father did to him all his life.

As for the time we spent together, it's always felt like so much longer than it was in reality. Maybe that's because of what happened with Doc. I don't know, but to this moment, I've never felt closer to another person in my life than Cason.

"So my son produced a boy. I guess I'm not surprised. Varens men always create the next generation," he says proudly and then takes another look back in at him.

"His name is Lukas."

My statement seems to surprise him, like he never considered my son to have a name before this moment. Why would he? Like his father, he means nothing to him other than just another person he can command to do his bidding.

But I won't let that happen.

Victor sits down and stares across his desk at me. "If you thought you were going to be able to keep this child from his rightful family, you're going to find out how wrong you were."

"I'm his rightful family. I'm his mother. That means more than anything else in the world. I carried him in my body and gave birth to him. I feed him and comfort him when he cries. Me. Whatever anyone else thinks they are to him, they aren't me."

As the words leave my mouth, I know somewhere in the back of my mind that any one of them may set this man off, and yet, I don't care. I don't know why he choose today to bring us here, but I have the sense that he's known for much longer that Lukas existed. We're likely just some useful pair of pawns to get Cason to do something for him. Nothing more.

"My first wife thought she was the most important person in Cason's life too. I can assure you I showed her that was an incorrect assumption."

"I know all about what you did to your first wife.

Cason told me exactly what happened to her. That doesn't change the fact that Lukas is only a baby and can't hold any worth to you, so why won't you let us go?"

Victor's eyebrows shoot up into his forehead at my reference to Cason's mother's murder. "One week and he told you that? I'm impressed, little girl. Not only did you turn the killer on another man but you got him to open up about something I would have thought he'd never tell a soul and leave the only life he'd ever known. That's nothing short of amazing, in my eyes."

His mention of what happened to Doc gives me the opportunity to explain the truth of that night, so I jump at the chance. "I didn't turn anyone on Doc. He tried to rape me, and Cason made him pay for it. As a killer, that's what he's supposed to do, isn't it? Kill people? I'd think you'd be happy he did his job."

For a long moment, Victor says nothing but continues to stare at me. I'm likely pushing my luck by being so mouthy with him, but Cason did nothing wrong.

"My son is only supposed to kill for me. By murdering Doc, he killed for you. An entirely different circumstance, unfortunately."

"How can you be so unforgiving of your own son? Doc was just an employee. Cason is your flesh and blood. Now that I've had a child, I can't imagine ever not forgiving him for anything."

I stop for a moment as what he said about Cason leaving his life behind echoes in my head. "Why isn't Cason here? Did you do something to him?"

My questions make him throw his head back in laughter. "Everyone is always so concerned that I'm going to do something to my son. You, his cousin, even my brother. Who knew so many people cared about a killer like Cason?"

A defense of him as more than just some killer bubbles up inside me, but I don't let the words out. There's no point. Victor Varens only sees the person he wants to see in his son. I can't change that if his own family can't.

That doesn't mean what he thinks of Cason is true, though. I saw something else when we were together. There's more to him than just what his father has tried to make him be.

CHAPTER TWENTY-THREE

*C*ason

Jaxon sits with Ryker in his office, the two of them silent as I step into the room. I felt tension in my father's office like this nearly every day I worked for him, but this is new at my uncle's.

The two of them look at me when I stop dead just inside the door. I want to ask what the hell is wrong, but part of me dreads hearing the answer.

"Cason, we need to go to your father's. Don't bother fighting us. It's something that needs to happen."

Ryker sounds like he's announcing someone's death he's so damn somber. Has my father died? The thought rushes through my mind, and as much as I know I shouldn't feel this way, I'm not unhappy.

"Fine. I won't fight you, but why?" I ask, silently letting myself imagine a world where Victor Varens doesn't exist anymore.

My uncle looks over toward Jaxon sitting on the

couch on the other side of the room and lets out a deep sigh. I wait for him to say something, but he sits there silently, so I turn to Jaxon.

"What are you doing here anyway? Why aren't you at my father's? If this is about going back there because of that bullshit between him and Duke, the answer is still no. Is that what this is about?"

Jaxon shakes his head. "No, that's not what this is."

"Then what the fuck are we all talking about? Someone want to let me in on the secret since the two of you clearly know something I don't?" I ask, my voice growing louder with each word as my frustration ratchets up notch by notch from not knowing what the hell is going on.

I turn to look at Ryker and see I won't be getting my answer from him. Looking back at the person who's the closest thing to a brother I have in this world, I ask, "Jaxon, what's going on?"

"Sit down. I need to tell you something."

My mind goes blank at the tone of dread in his voice. What could he need to say to me?

"I'm good standing, so let's just skip the bullshit and tell me what's going on, okay?"

After blowing the air out of his mouth, he says in a rush, "I haven't been honest when you asked me about Lily. I didn't know how to tell you, so I didn't say a thing."

Instantly, panic courses through my body. I have to go back to my father's and there's some problem with Lily? Fuck. If he hurt her, he'll wish he died because I'll fucking turn him inside out.

"What did he do to her? I swear to God, I'll kill him," I say, barely able to contain the rage that fills me.

My cousin quickly moves to calm me, shaking his head as he answers, "No! It's nothing like that. Just calm the fuck down. Christ, who jumps to conclusions like that?"

In a flash, I've got him by the collar and I'm holding him six inches off the ground. "Tell me what's wrong with Lily, or I'm going to practice what I plan to do to my father on you, Jaxon!"

From behind me, I hear Ryker say, "Cason, calm down. Your cousin went about this the wrong way, but it's going to be okay. Just calm down."

I release him and take a step back, already too wound up to think straight. I'm tired of riddles and getting no answers.

"I'll ask once more, and then even Ryker isn't going to be able to keep me from ripping you apart. What's wrong with Lily, and what does my father have to do with it?"

"She's fine. I just didn't mention she had a baby."

His words hit me like a punch to the face. A baby? He told me she wasn't with anyone.

As if he reads my mind, he adds, "It's yours, asshole."

For a moment, I don't know what to say or think, but then I remember what they first said as I walked in the room. "What does this have to do with my father and me going back there?"

"Your father wanted to see his grandson, so he has them at his office," Ryker says in a voice tinged with foreboding.

I turn to look at him and wish for the first time in my life that I could see his expression. "Why? What's he want with her and a baby?"

"He claims he wanted to see his grandson, but I think he plans to use them as a way to get you back with him. I'm not saying you have to do that, but I think you need to be there with her and the baby."

Grandson? I have a son?

Looking back at Jaxon, I shake my head at how he could have kept me in the dark about this for so long? "You've been watching her for the past year and knew about this the whole time? Why didn't you tell me she was pregnant? Why didn't you tell me I have a son?"

"I thought if you didn't know that she and the baby would be safer. I knew the second your father found out, he'd demand to have the kid in the family. Since you didn't want to have him be any part of your life, I figured you wouldn't want him to be a part of your son's either. Trust me, Cason, I wasn't trying to do anything that would hurt you or them."

"Jaxon was only trying to do what he thought was best for all of you, Cason. Don't blame him. We all know your father and what he's like. And it seems your cousin was right because once he learned of the little boy's existence, he had someone bring them to him. Victor called me about an hour ago to tell me she's there with him."

Rage and fear swirl around in a toxic mix inside me with hate for my father making me nearly explode. All this time I stayed away from Lily thinking that would keep her safe and thinking that by having Jaxon watch her that I'd know if she ever needed help, and now I find out none of that was true. She went through her pregnancy alone, giving birth to my son alone, and now she's sitting in my father's office likely being threatened by him all alone.

Barely able to keep my voice from shaking, I tell them what I plan to tell my father when I finally see him again. "If he touched one hair on her head or my son's head, I'll be that killer he so proudly likes to take credit for creating, and neither one of you will be able to fucking stop me."

THE FIRST STEP INTO THE HALLWAY THAT LEADS TO my father's office brings all those familiar feelings from when I worked for him rushing back. The rage and hate fill me again like always, and my chest tightens, making it hard to breathe.

I stop, unable to move as the reality of my life presses down on me. Once more, I'm forced to be back in my father's world, a place I thought I finally escaped. Inside his office just down the hallway is Lily, the only woman who's ever made me think I could be something other than just a killer, and our son, the child I didn't know about until only an hour ago.

As all these thoughts swirl around my brain, I see a figure rush out into the hallway to join us. I know instantly who it is.

Lily.

She's as beautiful as the last time I saw her standing in that motel room. My heart slams into my chest when she smiles at me, but I can tell her happiness is forced by the way her smile doesn't reach her eyes.

From behind me, Ryker says in a low voice, "I think we'll go in and see if we can defuse whatever your father is planning."

He and Jaxon disappear into Victor's office, leaving me alone with the woman I've never forgotten in all the time we've been separated. We walk toward each other, meeting in the middle of the hallway. For a moment, neither of us say a word, and then she breaks down, covering her face as she sobs.

I have so many questions, but I limit myself to the most important one. "Why didn't you ever let me know about the baby, Lily?"

When she looks up at me, I see confusion written all over her face. "How? I never heard from you again, Cason. I thought you could be dead. Who was I supposed to tell so you could know?"

She's not wrong. I kept away from her in the foolish belief that would help her stay safe from the world I live in. So much for that.

"I just wish I knew. How old is he?" I ask, struggling to keep the million questions I want to ask her from spilling out of my mouth.

Lily beams a genuine smile as she wipes away her tears. "He's four months old, and he's beautiful. He's the most beautiful thing I've ever seen in my life. To be honest, he looks a lot like you, Cason. And he's the sweetest baby that's ever lived. I love him more than I ever thought I could love anything in this world."

"What's his name?"

"His name is Lukas," she says before her smile fades away. "Cason, what's going to happen? What does your father want with a little baby? He took him out of my arms and won't let me hold him. I'm so scared."

"He wants me, and this is how he thinks he can get me back into his world, by holding you and my son so I have to come crawling back to him."

"Please don't let him hurt him," she says in a teary voice that makes my heart feel like it's being ripped from my chest. "He's just a defenseless baby."

That's my father's favorite type of victim. The defenseless kind. Like his ex-wife sleeping peacefully in her bed or a helpless child who can't fight back. I've done more terrible things than I want to ever remember, but I've never hurt a child. Even a killer has his limits.

Lily squeezes my hand, tearing me out of my thoughts, and I look down at her to see her struggling to keep from crying. She never agreed to this for her or Lukas.

"I've thought about the moment when you saw me again and saw our son for the first time. This isn't how I thought it would be," she says sadly.

Leaning down, I kiss her softly on the lips. "I'm sorry, Lily. You and Lukas shouldn't have to go through this because of me. I promise you'll have Lukas back in your arms tonight. Whatever it takes, whatever I have to agree to do for him, I'll do it. Trust me."

Tears fill her beautiful dark eyes as she stares up at me. "I do trust you, Cason. I just want to take him home and be safe. Can that ever happen now that your father knows about him?"

I don't want to tell her the truth, so I kiss her again and lie. "Trust me. You'll be back home with Lukas tonight."

Holding her hand, I take a deep breath in and lead her to the office where I know my father waits. I hear Lukas cry, and as Lily squeezes my hand in terror, I feel like someone's put my heart into a vice. If he's hurt one hair on my son's head, I'll kill him tonight without a second thought.

"Cason, he's crying. What did they do to him?" Lily sobs.

I can't answer her or she'll be terrified by the level of anger and hatred bubbling up inside me.

"Come in, Cason. Come see how happy your son is with his grandfather."

His very voice sickens me and makes me want to kill him right now, but I know he's looking for my rage. He wants to stoke it to make me become that man again tonight, the man he nurtured into a cold-blooded killer.

Victor sits behind his desk looking far too smug,

but thankfully, he doesn't have the baby in his arms. Lukas sits in a bassinette nearby like some stolen Moses, and a quick glance shows me he seems okay. Lily was right. He is the most beautiful thing in the world, and he does look like me.

She steps forward to take him, but my father holds up his hand to stop her. "Not yet, little girl. First my son and I have to talk."

"I'm his mother," she pleads, her voice full of fear. "He needs me. He's just an infant. Please let me hold him."

My father doesn't even bother to look at her as she begs to take her son into her arms. "Cason, your girlfriend needs to learn there are times to speak and times to keep your mouth shut."

I've heard him say that hundreds of times before, and the threat is as real now as it was every other time. But this time I won't let him get away with hurting her or Lukas.

Reaching out, I pull her close. She looks up at me, and I see by her watery eyes that she's trying so hard to be strong and not cry, even as everything about this situation makes her want to break down.

"It's okay. He's fine there. Trust me."

"Oh, definitely trust Cason, little girl," my father says, mocking me. "I mean, he's a killer, but if he says to trust him, go right ahead."

More goading. I know that, but it takes every ounce of willpower I possess to not snap back that I used to be a killer. In the past. A past he created for me and forced on my life by virtue of my being born his son.

But I'm not just that anymore.

We stare at one another, neither one of us saying a word, while Lily clutches my hand and never takes her attention off Lukas. It's a scene I never dreamed I'd be a part of. I thought I'd be alone all my life, a solitary killer trapped in a life that never felt like his to begin with.

My father's dark eyes so similar to mine, except for the lines around them, telegraph that he's waited far too long for this moment to get me back in his office and back in his part of the family business. He thinks he's won because I'm here.

He hasn't. I won't let that happen again.

Lukas lets out a tiny cry, and Lily reacts immediately, tugging on my hand as she instinctively steps toward him. I don't let go, though, because I see in my father's expression that no matter of crying is going to change what he intends to do here tonight.

"Not yet, little girl. We haven't had our discussion. First we talk. Then you can have your baby back."

"Lukas, honey. Mommy's here. Don't worry. I'm right here, honey," Lily says in a sweet voice that has no place in this setting.

"So, Cason. Do you know why I took your son and forced you here?" my father asks with a grin that's nothing short of evil.

I nod but refuse to give him what he wants. I know why he's brought me here. It doesn't change the fact that I'm not that man anymore.

"Jaxon tells me you don't want to be a part of this family anymore. You think you should abandon all you are. That's not how life works, Cason."

Standing on the other side of my father's desk, Ryker quickly jumps in to say, "He's still part of the family. I can promise you Cason is exactly what our father would want him to be since he's worked for me. He's still one of us."

But Victor ignores his brother's attempt to defend me. "He's not where he belongs. I'm surprised you don't understand that by now, Cason."

"By now? Why does being a Varens mean I have to work for you? I'm still in this family. I'm just in a better place doing things I want to do."

Victor rolls his eyes in disgust at my questions. "A better place? Why are you like this? This must be because of your mother because I've never given you any doubt about what you were meant to do. You are my son, a Varens through and through. We rule this world of ours because we aren't anything other than the kind of men you seem to want to look down your nose at lately."

I shake my head, refusing to believe what he says. "I'm your son in name only. I've never been what you wanted me to be. I became a killer because that's what you forced me to be, but I've never been like you."

"Much to your shame and my dismay," he says in a low voice.

Once more, Ryker tries to defuse the situation. "You have no reason to be ashamed of Cason, Victor.

He's exactly the kind of man our father would be proud to call his grandson."

But again, it doesn't work. My father glares at me with a look of hate so pure I have a hard time imagining he doesn't want me dead right now. That only makes me want to show him how much I don't want or need to be in his world anymore.

"No shame. You have another son to be just like you, and unless something's drastically changed in him, he's on track to be a junior Victor Varens. You aren't without an heir, so let me go continue to work for Ryker."

My mention of my half-brother does nothing to make him happy. I don't know why, though. Everything I said is the truth. Michael is just like our father, so why not be satisfied that he'll take over when the time comes and follow in the footsteps Victor so desperately wants me to follow?

"I'm not an unreasonable man. I'll let the little girl and her baby go, Cason, but you have to stay. Agree to that and they're free to leave right now."

He doesn't have to explain the tradeoff he wants me to make. I understand completely. I can't keep Lily and Lukas in harm's way any longer, so I'll stay. No matter how much I hate what I have to do.

"Swear you won't ever touch them again in any way. Do that and I'll stay."

Out of the corner of my eye, I see Jaxon slowly shake his head. He knows Victor. How much are my father's promises worth? Not much when it comes to me, but I can't take the chance that Lily and my son could be harmed because I didn't do everything possible to keep them safe.

My father smiles. "Done. They won't be bothered by me again."

Lily looks up at me with such hope in her eyes because she doesn't know what I've just agreed to. She doesn't understand that I've given him what he wanted in exchange for her and our son's safety.

Nodding, I try to smile to cover what's about to happen next as my heart feels like it's being ripped out of my chest. "Take Lukas home, Lily."

I lean down and kiss her softly before whispering against her lips, "You'll be safe now. Go."

And at that moment, I see by the sadness filling her eyes that she knows.

As I watch her hurry over to our son and take him in her arms, I don't blame her for leaving. This isn't her battle. When she stops in front of me with tears rolling down her cheeks, I gently run my palm over my son's tiny head and lean down to kiss his cheek for the first time.

"I'll make sure she gets home safely," Jaxon says in a low voice.

I nod my silent thanks and then return my attention to my father. He's gotten what he wanted. Now he'll make clear how much I'll pay for my choices.

A second later, Lily leaves and with her and Lukas goes my chance to be the better man I wanted to be. The better man I thought I could be.

CHAPTER TWENTY-FOUR

*C*ason

Alone with my father, I wait for him to give me my orders like I have hundreds of times before. I feel empty now that Lily and Lukas are gone, but at least they're safe.

That makes what I bartered away worth it.

"So much for me thinking you're my smart kid. You didn't negotiate that trade well at all."

"They're safe. You gave me your word you wouldn't touch them ever again. That's all that matters."

"But you gave in so easily," Victor says with a chuckle. "I thought it would take more from the way Jaxon was talking. He made it sound like you're a man of principles now. I guess he was wrong."

He's enjoying this. He wanted me back in the fold, back to where he could order me to do his bidding, and now that he's gotten all he desired, he's practically giddy.

"What would you know about principles?" I say, unable to stop myself from taking that jab at him.

He takes the bait and snaps back, "Oh, I forgot. You're like your mother that way. So full of fucking principles. And where did that get her?"

The way he says that, like something random got her instead of taking responsibility for his part in her death, makes keeping all that I've held in all these years impossible. Pulling my gun, I point it at him and yell, "Fucking dead! You sent someone to kill her knowing I was sleeping in a room just feet away, you son of a bitch! I was a kid and you murdered the only person who cared about me. Don't act like she suffered simply because she was a good person. What happened to her was because of you!"

It would take nothing to put a fucking bullet in his brain and be done with him. He deserves it. No one could argue he doesn't.

Fear fills his eyes, and he turns to look at Ryker. "Is this your influence?"

"Cason, we don't kill our own. No matter how much you may think he deserves it, don't. This isn't who we are."

I know he believes what he's saying is right. I've been brought up with that code to protect family above all else just like every other Varens.

But as my hand clutches my gun and I imagine how it would feel to finally kill my father, I don't want to obey some rule. All I want is to avenge my mother's death.

Ryker levels his gaze on me and shakes his head. "Don't do this, Cason."

I keep my aim on my father for a few moments more and then reluctantly lower my gun. "Fine. So you have me back. What do you want me to do?" I ask flatly.

"What you're meant to do, of course," Victor answers, smug again now that he doesn't have a gun pointed at his head.

"What's the name and where can I find them?" I ask, repeating the same words I've used every single time I've stood in this very spot all those times before getting my marching orders from my father.

I wait to hear which one of Duke's men he wants me to hit. Everyone else has had their turn in the two men's little war, so now it's mine.

"The name you know almost as well as your own. Michael. He's gotten to be a problem that can't be solved, so you get to take care of it for me. You won't have any difficulty, I imagine. You've hated him your entire life. I bet you've dreamed of this more than once. A little Cain and Abel job for you, Cason. As for where he is, you can find him out at the country house where you and that little girl stayed last year."

Ryker looks at his brother in shock, shaking his head as my father's order sinks into his brain and mine. "What the fuck are you doing, Victor? Michael? You expect Cason to kill Michael? I just told him that's not who we are and the next fucking thing to come out of your mouth is that you want him to kill Michael?"

My father nods and then gives a shrug, like none of this should surprise anyone. All Ryker can do is shake his head in disbelief.

I stand dumbstruck by what he says. Kill Michael? What could he have done to have fallen so far from favorite son to marked man?

"You want me to kill your son?" I ask, barely able to get the words out of my mouth. "I thought Jaxon said you needed me back because of this thing with Duke."

"Duke's being handled. I need you to take care of Michael for me," he says quietly, almost as if the profanity of what he wants done has finally dawned on him.

"I don't want to be your killer anymore. You know that. Now you want me to kill my half-brother. I'm not interested in being that man."

As much as I'm expecting a fight from my father, I don't expect what he says next. Nodding like he understands, he runs his hand through his hair and explains, "Then don't be. Do this last job and then go back to work for Ryker here. Or disappear into the countryside with that pretty little girl and her baby, if my brother has no use for you. Become a farmer for all I care."

Stunned, I stand there in front of him as his words filter through my brain. Just one more job and I can be done with him and everything his world entails? But that job is killing his son, my half-brother?

As insane as it sounds, it's all too easy. He's willing

to let me go after dragging me here if I'll do this one more job for him? Something's not right.

"Tell me why you want Michael dead. I won't do this if you don't."

Victor takes a deep breath and lets it out slowly, along with a growl that sounds like it comes from the depths of his soul. I watch as his expression twists into something horrific and beads of sweat begin to form on his forehead.

"He's been running things on the side and not cutting me in on them. He's been told about this and still insists on stabbing me in the back. So he has to go."

"And what about your wife? You don't think she's going to be upset when her son is killed?"

A look of utter dismissal momentarily crosses my father's face. "My wife is routinely upset. This will be piled on top of everything else that bothers her. And what do you care? She's the reason I did what I did to your mother, so I'd think you'd be happy to see her suffer."

"I don't give a fuck about her or him."

"Or me, for that matter. Isn't that right, Cason?" he asks, his voice verging on frantic now.

The way he says that, like he's hurt now that he's finally realized all his years of hatred toward me have come back at him, makes me chuckle. You created a monster, Doctor Frankenstein, and now you don't like the consequences?

"I don't give a fuck about anything anymore. I'm a killer, remember? We aren't supposed to care."

His face gets redder by the moment. He reminds me of how he looked that day he sent me out to the country house the last time all those months ago. Whatever madness is in him has only gotten worse since I've been away.

"This is crazy," Ryker says, leaning down on the edge of the desk to be eye-to-eye with his brother. "We don't kill family. Remember what our father told us? Have you forgotten that's one of the things you protect and rely on, Victor? No matter what you think you're doing by punishing Cason this way, you can't take out Michael."

Victor shakes his head and wipes his brow. "You're too much like your nephews, brother. It's probably that woman who's affected you and made you soft. Men like you and me, and Cason, for that matter, can kill anyone, including family."

"Is this some kind of fucking test? Like if he says he'll do it you'll be satisfied? This isn't the kind of business Dmitri Varens would have ever been a part of, and I won't be either. We don't kill our own. Period."

Nothing Ryker says sways him from what he wants me to do. Turning his attention back to me, he continues, "If you were really the killer I had hoped you'd become, I'd truly have to worry about you striking at me. But no, you aren't that man. You're just someone who killed, but you've never had the heart of a killer like I wanted you to. So take care of this last job and you'll be free to go back to Ryker's or to frolic in the countryside with that pretty thing and your kid."

"But won't that leave you with no heirs to this kingdom of yours?"

He throws his head back and a maniacal laugh explodes out of him. "You think you and Michael are my only sons? You're not even my only children, Cason. Don't worry about what's going to happen to this family once you're gone. We'll be fine."

I'd never thought about if my father had other children before this moment, and I have to admit I'm a little surprised this is the first I'm hearing about them. How is it they've escaped being forced into working for him, or are they just too young yet?

None of that matters, though. All I have is this one last job and I'm out of this life for good. More importantly, Lily and Lukas will be safe. It's all too easy, but it's too tempting to say no.

One more job and my life is my own.

"Then I'll do this and after you're out of my life for good. No more dragging me back in here. No more sending Jaxon to say I need to come back. I'm out."

"Right. Out. Enjoy the rest of your life."

He turns away and runs his thumb over the edge of the bassinette Lukas had been in as he mumbles something. No matter what he's promised, I'll never be able to leave Lily or Lukas unprotected again. Over my dead body will I let him do to my son what he did to me.

I leave my father's office as Ryker returns to his

attempt to convince my father that killing one of his sons is wrong. He won't be able to, though. Some people have no good in them, and the madness I see eating Victor alive makes talking any sense to him a useless cause.

Being related to him doesn't change the truth of who he is.

Or who I am. But if this will keep Lily and Lukas safe, I'll do what I have to do.

THE COUNTRY HOUSE LOOKS THE SAME AS THE night I left it to go rescue Lily from Doc. That Michael is staying here just adds a final level of insult to my life as Victor's unwanted son. The child of the woman who wanted my mother dead living in her house and now I have to kill him.

Everything has come full circle.

Michael's sports car in the driveway tells me he's here. If he's smart, he has a sense of what's coming. The problem is he's never had to think of anyone but himself, so I doubt he understands how little our father cares for him now that he's crossed him.

The front door is open, and I walk in to make my way into the living room where Michael sits. His dark head pokes just above the back of the couch, and I walk around the front of it to face him. I've never killed someone by shooting them in the back, and I don't plan to start now.

In his right hand, he holds a gun aimed directly at me. Fortunately for me, he's spent most of his time as a Varens being spoiled and lounging around at the island villa, so he's never become much of a shot. Taking my gun out, I point it at the center of his forehead.

"You should have just shot me from behind when you walked in, Cason. If you were any kind of brother, you would have."

His hand trembles as he tries to project all that bravado I know is pure bullshit. For the first time in his life, he's finally understanding what it means to be Victor's son.

"I'm not a coward. I don't shoot in the back."

"Maybe I'll shoot you and then Dad can go crazy when I disappear. Maybe I'll do that," he says, attempting to use that smartass tone he's always used when he talked to me, but it doesn't work now.

"How does it feel to not be the golden child for once, Michael?"

"Fuck you, Cason! You have no idea about my life, so don't hang yourself on the fucking cross like you've had such a hard life. Just fuck off and do what you came here to do if that's what you had planned for this little event of ours."

A cocky prick until the very end.

I stand there in front of him watching his hand shake around his gun and try to think of a single time he and I were ever nice to one another. Nothing comes to me. From the minute he came into this world, he's been nothing but a reminder that my mother and I were disposable, easily replaced by younger versions of us.

"You can't do it, can you?" he asks, his words tinged with a hope he shouldn't have. "You don't have to, you know. He's not the all-powerful being he thinks he is, Cason. We're men now. We don't have to be his puppets anymore."

As he talks, I watch him shrink in size right in front of me, but I can't let that change what I know I have to do. The memory of what Jaxon told me about how Michael wanted Tia to suffer merely for having the nerve to break up with him flashes through my mind. He's always been a petty fuck like that. Spoiled and thoughtless. That's Michael to a T.

"I'm not interested in whatever coup you're cooking up for Victor," I say quietly. "He and I have made a deal. I do you, and then the people I care about are safe."

Michael shakes his head faster and faster, like he can't believe this is how it ends for him. "We can take over, Cason. You know Ryker hates the way our father runs things. Victor is the past. We're the future —you, me, and Ryker. It's time for a changing of the guard. Time for youth to take over and make this family what it could be instead of what Victor wants it to be."

What's unbelievable is he actually believes what he's saying.

"We aren't anything. We've never been anything, Michael. You were my replacement, and from what our father said to me, now you'll be replaced by someone else. But my time living the life he made for me is over. As for you, be thankful he ordered me to do it. At least I'm not a savage fuck who wants to see you suffer."

I aim the gun at his head as he spirals out of control. Jumping up from the couch, he holds his hands up in surrender even as he turns to insulting me.

"You've always wanted to kill me. Admit it! Stop acting like you're doing this for some high and lofty reason, Cason, because you're not and you know it! This isn't for some girl or some kid who may or may not be yours. At least be honest and admit you've always wished I never existed."

Fear fills his dark eyes until I'm sure he's going to make some last ditch effort to stop me, like lunging for the gun or tackling me to the ground. But he doesn't. He just stands there with his hands up in front of him, as if that's going to stop me from doing what I have to.

"You were never my brother, Michael. You were always just one of the reasons my mother had to die so you could be more comfortable. Now you sit in her house—her house, you fuck!—and try to make me think I should save you? Why? Your very existence made mine a fucking nightmare. I became some fucking thing our father toyed with, nothing but an experiment he tinkered with in his attempt to create a killing machine he could use whenever he wanted. You shouldn't be surprised he ordered a hit on you. It was only a matter of time because you're just like him. Selfish. You took more than you deserved and now you get to suffer the consequences. He will someday too. Don't worry about that."

"So that's your plan? Take over the family after the two of us are gone? Do you plan to go after him next?" Michael asks in a shaky voice.

"See, that's why no matter what I say to you, you'll never get it. This isn't about getting to the top of the shitheap that is our family. What I'm doing here is about protecting people who shouldn't be hurt because of me. That's not something you will ever understand, but that's what this is about."

"You're just like fucking Jaxon. The two of you are suckers. A pretty piece of ass gives you a taste, and you put those bitches over your own family. You don't even know if that kid is yours, and you're willing to kill your blood for her?"

Inside me, something explodes and as he continues to talk shit about Lily and my son, I can't hear anything anymore, except the sound of my heartbeat pounding in my eardrums. I press my finger on the trigger, and a second later, Michael falls to the floor, finally silent.

But it's not over. I knew as soon as Victor ordered me to kill his favorite son it wouldn't end like that.

From behind me, I hear heavy footsteps and turn around to see Scotch. Sloppy fuck, he's practically winded from walking up the front steps.

"Sorry, Cason. You know how it is," he says in that husky voice of his that comes from being fat and smoking too many fucking cigarettes.

I do know how it is.

When he lifts his arm to aim his gun at me, my younger and healthier body moves faster. Like the killer I am, I don't think twice about how Scotch is about to get what he's got coming to him. Not that he ever had a choice. He must know I'm better at this than he is, but he couldn't say no to Victor. That's what life under my father is like.

You get to choose between the devil and the deep blue sea. Not really much of a choice at all, is it?

Before he can get off a single shot, the bullet explodes out of my gun, and a few seconds later, he crumples to the floor, his out-of-shape body just a heap of dead flesh. Another casualty of working for Victor Varens.

I look around at my mother's house and wonder for a moment if what I've just done has finally avenged my mother's death. Shaking my head, I know the answer is no. Michael didn't order the hit on her. Victor did. That he's still alive means the one responsible for her death hasn't paid for his crime yet.

But someday he will.

And Scotch just ended up where he probably always was destined to. Just a little earlier than he imagined, I guess.

When I walk outside, I see Jaxon waiting for me. A sudden rush of confusion courses through me, and for a moment, I wonder if he's been sent here to take care of me now, too.

"Strange meeting you here," I say, forcing a smile for my cousin.

With a shrug, he chuckles. "I thought maybe I

would get here in time to see it all myself. Guess I drove too slow."

"So now you're in the habit of watching hits? Seems like an odd hobby, but what do I know?" I say as I stop in front of him.

"I wasn't sure you'd do it, to be honest. Not that he didn't have it coming to him for years, but I didn't know if you could after the past few months."

His comment seems to reflect more about Ryker than me, and I laugh at the idea that somehow working for him has changed me. "Our uncle may not be like my father, but he's still a Varens. Ryker just goes about doing things differently."

Jaxon nods his agreement. "True. I just didn't know after all that different that you'd be able to step back into your job to take care of Michael."

"He got what he had coming to him. Whether it was you or me or any number of guys who did the job, his end was set in stone a long time ago. His time just came up."

"And that stupid fuck Scotch too. I sort of liked him," Jaxon says with a shrug.

My cousin doesn't respond to my attempt to be philosophical about my half-brother's end, so I take the opportunity to ask him about someone I do care about. "How was Lily? Is she okay? What about the baby?"

Lifting his hand to stop my line of questioning, Jaxon smiles. "She's fine. I watched over her until I left to come here, and Ryker is over there right now making sure she's okay. The little guy is fine too. I imagine he's dreaming of whatever babies dream of right now."

Relief washes over me. "Good. I'm glad you two kept watch over her. It's the least you can do since you kept me in the fucking dark about my own son, you asshole."

He hangs his head and gives me a tiny smile. "Yeah, sorry about that. In my defense, I thought I was doing the right thing."

As much as I could be pissed at Jaxon, there's no point in living in the past. What's done is done. I can only look at the future.

"I don't believe for a minute that my father is going to keep his word. This isn't over."

Jaxon shakes his head sadly. "No, I don't think it is. He's got some crazy obsession with you, and until something breaks with that, I think she and that baby are in danger."

I wish that wasn't true, but it is. Victor Varens isn't going to let me or the people I care about live in peace. My doing what he wanted hasn't changed his need to punish me. Why I have no idea.

"Be careful, Jaxon. I wouldn't be surprised if he ordered you to take me out now. He has no respect for family."

Patting me on the shoulder, he smiles. "No way. First, I have the get-out-of-jail-free card with Victor. A dead father gives you that with him. But second, if he comes at you, it will be him doing it himself now, so watch yourself, Cason."

I spent enough years around my father to know at

least part of what Jaxon says is right. That his father died helps him. That my father will strike at me on his own is something only time will tell.

But I can't live the rest of my life, no matter how long I have, in fear of him. I lived too long as that man already.

CHAPTER TWENTY-FIVE

*L*ily
       Peering out from behind the curtains on my front window, I see in the darkness that same man wearing that skull mask leaning against his car who's been there for the past two hours. He was at Victor Varens' office today, but I don't get the feeling he's like him.

At least I hope not.

But if he is, why is he just standing there on my quiet country road instead of coming inside? I think to myself that I should just march right out there and ask him why he's here. Of course, I don't. I can't be that brazen girl anymore now that Lukas depends on me. The Lily I was when I met Cason would do that, but she's gone, replaced by the mother of a baby who needs her alive.

Just as I begin to close the curtains to go back upstairs, I see another car pull up. My heart pounds in anticipation of who it might be as I watch for the driver's side door to open. When it does, I let out a sigh of relief.

Cason.

He stops to talk to the man in the mask and then hugs him, so I guess he's not like Victor. As if it's a changing of the guard, the man gets into his car and drives away, leaving Cason staring up at the window.

None of what's happened today was how I ever wanted him to find out about Lukas. After all we went through together, I dreamed of something sweeter for our reunion.

So much for dreams.

A few seconds later as I think about that fantasy I had about the three of us, his knock at the door brings reality rushing back. I make my way to the front door and open it, not knowing what to say now after all I heard back at his father's office. Did he kill someone to protect me and Lukas? I've never wanted that and don't know what to feel about it.

In the dark, he stands on my front porch looking equal parts ominous and gentle giant, something he once warned me he definitely wasn't. That only leaves him as someone dangerous, but I don't want to believe that.

"Cason, who was that man who's been watching my house for the past few hours?" I ask, needing to know if we were in any danger, even if I didn't know it for sure.

"That was Ryker. He's the other half of the Varens family. He was making sure you were safe while I had to be away."

His voice drops on the last word—away—before he reaches for the handle on the screen door. "Can I come in?"

A tiny part of me believes that if I make him stay away from us that we'll be safe. That's not true, though. I know that, so I push the door open to let him in.

He steps inside and stops just inches away, towering over me like he always has. When he looks down at me, I see in his eyes the same look he had that last day at the motel.

"I'm sorry, Lily. I thought if I stayed out of your life that you'd be safe."

"What's going to happen, Cason?" I ask, hating how scared I sound now.

"I won't let him do anything to you or Lukas. I promise. No matter what I have to do."

"But he said all you had to do was that one thing and he'd never touch us again. Why don't you or those guys who were watching the house today believe that?"

Cason steps forward and wraps his arms around me, pulling me to him. Instantly, I feel safer than I can ever remember feeling. His strength practically envelopes me.

Pressing his cheek against my head, he says quietly, "Because we know him. It's not you or Lukas he cares about hurting. It's me. You two are just a means to an end."

I tilt my head back to look up at him. "Why? What

would make him treat you like that? Is it because you killed Doc for me? Is that it?"

He shakes his head and sighs. "No. It's just how he is when it comes to me."

"So he doesn't want Lukas? I thought maybe because he's a boy he would."

Just the idea of that makes my blood run cold. I don't want my son near that man. Ever.

"When he gets older, if my father is still around, he'll try. He won't succeed, if I have anything to say about it. But for now, he's content to use you and the baby to get to me."

What Cason is saying makes me feel like all of this is hopeless. Closing my eyes, I let myself get lost in his arms again, wishing things were different for all of us.

"I'm sorry, Lily. Just know that I won't let anyone hurt you or Lukas."

That's the second time he's said that, but what does that mean?

"How are you going to stop him or anyone else?" I ask against his chest, too afraid to look up into his eyes when he answers.

"I'll do what I have to."

His words resonate inside him and against my cheek. I'll do what I have to. I know what that means. He'll kill for us.

"Is there no way to stop your father without having to hurt people? Won't he listen to anyone when it comes to you?"

Cason tilts my head back so I have to look up at him. I hate the way I know the answer just by the darkness in his expression. There is no way other than killing. But will this be our life forever? Will Lukas and I never have a moment of peace without Cason having to be that killer?

"I've spent my life trying to be what he wants. I'm done with that. I don't want to think about him anymore," he says with pain in his eyes.

"I'm sorry."

Shaking his head, he tries to smile. "You don't have to be. Some things are just the way they're always going to be."

We fall into silence, neither one of us knowing what to say. He feels so foreign holding me, even as I revel is how familiar his touch is. We only knew each other for such a short time, but it feels like I've waited forever to have him back.

Cason cups my cheek, and I lean into his palm and close my eyes. "I've missed you," I whisper, afraid to look up at him when I say that.

His thumb traces the outline of my lower lip, making my body come alive. Still, I keep my eyes closed, unsure he feels anything close to what I feel.

"All this time, I've wondered what happened with you, Lily," he says in a deep voice as he drags the tip of his thumb over my upper lip. "I guess I figured you met someone who..."

I wait for him to finish and after a few seconds open my eyes to see him staring down at me with that pained look from before. Shaking my head, I smile. "No. There's been no one."

No one since him.

And then in a flash, the pain in his eyes is gone, replaced by a hardness I don't understand. When he speaks again, that hardness comes out in his words, too.

"You deserve to meet a nice guy who can live here with you."

Why would he say that? Is it that he doesn't feel anything for me other than the urge to protect me and our child like some kind of guardian angel who sees it as his job?

"Maybe I don't want a nice guy."

Turning his head, he slides his arms from around me. "Well, that's what you should have."

"Have anyone in mind?" I ask, trying to hold my emotions together as he feels like he's disappearing right in front of me.

"No," he says in a low voice tinged with an edge that unnerves me.

Why is he acting like this?

Hurt courses through me. So I mean nothing to him, and this is how he shows that?

"Well, I guess that's that then. I think it's time for me to go check up on Lukas. Make sure the door is locked when you leave."

He doesn't stop me when I walk away toward the stairs, but as my foot lands on the first step, I hear him say behind me, "I'm not a nice guy. I never have been."

Something about how easily he lets me go makes rage explode inside me, and in less than a second, I'm standing in front of him unwilling to let things die between us like this. He looks away, but I step to my right to get into his line of vision again.

"Look at me! Stop avoiding me, Cason!" I scream, startling him.

When he does as I want, he stares down at me with that same hard glare from just a minute before. He says nothing, though, forcing me to say the words he won't give me.

"So I mean nothing to you now? You're just that heartless killer you've always been, a man who never meant a thing he said to me in that motel room?"

"I've never been anything but a heartless killer. You knew that."

Shaking my head, I swallow hard and try not to let my emotions overwhelm me before I get to say what I need to. "No, you weren't, Cason. You were and are more, whether you can see it or not."

"You deserve someone nice now, Lily."

Now? Why now?

Then it dawns on me what he means. Now that I've given birth to Lukas, I'm some untouchable to him.

Once again, something inside me explodes, but this time I don't try to stop my rage and lash out at him with my fists against his chest as I scream, "Oh, so now I'm not good enough. Like I'm not the same Lily who spent days with you in that bed? Or the same woman you killed Doc for?"

Cason grabs my wrists to stop me, holding them in front of him as he shakes his head. "Stop before you hurt yourself."

"Fuck you! This thing you are now is worse than a killer. What's wrong? Do you have a Madonna and whore problem with me now? I'm the mother of your son, so now I'm not attractive anymore? Not sexy enough now, Cason? Is that it?"

My verbal attack stuns him for a moment, and when he releases my wrists, I slap him hard across the face. Instantly, his rage meets mine, and he pushes me back against the wall.

Pinning my hands above my head, he stares down at me as he breathes heavily, like he's using all the strength he has not to lash out at me. The hardness in his eyes is gone, replaced by the sensual look in them I've waited to see.

"I'm not breakable now that I've had a child. Is that what this is? Is that why you're trying to push me away and saying I should find someone nice? Or is it that you just don't care for me anymore?"

My heart slams into my chest as I wait for his answer. I feel vulnerable and exposed, almost more than I can bear.

Sliding his hand down my arm, he reaches my neck and presses softly against my skin. "I kill people with these hands. They don't belong on someone like you now."

"Why? What makes me different than before?"

He winces and then answers, "Because you're someone's mother. It's like I'd be defiling something sacred. I'm too cruel, too hard for you now."

"Oh, baby. They fucked you up, didn't they? You

deserve me as much as you did before. There's nothing I want more than to feel your hands on me."

But still he shakes his head, unwilling to believe me. "No. You're sweet and beautiful, and I'm nothing but a killer."

Tears begin to fill my eyes. "Then go. Do whatever you have to so our son is safe. I'll find that nice man who can see me as something other than some untouchable thing, and he'll be in charge of keeping me safe and making me happy."

Cason shakes his head again and looks away. "I don't want to hear that."

Yanking my hand away from him, I step to move around him. "Well, that's the way it has to be. You made that choice."

Before I can walk away, he slides his arm around my waist and pulls me against his body. I look up and see pure need in his expression.

"I can't stand the thought of you with anyone else. I don't care if he's a nice guy like you deserve. I hate it."

An edge in his voice makes it sound like every word is being pulled from deep inside him. He's barely holding on.

"Isn't that what I deserve? That nice guy who will come home every night from his nine-to-five job and eat the dinner I cook?"

His eyes narrow to slits, and his breathing becomes ragged. I sense he's close to finally getting over whatever he's convinced himself about me.

"You know, the nice guy to fuck me but who I

have to pretend to love as much as I loved being with you."

The mere mention of me with this nice guy he's created in his mind for me makes him lose control, and he stuffs his hand into my hair to tilt my head back. "I don't want to hear another word about you and some guy. Do you understand me?"

I see the need in his eyes and push even further. "Why? Am I not supposed to ever have sex again? Just because you don't want me doesn't mean there aren't many men in the world who'd be happy to have me every night."

Cason lets out a sound like a growl and shakes his head. Tightening his fingers in my hair so streaks of pain dance across my scalp, he leans down and whispers against my lips, "You have no idea how much I want you."

With a brush of my thigh against his crotch, I feel how hard he is. "As much as I want you. I've thought about you and how much I want you for months. Did you think about me, Cason?"

He nods but says nothing as he tugs my T-shirt over my head. Staring down at my body like he's seeing it for the first time, he shudders and takes a deep breath in.

"What did you think about? That first night when I seduced you and willingly dropped to my knees to suck your cock? Or later that night when you fucked me from behind and I felt like I couldn't breathe every time you slid into me? Or did you think of something else?"

My questions hang in the air as I arch my back to tease him with my breasts. Bigger now after giving birth, they practically spill out of my bra. Like that first night, I want nothing more than for him to fuck me. This time, though, it isn't to save my life.

It's to save us.

His hands make quick work of my bra, and he reverently cups my breasts, pinching the deep pink nipples as he answers me. "I thought about every moment with you. The taste of your skin when I ran my tongue over your stomach and licked your pussy. How you felt with your mouth on my cock. The feel of your cunt when I fucked you that first night. The way I felt when I opened that cabin door and saw Doc hurting you. Over and over, I replayed every second we were together thinking that's all I'd ever have with you again."

When he finishes talking, he kisses me hard and I feel his cock against my hip. My fingers fumble with the button on his jeans and then the zipper, but finally I free it from behind the fabric to hold it in my hand. He's heavy in my palm, and when I stroke him from balls to tip, he seems to grow even bigger.

I lower myself to the floor and look up to see him watching me as I grip his cock and lean forward to take him into my mouth. Thick and long, he slowly moves over my lips until the head nudges up against the back of my throat. When I slowly ease him out of me, I smile up at him. He's power personified, and I love it.

"Fuck. You feel so good on me, but that's not going to be enough for me tonight."

Butterflies flutter inside my belly at his words, and he pulls me up to stand on my feet again. His hands peel off my yoga pants and underwear, leaving me standing naked in front of him.

As his gaze roams over my body, he groans, "I've missed you so much, Lily."

"Show me how much you missed me," I whisper into the space around us and move my hands to push down his pants.

He tears his shirt over his head and tosses it aside before stepping out of his jeans. I'd forgotten just how beautiful he is. His body with its taut muscles, all those tattoos, and the two silver barbells in his nipples makes my mouth water in anticipation.

Lifting me by my waist, he positions me perfectly above his cock and holds me there for a long moment, making my need to feel him inside me grow more. I wrap my arms around his neck and lean in to kiss him long and deep, flicking my tongue against his before I say with a moan, "God, don't make me wait any longer, Cason."

As if my plea unlocks something inside him, he gives me what I so desperately want and slides into me in one smooth movement that takes my breath away. He's so full inside me, stretching my body to take all of him, and I tilt my hips to ease the last delicious inch in.

"Oh, God…"

I can't control the tiny whimper that escapes from my throat when he begins to fuck me in earnest, and he stops, staring at me with a look of fear in his eyes. He doesn't say it, but I know he thinks he's hurt me.

But nothing could be further from the truth.

"Don't stop," I plead, practically crawling up his body to get him to move again. "You feel so good."

"I don't want to hurt you."

With a smile, I shake my head. "You won't. Just don't stop. Fuck me like you did that first night. I've wanted that for so long, Cason. Please."

His mouth crashes against mine as his hips push forward and he plunges into me. I claw my fingernails over his shoulders, and with each thrust of his cock, I dig my heels into the small of his back, needy for every inch of him.

"Lily, I'm not going to be able to hold back if you keep doing that," he groans in my ear.

"Don't hold back. Please, don't."

Cason leans back to look into my eyes, as if he seeks confirmation of what he just heard, and then all his control evaporates. His restraint gone, he fucks me like an animal, his only focus burying his cock into me.

Every inch of my body becomes his to do with as he likes. His right hand cradles me under my ass while the other one steadies us against a doorframe. I feel safe in his hold, and when he pushes my back against the wall, I cling to him as he jackhammers into me.

I ride his cock, fucking him as well as he fucks me. My hands slide over his shoulders damp from perspiration, and I clutch the back of his neck, desperate to hold on so he won't stop.

But he doesn't even notice, his attention only on

thrusting harder and faster. I'm sopping wet, my body fully surrendered to him.

I can feel my orgasm making its way through me, and in his ear, I beg, "Oh, God, I'm so close. Don't stop. Fuck, don't stop."

He grunts in response, groaning my name. "Lily, oh, God..."

And a moment later, every nerve in my body feels like it's on fire. I buck my hips against him to feel his body against my clit and my release makes me feel like I'm flying.

I rip my fingernails into his skin on the back of his neck, and he howls before thrusting into me one final time. He stills fully nested in me, filling me.

Cason sags against the wall, covering my body completely. We're both drenched in sweat and exhausted. I kiss his neck and taste his skin. It's a mixture of salty and clean, sweat and soap and water.

"Are you okay?" he asks in a low voice as he searches my face for the answer.

Smiling, I know what he means. "I'm more than okay."

And when he kisses me, the feel of his soft lips against mine makes me sigh. Okay isn't the word for how he makes me feel.

CHAPTER TWENTY-SIX

*C*ason
      I watch as Lily sleeps, her head resting on my chest and her hand settled over my heart. She's small and beautiful, and it's all I can do to try to find a way to keep her and my son safe. But I've never been able to do this. The one person I wanted to keep safe I couldn't. I can't let that happen again.

The irony of who I am and what I'm trying to do doesn't escape me. I'm a killer who never shed a tear over my victims. Now, suddenly, I need to find a way to ensure Lily and Lukas are kept out of harm's way, and I don't know how.

A tiny chuckle escapes from my throat at the idea of harm's way. I'm harm's way. Maybe they should be protected from me.

Shaking my head, I push that thought out of my mind. No. That leaves only finding a way to make sure Victor never touches them.

His text replays in my mind like some sadistic loop

I can't stop. I should have never read the damn thing. Not that it would matter. I know how this business works.

I'll be expecting you today to let me know about Michael. Things between us won't be finished without that first. Whatever else I am, I'm still your father, and with that comes rights.

Rights. I know what that means. That's his way of saying he'll never let me go.

I've sat here for hours trying to escape the obvious answer how to change that. I swore never to turn on him. He's my father, the head of the Varens family. He's blood. Not like Michael was related to me by some miserable coincidence but my father, the man who raised me.

And even with all of that, I know what I have to do. If I can't kill him, at least I can stop him.

Lily moves, and I feel her warm breath skitter across my skin. As I watch her, she tilts her head toward me and smiles.

"What time is it? Did Lukas wake up yet?" she asks in a dreamy voice.

"Around seven. I didn't hear him."

She sits up off me, and the last touch of her body leaves mine. Pushing her hair off her face, she tries to wake up. "How long have you been up?"

With a shrug, I lie. "Just a few minutes."

Lily's gaze scans my face. "Then why do you look like you've been awake for hours?"

"Clean living? Healthy diet?" I say with a chuckle.

But my joke falls flat, and her beautiful mouth turns down into a frown. "Were you up all night?"

My smile fades to a frown to match hers, and I nod. "Sleep is overrated anyway."

For a moment, she's silent and I know she's listening for the baby. When she doesn't hear anything, she throws her leg over mine and straddles my hips. The sadness in her expression is gone now, replaced by a sweet look in her eyes.

She cradles my face and then leans down to place a small kiss on my lips. Against them, she says, "I'm sorry."

"You have nothing to be sorry for. Of all the people in our little drama, you never did anything wrong."

And right there is the painful truth of all of this. My father did wrong. I did wrong. Lily never did a single thing wrong, but she and our son are forced to pay.

"I wish a lot of things never happened, Cason, but not us. Not us. Don't ever think I regret being with you."

Looking away, I say what I know is the truth, even if I don't want to believe it. "You should."

"Oh, Cason, they really did fuck you up, didn't they?"

I hate the sadness in her voice. Cringing at how she sees me, I shake my head and try to play it off as nothing. "Just who I am."

"No, it isn't. Don't believe that."

Fuck. She's too close and too real right now.

"Look at me, baby."

"Stop."

Her fingers grab my face to make me look at her. "Cason, please."

The way she says that makes me feel like she's got my heart in her hand and she's squeezing the life out of me. I fight her for a few moments more and then turn to face her.

"Don't do this."

"Do what? Try to make you see you're not just that killer your father wants you to be? Why?"

Her dark eyes stay fixed on mine, and right there I'm laid bare for her to see. "Because it's like you said. I'm fucked up."

I don't know why I don't stop this whole thing right now. She does something to me that makes me think everything will be okay, but then when I know she sees me, like she can look into my soul, I can't stand it because if she sees the truth, then we can never be okay.

"Do you love me?"

She asks that so plainly, so honestly that I don't know what to say. Maybe I don't know what love is. I thought about her every day and every night for all those months we were apart. Is that love? I killed my half-brother for Victor because I wanted to believe she'd be safe, no matter how much I worried that wouldn't be enough. Is that love? Whenever she's around me, I wish I wasn't the man I am and we could have that happily ever after she deserves. Is that love?

I don't know, so I look away and shrug like love

means nothing to me. "I don't know what love is. You can't be a killer and be loving people."

My words are fucking lies.

"I don't believe any of that, so I'll ask you again. Do you love me?" she asks, this time more insistently.

When I don't answer, she balls her hands up into fists and pummels my chest. "Why can't you just answer me, Cason?" she screams. "Answer me, damnit! Do you love me?"

Her punches feel like tiny taps against me, barely registering, but the hurt in her words stabs into me. I turn to look at her and see tears rolling down her cheeks, shredding what's left of my defenses.

"Is being willing to die to make sure you're safe love? Then yes, I love you. You take up all the fucking space in my brain. You have since the day I met you. But I am that killer you don't want to see in me, so maybe I don't get to feel love like you do."

When I stop talking, she smiles and kisses me. Her salty tears roll onto our lips, but she doesn't stop to dry them.

"Cason, I know what you are and still I love you. Please don't shut me out."

I push her hair off her face and stare into her eyes red-rimmed from crying. "I don't know if you want to be inside me. It's all hardened over in there for so long that I don't think someone as soft as you could survive. Then I think about you with someone else and I feel like everything is falling away and I want to be the kind of man you need. But what if who I've been for so long means I can't be that?"

"Do you think I fell in love with you and didn't know what you were? But I also know what you are with me. Somewhere inside you is kindness. I've seen it and felt it. Don't take that away from me."

"I promise I'm going to do whatever I have to so you and Lukas are safe."

Because she's good, she believes that's my way of saying I'll stay with her and our son. It's not. It's just the promise I plan to keep, do or die.

Now that I know what I have to do, it could be either.

Lukas makes a noise in his bedroom down the hall, so Lily rolls off me to go to him. I catch her by the hand to stop her before she gets away and force a smile.

"I have some things I have to do today. I'm going to have my cousin Jaxon watch over the house. Don't go anywhere without telling him."

Worry draws her eyebrows in toward her nose, but all she does is nod. She's learned not to ask what those things are that I have to do. All the better. She's too good to be tainted by the reality of them.

"Will you come see Lukas before you go?"

"Yeah. I'll be right there."

As she leaves me sitting alone in bed, I take a deep breath in and resolve myself to the fact that this morning may be the last time I ever see my son and Lily, and all I can wonder is what she will tell him about me when he's old enough to ask about his father. Knowing her, the answer will be far too sweet to be honest.

RYKER ANSWERS HIS PHONE IMMEDIATELY, A HINT that he's been waiting for me to call. "Cason, where are you?"

"I'm in my car. I need you to meet me at Victor's estate. Things are going to be settled one way or another today with my father, but as the other head of the family, you need to be there."

My words are met with silence for a long moment before he says, "Okay. Feel like giving me a clue about what's going to happen?"

I put my foot on the gas and pass a car out on the country road leading from Lily's house as I try to think of how to tell him. Better for Ryker to hear it when Victor does. "No, but trust me. I've got no other choice."

Another pause tells me he understands, or at least he thinks he does. He's known my father longer than I have, so maybe he does realize how he pushes people to do desperate things.

"Okay. I just want you to remember that no matter what it feels like now, Jaxon and I and the rest of the family are behind you on this."

"Thanks. I'll be there in an hour."

The phone goes dead, and I toss it on the passenger seat. If I know Jaxon, he'll be calling me in less than a minute after hearing what's going down. He'll probably want to be there, but I need him to watch Lily and Lukas for me.

As if on cue, my phone rings seconds later, and I

see his name flash on the screen. We may only be cousins, but we're more like brothers and he's not going to want to see me go through this without him around.

I answer the call, but before I can even get the word hello out, he's talking. "Ryker just called to let me know you're going to see Victor. I should be there, Cason. He needs to see we all think what he's up to is bullshit."

"No. Someone has to watch over Lily and the baby. You're the only one I can trust to do that."

"I know. I'm five minutes away from the house, so don't worry. I just feel like this is something he needs to see is an entire family thing. You know he's going to try to pull that big brother crap on Ryker. He always does."

Smiling because I know he's right, I shake my head. "Ryker will remind him that he's not ten anymore. It'll be fine. Just promise me if anything happens that you'll get Lily and Lukas to a safe place."

"I promise, Cason. I know exactly where I need to take them to. You just be careful. Even with Ryker there, Victor isn't going to take you defying him lying down. Michael and Scotch were a message, and you know it."

His mention of my half-brother makes me wince. I know full well what Michael was. What he has always been in my life.

"Remember, keep her and Lukas safe, no matter what. If this goes sideways…"

The words get caught in my throat. I want to say

tell her I love her, but she knows. I want to say make sure my son knows who I was and why I did what I did today. I don't, though.

"Just fucking stop with the maudlin bullshit. Jesus, Cason. I think you read too much and it makes you like this. Just cut it out, all right?"

Jaxon can't hide the worry that hangs off his words. I know how he feels. I'm going up against a giant and I barely have a fucking slingshot to fight him with.

"Okay. I know. Too much reading and too many documentaries. Got it. In the future, I'll stick to working on being illiterate," I joke, trying to break the tension of the moment.

He lets out a genuine laugh. "Exactly. No more books, you asshole. Stay stupid like the rest of us." After a pause, he adds, "But stay smart today, okay?"

"Bye, Jaxon."

Obstinate as ever, he chastises me for saying it like that. "Fuck that goodbye shit. Just say you'll see me later, asshole."

I smile at how much like a brother he is to me. "I'll see you later, asshole."

One more laugh and the conversation ends. Hopefully I do see him later.

I SEE RYKER'S CAR WHEN I ROLL UP THE LONG driveway to the house on Victor's estate. My heart begins to race at the sight of it, the reality of what's about to happen pressing down on me. There are a few cardinal rules in our world, and I'm about to break one of them. Then again, killing family members is one of those rules, and Victor's hit on his own son shows he doesn't give a fuck about rules.

Stopping the car, I shut off the engine and take a deep breath. This is the way it has to be. Rules or no fucking rules.

I watch Ryker open up the driver's side door and then see the passenger side door open. Did he bring Kane to this meeting? But he's not family.

A dark haired man gets out, and I stare in shock to see him here. My Uncle Joseph may be a Varens, but he doesn't get involved in family matters like this. He left the business years ago when he and my aunt had my cousin Sophie, and from what I've always heard, he swore to never be a part of it ever again after that.

I slam the car door shut and walk over to join them, unsure of what's going on. My mind races with possibilities. Did Ryker bring Joseph to support me or to back up my father? He is, after all, his brother.

"Cason, I thought instead of having Jaxon here that we needed to bring out the big guns. How long has it been since you saw your Uncle Joseph?"

Studying the man standing next to him, I nod. "I was a little boy the last time, I think."

He extends his hand to shake mine and returns my nod. "Your mother's funeral, I'm sorry to say. You grew up to be just like Ryker here. Sorry to hear your father is acting like he is. I'm afraid power must have gone to his head."

Turning to look at his brother, he smiles. "Not that

either of us is surprised, but when it comes to an innocent girl and a baby, we have to draw the line. With any luck, he'll see today that what he's doing can't go on."

"He doesn't know I brought Joseph, so the element of surprise belongs to us. Maybe that will be good," Ryker says hopefully.

My uncles have no idea how much surprise will play a part in this meeting. I consider bringing them in on my plan, but this isn't their choice. It's mine and only mine.

Once again, that same dread covers me as I walk to my father's office. Ryker and Joseph follow behind, but like always, I'm truly alone in how Victor treats me.

With a final deep breath, I step into the office and see him sitting behind his desk, the bassinette Lukas lay in still a few feet away beside him. I know what that means, and my dread morphs into simmering anger at the thought that he thinks my son will someday return to this place. No one else is in the room with us, but I know from experience it would take mere seconds for one of his men to join us, his gun drawn and aimed at my head.

My father's eyes open wide when he sees his brothers file in behind me. His mouth falls open, but no words come out for a few seconds, a sign he truly is surprised.

"Are we having an intervention? Joey, they brought you out of retirement for this meeting? And Ryker, ever the doting uncle, I see."

"Still the same man you've always been, aren't you, Victor?" The way Joseph says that tells me there's no love lost between these two brothers.

My father regains his composure quickly and grins as he asks, "How is Isabella? I was just thinking of her the other day."

I glance over and see Joseph's expression harden. "She's fine, as always."

"Be sure to tell her I said hello. It's been too long since she and I saw each other."

Joseph seethes at his suggestion. I'm not sure what about that upset my uncle, but it's clear my father knows how to rankle him like he does with me.

Ryker and Joseph take their seats along the wall, and all I can think of is that's how everyone looked at my mother's wake. People seated in black chairs all along the side wall of the room at the funeral home quietly talking about how wonderful dear Cecelia was and how terrible it was she died so young from that horrible home invasion.

As if every person in that room didn't know exactly what had happened to her and who did it.

"So, Cason. I'm intrigued about why your uncles are here with you since it's quite obvious they aren't here to catch up on old times with their brother."

His words tear me from my memories of that night, and I focus on his face, the face of my mother's killer and my tormentor. Whatever surprise he felt at seeing his brothers a minute ago has vanished, leaving that smug expression he so often wears when he deals with me.

"I did the job you wanted me to do, so our deal is set. You don't bother with me, Lily, or Lukas ever again."

The flat sound of those words shocks my ears. I know he doesn't intend on living up to that deal, and what I have to say next is more explosive than anything I've ever considered uttering in my life.

Just as I expected him to, he shakes his head and laughs at my claim. "It never fails to surprise me that you're so trusting, Cason. I would have thought my having your mother killed just a room away from you would have forced that out of you at a very young age. You're my son, and no matter what my brothers here seem to think, I don't plan on giving you up any time soon. With Michael's untimely demise, you're going to be more important than ever to the operations of this family's business."

I hear the shock register in my uncles, and a second later Ryker answers my father like I knew he would. "Cason is a Varens and works for this family. I'm not sure why that seems to escape your notice over and over. Whatever he is or isn't to you, he's still a loyal part of this family."

My father scowls at him. "I'm so fucking sick and tired of hearing how wonderful Cason is since he's started working for you. You don't even have him killing, for fuck's sake. How is that wonderful?"

Turning to look at me, Victor grimaces. "But you worked overtime yesterday, now didn't you, son? I guess I should have known Scotch wouldn't have been able to take you."

"I have other men to do that," Ryker answers, his tone utterly devoid of emotion. "Cason is family, so he deals with other work more suited to his place as a Varens."

As much as my uncle is merely telling the truth, I can't help but be thankful to hear him describe me like that. Victor has never in my entire twenty-eight years said anything like that about me.

"How nice," my father says, rolling his eyes. "And let me guess. Joseph, you're about to try to tell me how to run this family's business, even after you've been gone from it for over twenty years. Am I right?"

"I left because of you, but all my time away doesn't mean I don't understand what our father would think of how you're treating Cason. Even when Dmitri Varens forced me to work for him, he never treated me as badly as you do your own son. I guess I shouldn't be surprised since you had the other one killed. You're a real fucker, Victor."

"I thought you left because of that pretty little Isabella. At least that's how I remember it."

Joseph jumps up from his seat, but Ryker restrains him and shoots my father a nasty glare. "There's something wrong with you, Victor. Going after women and children isn't how we Varens do business. Enough of this bullshit. Pledge that you'll uphold your end of the deal with your son and walk away from all of this before it's too late."

"Is that a threat, Ryker? We may be equals in this family, but I'm still the oldest son of Dmitri Varens. Don't think I've forgotten that."

"I'm not that little boy you bossed around anymore, Victor. I may not run the business like you do, but never underestimate my devotion to family." He stops and then adds, "Excluding some members at this moment."

For all the years I worked for my father, I've never heard anyone challenge him like that. The shock in his face tells me he's surprised by Ryker's challenge, but now I need to do like my uncle has done and show him he can't fuck with me anymore either.

"Enough!" I bellow, forcing Victor to focus on me. "If you won't swear to live up to our deal, then you leave me no choice. I've worked for you for years, and I've seen more than I need to that would put you away for life. Come anywhere close to me, Lily, or Lukas ever again, and I'll turn state's witness and they'll bury you so deep in the hole you'll never inhale a breath of air as a free man again in this lifetime. Your choice, Victor."

Nobody says a word for so long that I wonder if I really said those words. I've rehearsed them so many times in the past, but never before did I believe I could go through with my threat. Now that Lily and my son's safety is on the line, it felt more natural than I thought possible.

"You're bluffing. I know you, Cason. You're your mother's son. She never had the strength to take me down, and you won't either."

My father's words come out shaky, like suddenly I'm someone he fears. Good. He should fear me. I have nothing to lose now, so I'm more dangerous than he can ever imagine.

"No bluff. I'll do it and won't even think twice."

He laughs, but it's forced. Beads of sweat break out on his forehead. Looking past me, he says, "You won't do it because you'd bring Ryker down with me."

Before I can say a word, my uncle answers, "I won't be going down. The moment Cason tells me he's going to the authorities, Kaia and I will be on a plane and leaving all of this behind. I've always been ready to disappear. That you aren't shows you love this too much."

"You son of a bitch," my father mutters under his breath as all the blood drains from his face.

"It's your choice. You can continue living your life and let me go free and clear, or you can wonder when the world comes crashing down around you if you ever bother anyone I love again."

Victor's mouth settles into a deep frown as he glares at me. "I bet you think you've got me cornered, don't you? You turned my brothers against me, and now if I don't promise to leave that pretty little thing and her baby alone, you'll ruin my entire life. You really think it's going to be that easy?"

"I think by the way you're acting that you know I'll do it."

He thinks for a few moments and shakes his head. "You think they'll give you a free ride after all you've done?"

"No, I don't. But at least Lily and Lukas will be safe, even if I'm locked away."

Ryker quickly adds, "You have no choice if you want to keep the life you love so much, Victor. All you have to do is let him go and never bother the girl or the baby again."

"You all know all I have to do is press a single button under my desk and my men will be in here in a few seconds," my father says, his voice shaky.

The bravado act isn't working anymore.

"And you know that Ryker and Joseph didn't come here unarmed, and I have my Glock ready to go. You don't have another man who can kill like I can, and I don't think you want to take a chance that the other two sons of Dmitri Varens don't know how to kill. So what's it going to be?"

"What makes you think I haven't already sent someone to get the girl and the kid?"

For a moment, I freeze in terror. I can't let him think he's frightening me, though, and I know if any danger appears out at the house, Jaxon will keep Lily and Lukas safe.

"I may not want to be like you, but I'm not stupid. I've got them both under watch, so unless you plan on having your men kill your nephew, they're safe."

All Victor can do is shake his head. Looking past me, he focuses on his brothers and sighs in defeat. "Our father is spinning in his grave right now. My own brothers turning on me."

"If only we could have Maxim here, maybe you'd understand how fucking far you've strayed off the path," Ryker says.

The four of us remain silent after the mention of

Jaxon's father, and I see in Victor's eyes he finally understands what's happening. I know he doesn't like it, but that means nothing now. His life and all the comforts it provides him mean more than his determination to make my life miserable anymore.

Shrugging, he sits back in his chair and tries to act like none of this matters. "Fine. I'll live up to our agreement. Enjoy your life, Cason."

Before I turn to walk out, I step forward toward his desk and stop just a few feet away from him. "Remember, if you ever try to get to either of them or me, I'll do it. Don't test me."

"As will I, Victor. I can give this life up in a heartbeat. If you do anything to break your word on this, I'll do it if Cason can't. This vengeance on your son for whatever twisted reason you have ends right now," Ryker says from behind me.

With one last attempt at hurting me, Victor forces a chuckle. "Thank God I have other sons. Maybe they won't be such a disappointment."

But his judgment of me stopped meaning anything a long time ago.

CHAPTER TWENTY-SEVEN

*C*ason

By the time I reach my car, I feel like I'm about to explode. Ryker and Joseph talk behind me about arranging a date when the two of them should get together for dinner with Kaia and my aunt. To them, standing up to Victor is something commonplace, I guess, but never before in my life have challenged him.

Patting me on the shoulder, Joseph smiles. "Your grandfather would be proud of you, Cason. I see a lot of him in you. Thanks for letting me watch that today."

Ryker nods, beaming his happiness at what's happened. "Me too. I was a little surprised when you pulled that turning state's evidence thing out of your hat, but I didn't lie when I told your father that if you can't take care of business with him, I will. No one is going to let Lily or your son get hurt."

"Thanks. The two of you didn't have to back me

up in there, so it means a lot that you did. I don't know if I'll ever be able to believe he'll stop with whatever obsession he has with making my life a living hell, but he better not push me to do something to him. He has no idea how good it would feel."

Joseph extends his hand to shake mine. "You can't choose your family, Cason, but that doesn't mean you can't live your life like you choose. I'm proof of that. Take care and come see your aunt and me sometime. I'm sure she'd love to see how you turned out."

"I will. Thanks again, Uncle Joseph."

After he leaves, I turn to Ryker. He's the one who truly deserves my appreciation. "Thank you for standing up for me in there. I'll never be what he wants in a son, but it was nice to hear you say you're proud of me."

"I am, Cason. You understand loyalty is earned, and you've shown me time and again that I can trust you. I don't know why your father never saw that in you."

My phone buzzes in my pocket, and when I take it out, I see Jaxon's name. Quickly, I read his message and see my father sent one of his men out to Lily's.

I lift my head and say to Ryker, "That fucker wasn't lying. Jaxon says Victor sent someone out to the house."

"Is everyone okay?"

"Yeah. Jaxon got them to safety, but I don't think we can go back there ever again. Son of a bitch. He just can't let us be."

"He won't be able to get to them now. I guess this

means we're neighbors," Ryker says with a smile. "See you there."

I nod and pretend like any of this is okay, but once more, my father has made sure someone lost because of me. For that, I'll never forgive him.

THE CARRIAGE HOUSE ON RYKER'S ESTATE SITS AT the back of the grounds, hidden away from view behind tall trees. He offered to let me stay there when I first came to work for him last year, but I chose a room in the main house instead because it was only me and a bag full of clothes I needed space for.

Now things are different. Lily, Lukas, and I can't fit in that single room, so just like when he gave me the chance to start over after I found out my father put a target on my back, now he's giving the three of us a chance to be together and safe here.

My hand stills on the doorknob as I try to imagine what I'll say to Lily now that she's lost the one place she dreamed of having. She bought that house with her father's money, and because of my father, she was forced out.

Just another reason to hate him.

I open the front door and see her standing with Lukas in her arms. Worry fills her eyes when she looks at me. That worry is because of me.

"Oh, Cason! Your uncle and cousin told me everything was going to be okay, but I didn't believe it until right now. Are we really going to be safe here?"

Closing the door behind me, I force myself to

smile. "We're safe here. Nobody gets onto this estate without security checking them first."

"Are you okay? What happened?"

Lukas lets out a tiny cry and yawns as I walk over toward them. I don't want to talk about my father now. All I want is to apologize for everything that's happened to make Lily and our son end up here, torn away from their home.

I look down at the baby and run my palm over the top of his head, loving the softness of his dark hair against my skin. Like his mother, he's innocent in all of this, and I regret so much of my life at this moment.

"I'm fine, but we can't go back to your house. I'm sorry, Lily."

When I look up and see her dark eyes fill with tears, I can't stand how all of this is because of me. I can blame my father, but Lily is suffering because she gave birth to my child.

"Never?" she asks, her voice trembling as she holds back tears.

Hanging my head, I tell her the truth of what her life is forced to be with me. "Never. I need to keep you safe, and this is the only place I can be sure he won't get to you or Lukas."

"Will you stay here with us?"

I lift my gaze to see her waiting for my answer with hope in her dark eyes. "Yes. If you'll have me here, I want to live with you and our son. I'll be working for Ryker, but I want to come home to you."

"How can I say no to the man who protected us? Of course, I want you here with Lukas and me. How could you think I would ever say no?" Lily says as her attempt at keeping her tears at bay finally fails.

"Because I'm the reason you two were in danger in the first place. It's my fault you lost your house. I wouldn't blame you if you hated me."

Standing on her tip-toes, she kisses me softly and smiles so she looks like an angel. "Hate you? I love you, Cason. I want you to be around your son, where you belong."

I turn my head to scan the carriage house around us. Like the main house, it's got the best of everything. Ryker spared no expense decorating it. But it's not the home Lily loved.

"Do you think you can be happy here? I know it's not your house in the country, but it's pretty nice, don't you think?"

Lily looks around at the opulence all around us and shakes her head. "I've never lived in any place as great as this, Cason. Do you remember my father's house? And as much as I loved my little house in the country, I don't care where the three of us live, as long as we're together."

My heart swells at the news that she can forgive me, and I lean down to kiss her forehead. "I do love you, Lily."

She sets Lukas into my arms and beams her happiness. "It's time for your son's bottle. Ready to try your hand at feeding him?"

I don't get a chance to answer her before she walks away into the kitchen, leaving me standing with Lukas as he stares up at me. He truly is the most beautiful thing I've ever seen, next to his mother.

"Looks like you're stuck with me, Lukas. I hope when you're old enough to know who I am that you're not disappointed. But I promise I'll never do to you what my father has done to me. You can trust me on that."

Lily hands me his bottle and kisses me. "He'll love you like I do, Cason, because deep inside you is goodness. Your father tried to force it out of you, but it's there."

As I watch my son drink from the bottle and he squeezes my forefinger in his tiny hand, I think about how my goodness can only have come from one person. Maybe that's the way I'll finally avenge her death because my father hates nothing more than my not being as cruel as him.

I pull my gaze away from Lukas and smile at Lily. Maybe goodness can exist in a killer.

A knock at the front door makes that thought vanish, and Lily freezes in place. "Cason?"

I hand the baby to her and press a kiss on her forehead. "It's okay. I swear."

My feet feel like lead as I walk to the door to answer it, and for a moment, I worry maybe the three of us will never be truly safe ever again. Slowly, I pull the door open and see Jaxon's smiling face.

Relief washes over me, and I shake my head. "Asshole. What do you want?"

He rolls his eyes and laughs. "Who talks to their family like that?" Looking around me, he says to Lily,

"We need to borrow your man here for a little while. Just family stuff. Nothing bad, I swear."

"Jaxon, can't this wait? I just got here."

Shaking his head, he waves me outside. "It's waited long enough."

I walk back to Lily and Lukas and kiss them both. "Don't worry. We're safe here. I'll be back as soon as I can."

She lifts herself onto her tip-toes and softly kisses my lips. "I love you."

"I love you, too," I say before looking down at our sleepy son cradled in her arms. "And you, too."

"We'll be here when you come back."

The worry in her eyes remains, but she doesn't have to fear. I won't be gone as long as last time.

I walk into Ryker's office and see him and Kane waiting for me, along with Seymour, the doctor we call whenever anyone's hurt. Jaxon slides past me to stand next to them, but nobody looks like they need medical attention. In fact, I don't think I've seen any of them look this happy before.

"So what was so urgent that it couldn't wait?" I ask as I look around the room for any clue why I'm here.

Ryker steps toward me and points at the table along the far wall. "Time for us to do something that should have happened a long time ago."

Still, I draw a blank. "Which is?"

Jaxon pushes against my arm and laughs. "You

really are the biggest asshole in the world, aren't you? Do you think we're all gathered here to watch you get a massage, for Christ's sake? Lay on the damn table and get your rightful rewards already."

Still confused, I look over at Ryker and shake my head. "What's this about?"

"You should have been given this honor years ago, and if your father had been a decent leader of this family, it would have happened right after mine. It's time for your brand, Cason. So lay down and remember the pain only lasts for a few seconds before you can't feel a thing."

Every man in the Varens family going back to my grandfather's grandfather worked in the family business and got the brand on his skin once he proved his worth. My father wore it like a mark of pride, and I remember watching Ryker get his when I was still a teenager. Victor gave Jaxon his last year, and I stood by in his office struggling to understand why I still hadn't gotten mine.

Then again, what worth is there in simply being a killer?

Hanging my head, I quietly say the only thing on my mind at this moment. "I killed my own brother. There's nothing honorable in that, Ryker."

He pats me on the shoulder and sighs. "Your father had no right to put you in that position. Michael's death is on his head, not yours. You did what you did to protect Lily and your son. You've protected your family since you began working for it. No one deserves this more than you, Cason."

I look at him and smile. "Thanks, Ryker."

"Now take your shirt off and lay down on the table. And remember, it's only blinding, unrelenting pain for a second or two and then you won't feel a thing," he says with a laugh.

Tossing my T-shirt onto the couch, I take a deep breath in, suddenly a little nervous. Jaxon sees my fear immediately and seizes on it. "Thank God Seymour is here just in case Cason goes all pussy and passes out the second he feels the iron on his skin."

"Fuck you, asshole," I say with a smile.

"Right back at you, asshole."

Kane jumps in and points at my nipple piercings. "You'll be fine if you could handle getting them. I got my dick pierced and it didn't hurt anywhere as much as the nipple one."

Everyone, including a very wide-eyed Seymour, looks over at Kane. Suddenly the focus of all the attention, he shakes his head. "What? Women love it, so go fuck yourselves with your opinions."

Ryker says nothing for a long moment and then merely shrugs. "You think you know someone and then they say something like that."

"I may be your right hand man, but I don't have to share everything I do," Kane says with a chuckle.

"Well, assuming you don't have any more true confessions, let's get this going. I have a feeling Cason is having second thoughts," Ryker says and then points at the table. "Time to do this."

A little more relaxed now, I lay face down on the

table. In front of me, Jaxon puts his face close to mine. "Hang on to the table. Seriously."

I do as he says and he covers my hands with his as Seymour wipes something cold and wet across the top of my back. I watch as Ryker is handed the branding iron with the Varens family mark, and when he stops next to the table, he pats me on the shoulder.

"Cason, I'm proud to be the one to give you this honor. You've deserved it for too long."

Even if I had the words to thank him for all he's done for me, I don't have time to even attempt to form them in my brain before the red-hot iron sears into my skin. A strangled cry escapes my throat, and then all I feel after the pain is the pressure from Jaxon's hands pressing down on mine.

When it's over and I can focus again, I blow the air out of my lungs and smile at Jaxon. "Thanks."

He lifts his hands from mine and smiles back at me. "I thought you were going to toss me across the room for a moment there. You're still an asshole, though."

I sit up on the table and see Ryker pouring everyone glasses of whisky. Kane hands me one and gives me a nod. "Was I right? I bet those nipple piercings hurt more."

To be honest, I don't know because I can't remember that pain like I can't remember most of the pain I've suffered throughout my life. "It's all the same, I guess."

Raising his glass, Ryker makes a toast to me. "To Cason, a Varens through and through."

Everyone agrees and as they drink, all I can think is after all my life feeling like I had the worst family in the world because of Victor, now I feel like I have two of the best with Lily, Lukas, Ryker, and Jaxon.

I nod at my uncle and raise my glass to toast all of them. "To family."

WHEN I GET BACK TO THE HOUSE, I STOP AT Lukas's bedroom door and watch him sleep in his crib, lost in amazement that I somehow had a part in creating this person. Me. Cason Varens. Killer. Looking down at him, I see how much he looks like me with his dark hair and silently swear to God he'll never go through what I did growing up.

"Whatever it takes," I whisper into the dark room, "you won't know what it feels like to lose your mother because of your father, Lukas."

Moving on to the next bedroom, I see Lily sleeping, her hands tucked up under her cheek in that way that makes her look so small there in the bed. I don't know why, but I need to tell her what I am just in case she doesn't know it by now.

Crouching down beside the bed, I gently brush her hair off her face. Her eyes open and slowly focus on me, her expression softening when she realizes I'm there.

"Is everything okay? What did your family want?" she asks with a tiny smile.

"It's fine. I just wanted to make sure you understood why I didn't answer you right off when you asked me if I loved you. I didn't know if I could. Love, that is. It's been so long since I felt that, or at least since I thought I felt that once my mother was taken from me. So that's why I didn't know how to answer you."

Lily sits up and shakes her head. "It's okay, Cason. You don't have to say anything. I get it."

I take her hands in mine and hold them as I continue. "I thought that maybe I wasn't capable of love because of what my father did to her and not having anyone who showed me any kind of love after she died. But I realized tonight that I was wrong. I had love, even if it didn't come from my father all these years. I had love from Jaxon, who's like a brother to me, and from Ryker, who's like a father to me. It isn't the same as growing up with a father and mother who loved me, but it's still love."

She brings my hands to her lips and kisses my knuckles as her eyes fill with tears. "I know you can love, Cason. I saw it back when you held me in your arms in that motel room after you saved me from Doc. I saw it when you were willing to do anything to protect Lukas and me in front of your father. I see it in you right now."

"I didn't want you to think I wasn't sure what I feel, Lily. I know things between us went fast at first last year, and then everything's happened fast again this time, but that doesn't mean it can't be real," I say, still unsure I'm getting across what I feel.

Her smile grows, lighting up her beautiful face, as she nods. "Nothing's been normal with us from the very beginning, but that doesn't mean it can't be love, Cason. Maybe ours is just a different kind of love. A rare kind."

As I slide into bed next to her, I wrap my arms around her shoulders and sigh. I want to tell her about the brand and show her how it looks, but for right now, what I want most is to show her that love I know I have in me now.

Keep reading for more on Beyond The Lies, the third book in the Captive Hearts series, coming May 2020!

BEYOND THE LIES

I'm not who I appear to be. Who I am is a lie.

I have a job to do, but in one night that all changes when a beautiful girl turns my world upside down.

She has no idea how much danger she's in, but it's too late now. Because once we start on this path, there's no turning back.

Everything I am is a lie. Except when it comes to her.

COMING MAY 2020!

WANT TO ALWAYS BE IN THE KNOW?

JOIN ABBI'S READER GROUP, ABBI'S TWISTED ANGELS, ON FACEBOOK TODAY AND BE AN INSIDER!

ABOUT THE AUTHOR

Abbi Cook grew up wondering if she was different because she always wanted to know more about the villain than the hero in the stories she read. When she got older, she found there were others in the world like her and devoured their writing, loving every dark word. She's written her own tales for years, but in 2019 she decided it was time to take the next step and publish them. She's never looked back since that day.

Readers can find her at her website at abbicook.com, on FB and IG, and through email at abbicookauthor@gmail.com